FROG PRINCE

Dyanne Davis

Manufactured in the United States of America
First Edition
Cover Design: A.M. Wells

ISBN:978-0692253991

<u>Acknowledgements</u>

As always, I give thanks to the Creator.

To Bill and Bill Jr. love you always.

To A.M. Wells, thank you for all that you do. I am assured that you will become a well known writer and cover designer.

To my family, friends, and readers, thank you for your continued support.

Dedication

This story is dedicated to all the heroes, in whatever form they might take. Without heroes, romance writers, would be lost. And the readers would miss your heroic deeds.

Dyanne Davis TITLES:

Full Circle (Book III in the Undying Love Trilogy)
The Gift (Book II in the Undying Love Trilogy)
Giving It Up
An Imperfect Life
Hitting The Right Note
The Affair (Book I in the Undying Love Trilogy)
The Critic
Another Man's Baby
Many Shades of Gray
Two Sides to Every Story
Forever And A Day
Let's Get It On
Misty Blue
The Wedding Gown
The Color of Trouble

Novellas:

Santa Baby
Taming the Bad Boy
Forget Me Not
It's The Little Things
Rebound Love
Flight 22

Anthologies:

Continental Divide (Lotus Blossoms Chronicles 11) Anthology
On My Knees (Destination Romance) Anthology

Titles under F.D. Davis:

In The Beginning
In Blood We Trust
Lest Ye Be Judged
The Good Side of Evil (Carnivale Diabolique) Anthology

"You're a freak."

"I'm an artist. I want to put every movement of your fingers into my memory. I want to see how the clothes fall when you take them off. I even want to look at the way they crease. Call me crazy."

"You're crazy."

"Perhaps. How about we go at this a bit differently, a little slower perhaps. How about if you just undo the button of your slacks and perhaps the zipper."

"Just the button?"

"Okay, go ahead, the button."

She did that.

"Now the zipper."

FROG PRINCE

Rebekah Johnson, AKA, Rebe, had to finally admit her desperation was getting a bit out of hand. Trying to find a man to take her to a dance at the last moment was proving to be downright impossible. For one thing, Rebe had a checklist for her would be date: The man had to look the part of the fantasy hero. If only she'd thought about the timing before she'd dumped Chase.

What was she thinking? If only he'd thought before he'd cheated once again, and with no regards to public displays of affection. Couldn't he at least have had the decency to wait until after her event to get caught? How rude.

Rebe stared into the heavy ornate mirror on the wall across from her at her reflection. Wondering what picture she would portray if she showed up alone. That would make for one desperate heroine and no doubt it would feature somewhere in a romance novel or two. *Romance writer couldn't get a date.* Sure that would make good reading, and it would profit someone, just not her.

"Kandi, why in the world do you have a mirror in your kitchen?"

"To keep me from over eating."

"Your body is perfect?"

"And I want it to stay that way," Kandi laughed.

For a nano second Rebe narrowed her eyes and frowned as she critiqued her friend's body, model perfect TV meteorologist body with a critical eye. Where Rebe was tall and statuesque, Kandi was a bit on the petite size and her pixie haircut gave her a fairy look. Rebe on the other hand kept her thick hair, long, and even added in extensions for more length and fullness. And where Kandi kept her natural brown eyes, Rebe was constantly changing the color of her contacts depending on the outfit she was wearing. As different as day and night, the women had been best friends practically since birth

With a groan Rebe propped her elbows on the kitchen table where she and Kandi were seated. Then she cupped her face and groaned again, only louder this time, in order to elicit a bit of sympathy from her friend. At the sound of Kandi's chair scrapping the ceramic tile floor, Rebe peeked between her fingers and hoped. Then Kandi said the unthinkable.

"I can set you up with Sam."

An image of tanned legs, a great behind and rock hard abs filled Rebe's mind, but she brushed it away. She would never venture down that path. Instead she glared at her friend. Surely she was kidding. Sam Adam, was what—about five feet tall? He was clumsy as all get out, and he was grossly overweight. Sighing trying to decide exactly how to word it so it wouldn't come out making her look bad, Rebe blurted out the same sentiments she'd thought.

"Kandice Kane, how dare you suggest Sam?"

Turning to give her a frown, Kandi said, "It's a good thing you chose two professions where fiction is a part of your work. Besides, I was trying to do you a favor. I think since you want to call me Kandice, I'll just leave you to your own devices."

"What? That is your name."

"And you know how much I hate it. Why didn't my parents think of the jokes people would make of my name. Kandi Kane, indeed.

"Your parents named you Kandice, so I don't think they were trying to make you the butt of jokes."

Kandi stopped in her track and mock glared at Rebe. You're right; you're the one who started calling me Kandi. What were we, three?"

"I like Kandi. Besides you also gave me a different version of Rebekah."

Rebe and Kandi laughed together grateful for the bond they shared. They were both the only girl in their family. Rebe had had the most wonderful big brother, Jamie. While Kandi's three brothers, had played surrogate for both her and Jamie. Moving to hug Kandi, Rebe gave a noisy sigh. "Now let's go back to Sam. This isn't fiction. He's shorter than I am."

"He is not and you know that. He's also not clumsy or overweight."

"Whenever he's around me, he's always tripping over something."

"Even if he were, so what? He's crazy about you."

"How would you know that?"

"Trust me. I know."

"Sam glares at me so much, to even think he cares about me is crazy."

"Anyone with eyes can tell how he feels about you, except you obviously. In addition to caring about you, he'd make the perfect date for you to take to a romance event. He's smart. He's a fantastic dancer. He has great conversation, and might I add, he's very handsome. There is however one very important qualification. He's very nice."

"And there's one thing that disqualifies him. He's my friend. Rather, he used to be my friend, until he decided I was lower than dirt." Ignoring Kandi's laughing, Rebe continued. "Granted, Sam is smart and he's nice, at least to other people. And just maybe he's a wee bit taller than five feet. But let's not forget, he's still shorter than I am. Seriously, he is. And that's with me wearing flats. Do you really think I'd go to the biggest event of the year in flats? And with Sam?"

Rebe had no choice but to ignore Kandi shaking her head indicating she thought Rebe was judgmental, condescending, and perhaps a bit superficial. Hmm. Perhaps she was. She'd fess up to the superficial rap. She'd always admitted to that. Why shouldn't she be, it seemed to be the only area of her life she'd had any real control over.

Her life plans had been made since before she was born. Her parents had determined she'd be a lawyer. And she'd done that…was still doing it. But her secret career was writing. She produced fantasy for women. If she were a slight bit superficial, romance had made her so. Writing it and reading it had made her look for certain qualities in a man. The more she wrote, the more she was on the lookout for heroes.

That's right, she thought proudly, she was a romance writer. And she'd learned a few things about women and romance. Women did not read romance for the realism, or to see themselves and their own lives reflected back to them by the characters on the written pages. They didn't want the heroine to make stupid choices, or to not know what to do in a given situation. They had lots of demands for their fictional heroine. She couldn't be a 'B', couldn't be selfish, spoiled, or one of the favorite expressions of romance readers: She couldn't be too dumb to live. They wanted the heroine to be what they themselves wished they could be in their real lives, brave, resourceful, having all, or at least most of the answers, having a man, though not needing one. Women read romance for the fantasy of it.

If readers required a lot from their heroines they required even more from their heros. They want the hero to be tall, rich, and incredibly gorgeous. He had to be a take charge kind of guy, the typical alpha male. Actually Rebe didn't think any woman would want a real alpha male to live with twenty-four-seven. She thought women would tire of them quickly. But she was in the fantasy business, so she adhered to the rules, and the dream of the perfect man. The hero. His body had to be muscular, broad shoulders, kissable lips. Oh, he could have a tiny flaw, but he definitely couldn't be a short, overweight guy. What would be the fantasy in that? And here was her best friend telling her to date a romance, 'no no', and to take him to the largest romance ball of the year.

What she needed was…dare she say it? Eye candy. What a name. But it was what it was. Romance writers brought out the heroes to the event that women had wet dreams about. And the fans went home happy to know that their heroes existed, that the writers, who wrote about such yummy men as their lead characters, had them in real life. Never mind that the men the authors took to the event were generally hired from a modeling agency and paid to be adoring. Or the fact that more than likely fifty percent of them were gay. The fantasy was in fact intact. Rebe owed it to her readers to wow. Her attention suddenly refocused on Kandi when her friend snapped her fingers beneath her nose. Of all the nerve.

"Look, Rebe, I'm only trying to help you. You had the hunk primed and ready to go. Chase even called me to relay the message to you since you weren't taking his calls, nor were you talking to him at work. He said he'd still go with you because he knows how important tonight is to you. And you told him no way in hell. Perhaps you want to rethink your position."

"Rethink if I want to take a man who has cheated on me more times than I can count, to an event where I'll be judged by the man on my arm. You want me to take a dog to a pet store and turn him loose. I don't think so."

"Then are you going to join in the hunt and call around and see if you can get a guy?"

"I already did. I even asked my cousin Evan to go with me. I was going to pay all of his expenses to fly here. I even offered to pay him to take me. But he said no way in hell would he go with me and pretend to fawn over me."

Rebe laughed as she thought of Evan's swearing. She'd had to hold the phone from her ear. Disheartened or not, she had to admit he had a point. She glanced at Kandi deciding to ignore the smile on her face. "I'll admit my even asking him could be seen as creepy, but I'm desperate."

"Then let me ask Sam."

"I'm not that desperate."

"Suit yourself. It's your money. How much is that again?"

"It's not so much about the money. Besides, all the authors put in the same amount. It's our way of saying thank you to our fans. There are more than enough conferences where they can go and spend a ton of money. We wanted to do this and have them eat a nice dinner, dance, win prizes and have a good time." The look Kandi was giving her couldn't be ignored.

"Okay, and we want them to buy a few books."

"Why don't you just give the books away too?"

"We do give away copies of our backlist, but the book signing is also a tribute to the booksellers, well one in particular. Sue Peterson always makes herself available for selling books at chapter events and even single author events. The dance allows her to make a little money and yes, before you ask, the authors make money from the book sale. We had thought to give the money to charity, but none of us could agree on just one or two. In the end we decided it didn't much matter. Most of the money we make goes back into the prizes we give away. Why are you asking me so many questions? You went with me once. You know what it's all about. Hey—"

"No, before you ask, I feel the same as Evan. I'm not going as your date. Once was okay, but twice and we'll start rumors. I'm sure that's not the fantasy you want to present to your fans. Granted, there's nothing wrong with it but..."

"Stop that." Rebe sighed. "A couple of years ago bringing a friend was no big deal until someone decided to turn it into a contest of which one of us could bring the hottest guy."

"I think the lot of you are crazy. Love doesn't come in a preconceived package."

"That is so not true, at least not for romance readers. Pick up a romance book by any author, it doesn't matter the genre. The heroes rival the gods from Mount Olympus and have swagger down to a science."

Gods?"

"Don't get technical with me. Besides, as a kid I loved the whole Greek gods' thing. Matter of fact I still watch any movie with a Greek god. And I am talking little 'g' god. Its fantasy and I love it. As a result I totally understand what the romance fans are looking for."

"Then you have to go. What am I saying? You have no choice. You also have a speech to give, my friend. Your choice. Go dateless, or go with Sam."

Sighing deeper this time Rebe weighed her options. How the heck she'd ever become involved in the unspoken competition with the other writers of trying to fulfill the romance readers' idea that women who wrote of the perfect couples lived a perfectly romantic life was a mystery? But she was involved in it and she needed a date that would wow.

"I'll talk to you later," she said absently, reaching for her purse and heading for the door. "I need to go home and think."

Out in the hallway Rebe stared at Sam's door, wondered for a moment and did her best not to think of him in any other way but the picture of him she'd conjured up to replace who he really was. Her imagined image was best for all concerned. She couldn't do Sam. She wouldn't do Sam.

By 6: p.m. there was no choice but to admit defeat. She was giving a speech and there was no way she was going alone. She thought about Sam and groaned. Better she went with him than go dateless she supposed. Reaching for her cell she was prepared to take a fair amount of ribbing from her friend. Without preamble she asked Kandi, "Do you think Sam will go with me?"

"I thought he was too short."

"Look, I'm frantic. Will you give him a call?"

"Only if you promise to be nice to him."

"What is that supposed to imply? I am not a mean person. I would never be mean to Sam. Tell him, I'll pick him up at 7:30."

"You're not even going to wait for me to let you know if he can make it."

"Like he's busy. I'll be there at 7:30. And check to make sure he...well... looks presentable."

"You know, Rebe, I'm thinking about not asking him. It would serve you right to go to this thing alone."

"I'll be there at 7:30. Now go see if you can help Sam scrub some of the paint off his body. See you soon."

Sam glared at Kandi. "Are you serious? Do you really think I want to go to a romance dinner dance? And with Rebe? You've got to be kidding. The woman is a snob. Besides she doesn't like me, or any man she thinks isn't up to her standards."

"You'd be helping her out."

"Why on earth would I want to help her? I don't even like her. You could say, I can't stand her."

"You made a promise."

"That's blackmail and so not fair."

"Desperate times calls for desperate measures."

"Why can't Rebe be more like you?"

"If she were she wouldn't be…oh darn it." She'd nearly blown it. If Sam for one moment thought she knew his true feelings concerning Rebe he wouldn't go.

"What were you going to say?"

"Rebe makes life interesting."

"That doesn't mean I want to date her. I'd much rather have a beer and sit with you and watch a movie."

Kandi didn't say that was the point of the date. Neither of her friends needed to know she thought they were what the other needed. She could have sworn a couple of years ago they were headed in that direction, and then something happened to change that. Rebe's brother, Jamie, died and Rebe hadn't been the same. And poor Sam, Jamie had been his best friend. It had been nearly as hard for him losing Jamie as it had been for Rebe and her parents.

Things had been made harder because of the transformation Rebe had made toward him. Sam had gone from being her friend to…she didn't even know. She only knew it made no sense and try as she might; Rebe had refused to discuss it with her. So had Sam.

He'd said Rebe was finally showing her true colors. Kandi knew for a fact that wasn't true. They'd been best friends their entire lives. There was only one person Rebe treated with disdain and that was Sam. Kandi was determined to find out why and to repair the riff in Rebe and Sam's friendship. If she couldn't make a love match, she'd settle for them being friends again. She loved them both and the past two years had been more than awkward with their strained relationship.

She looked Sam over wondering why Rebe had never seen him for who he was. He had soulful green eyes with tiny hazel specks and they sparkled with his emotions. She'd long ago noticed anytime he was around Rebe, spoke her name, or even complained about her, his eyes would light up from within with green fire.

Kandi almost laughed knowing she'd been around Rebe too long while she wrote her descriptions of the heroes in her book. She was starting to sound like her. Though her description of Sam was right on point. In fact, if her friend would stop whatever vendetta she had against him, she'd see that in his own way he was every bit the romance hero as Chase. She stood back to peruse Sam. *Not bad, not bad at all,* she thought.

"Kandi, is something wrong?"

With nothing more than a grin, Kandi continued her inspection of Sam. Looking at his long wavy brown hair she gave a tiny sigh of appreciation. Despite the tiny splatters of paint, his thick hair looked so silky that if she was into him, she'd have her hands twisted in his hair all the time. She grinned as he frowned at her.

But she was not yet finished with her assessment. His dimples were to die for. And Rebe loved a man with dimples. Sam's were the deepest she'd ever seen. Pair that with his strong jaw line, and beautiful smile and he'd hold his own with any of Rebe's fictional heroes, any day of the week. Besides that, he was brilliant, funny, and very respectful of women. He was fiercely loyal and a man she trusted her friend's safety too. Of course she realized he didn't have much use for Rebe. But then again, Rebe didn't have much use for him either.

"You've been staring at me as though you're trying to decide if I fit the bill. If you were any other woman I'd think you're checking me out, but since it is you and you're in my apartment asking me to do the most ridiculous thing I could have ever imagined, I'd have to think you're trying to see if I'll measure up for Rebe. Who cares if I do or not? Apparently I'm the only man left on planet Earth, since that would be the only reason she'd want me to take her to this damn dance."

Kandi smiled at Sam. "Do you own a suit?" When he glared at her, she laughed. This was going to be fun.

Pulling up to Sam's and Kandi's apartment building, Rebe took in a couple of deep breaths and exhaled. She'd blown the horn several times already and Sam had not come down. Pulling out her phone she called first Kandi them Sam. Neither one of them answered.

Now she was forced to get out and ring the bell. When the buzzer sounded she yelled into it. "Sam, come down."

"If you're here to take me on a date, you can damn well come up and get me, Rebe. Honking your horn for me is just plain rude, even for you."

Darn it, why couldn't Kandi have made sure Sam was ready and waiting downstairs for her, instead of behaving like a Prima Donna? She wondered, as she stomped toward the elevator and pushed the button for the second floor. This was wasting valuable time she didn't have. She banged on Kandi's door. When she didn't answer Rebe threw up her hands. Her plan had been to ask her friend to go and collect Sam. Now she'd have to go to his apartment, which she didn't like doing because he had too many reminders of her past on his walls.

Taking a slow ten count Rebe stared at Sam's door. Now she didn't have a choice but to proceed to his door and knock, she thought as she made her way across the hall to Sam's apartment. When Kandi opened the door, Rebe refused to cross the threshold preferring to stand on the other end of things that would make her sad, namely the pictures on Sam's walls. With her hands on her hips she glared at Sam who stood just inside the door glaring back at her. "Sam, come on, you're worse than a woman. Why aren't you ready?"

A scowl was added to Sam's glare. Rebe tilted her head at the transformation, inspecting him from a distance for paint splatters. He'd pass. Now if she could get him to move his butt. "Sam, come on, you're going to make me late."

"How about a thank you, Rebe? You actually have a lot of nerve thinking I had no plans, and would be here at your beck and call."

Whoa what the....glancing toward Kandi, Rebe noticed her friend merely shrugged. Something was wrong with Sam. Why wasn't he fawning over her, grateful to be seen in her presence? *Oh right.* That was what happened in the books she wrote, not in real life. Now she remembered why he wasn't fawning. He hated her. For a moment she contemplated going to the dance alone.

"Well, Rebe, do you even know how to say thank you?"

"Sam, why the hostilities? Kandi led me to believe you'd be happy to go with me."

"Did she now?" Sam frowned and looked toward Kandi who just shrugged.

"Did you have plans for tonight?" Rebe asked, though she should have asked the question without the smirk, but it wasn't going to happen. When Sam made a move to undo his tie she gave in. "Okay, okay, stop, don't go getting undressed. We don't have time for histrionics. Thank you for going with me tonight. I should have said that already. You're right. It was rude of me to ask you at the last moment. You look very nice by the way."

She was taken aback when Sam scowled at her and rolled his eyes. Okay, there was no way he was going to play the role of adoring, fawning boyfriend. She wondered would going to the dance with a man who looked as if he'd like to kill her, be better than going alone. She knew the answer, yes. The women would more than likely attempt to imagine their hatred was unfulfilled love, or at least unbridled lust. Hmm, perhaps they'd assume they'd had a fight. Ooh yes, that would be good, and then they'd more than likely imagine the torrid sex they'd have later.

Just like that an image of her and Sam, in bed, wrapped around each other's naked sweaty bodies came to her. She was as bad as her readers in thinking about the romantic mushy stuff. She ought to know, that was what she wrote, what she wanted romance reader to believe. Why wouldn't they think it could happen in real life?

"Sam, if you're ready to leave, I'm parked downstairs."

"We'll take my car," Sam spoke quickly. "That way when I become bored and want to leave, I can."

"Fine, but you can't leave until after I give my speech, okay?" She finally asked him in a much nicer tone of voice. "Please." He didn't answer her, just gave her a look that could have meant anything from he'd suddenly tasted something rancid, to, he was heading for the worst night of his life. Without nothing more than a gruff, "Come on," Sam headed for the elevator, not even bothering to lock his door. Rebe looked behind them and saw Kandi was taking care of that. When she turned to face them she was laughing.

Thanks a lot, Rebe wanted to say. *Had a thing for me. Yeah right.* Sam didn't even look her way from the moment they were in the elevator until they were standing by the curb, and he took his keys from his pocket

When she heard the beep of his alarm she hadn't expected the shiny green SUV to belong to him. Nor did she expect him to hold the door open for her. He'd been sort of…well rude and it appeared as though he didn't like her very much. Taking another look at his car, she saw it was new. His last car, as far as she knew had been a black Toyota Camry, the one he'd driven her home to Atlanta in. She shook her head wanting to let go of the reason for that particular road trip.

CHAPTER TWO

Rebe watched Sam as he made his way around to the driver's side. He didn't appear quite as short tonight. She smiled at his back. But he was still short, at least two inches shorter than her. And she'd have to admit he wasn't exactly grossly overweight. Hmm taking another look she noticed he did have very broad shoulders. Where the heck had those come from? Perhaps he was using padding. Before she could stop herself, she was eyeing him as though he was a caramel pecan sundae from Andee's Frozen Custard.

"Have you been going to the gym, Sam?" she asked. For an answer she received another eye roll. Okay, this evening was definitely starting out to be less than fun. Perhaps it was time to bring whatever the heck was bothering Sam about her out into the open. Heck they used to be friends. She'd never intended the friendship to turn so hostile. She had no desire to be Sam's enemy, or for him to want that either. Perhaps she should do as Kandi suggested and try being nice to him.

"Is there a problem, Sam?" She asked as sweetly as she possibly could, making sure to put her southern upbringing into the question.

"No problem. Why do you ask?"

"Because you keep scowling at me. And you're refusing to answer me."

"You're asking me rude questions. What would you do if I asked you if you'd been on a diet? Or if you'd dyed your hair? Or if I just happened to mention the addition of the extra hair extensions? I could even ask you why you aren't wearing as much makeup as you usually do."

"You don't like me very much do you?"

"No, I don't. You're rude, don't care much for the feelings of others, and you're extremely shallow. Did I miss anything?"

"Just that you've proven something to me. Fairytales are just that. There is no way to make a prince out of a frog. Once a frog prince, always one." To her surprise Sam laughed.

"Am I the frog prince?" He laughed even harder. "Okay, Rebe, since I've agreed to accompany you tonight why don't you tell me what you're expecting. As long as you don't ask for anything ridiculous, I think I can fake it."

"It would be nice if you could pretend to be in love with me, you know, with the furtive looks, and secret little touches. If you could fawn over me a bit and keep your eyes and your hands off the other women in the room, I'd really appreciate it. You might say, I'd be in your debt."

"You ask a lot of a man that doesn't much care for you." Sam glanced her way and chuckled.

For a long moment Rebe stared at Sam before she felt the catch in her throat. And when she opened her mouth to speak, her voice came out wispy and soft. "Perhaps you could remember back to when we were friends, before you didn't care for me much." He glanced quickly at her before diverting his attention back to the road. A weird thing happened to Sam's eyes as he glanced at her. He toyed with his lips then pulled in a breath and sighed and toyed some more with his lips. Rebe watched in fascination. *What beautiful lips, very kissable lips*, she thought.

Sam's eyes were on the road, but the dimple in his cheek was evident. He was still laughing at her. Her gaze remained on the dimple. Wow! Had it always been so deep? An unbidden sigh of pleasure that sounded more like a woman moaning while in the throes of love making came from her throat. Darn it. Before she could even lower her eyes, Sam had glanced once again at her. If he were any kind of gentleman he wouldn't mention the sound she'd made. He'd just let it go. But he cleared his throat and she knew he wasn't about to let it go. She didn't exactly blame him.

"I gather you're checking me out and approve," Sam teased.

"Get real. I was writing a scene in my head. You weren't in it," she lied.

This date was going to be a lot different than what she'd expected. And why the heck had Kandi practically told her that Sam was in love with her. Maybe not those words, but it was definitely what she'd gotten out of the conversation. That had to be the reason she was behaving as a sex starved…hmm. Was she the heroine in this little drama of hers? And if that were the case, what would that make Sam? It was time to stop this nonsense, stop imagining kissing a man she couldn't have. A man who hadn't liked her for more than two years. She couldn't think that because of him helping her, he'd changed his opinion of her, not that quickly anyway. Okay, she'd been in a bit of a pickle and he'd helped her out. No heroine should have to go into an event unescorted, so she was grateful.

"Thanks for coming with me tonight, Sam. I really do mean it this time. It was very last minute, and you certainly didn't have to do it. For the past week I've been in a panic about this dance. I'll admit I've been at my worst. I've been rude and maybe a little bit nasty." Rebe was watching him when she saw him swallow as though …perhaps he wanted to let her off the hook. "Will you forgive me, Sam?"

"Are you asking for my forgiveness to ensure I behave at the dance?"

This time it was her turn to laugh. "Of course not. Naturally I'd be thrilled if you just don't show how much you really can't stand me. I know asking you to fawn is a stretch…open dislike though would be a bad thing for this event. No matter how it plays out tonight, fawning, or out and out hatred, I wanted to let you know that I'm sorry if I hurt your feelings."

"Rebe, I can't believe as many years as we've known each other, you really don't know me at all do you? Just so you know, regardless of my feelings for you, I'd never deliberately embarrass you in public. You don't have to worry about that."

"Thanks. I wasn't kidding before when I told you to consider me in your debt."

"I didn't do this so you'd owe me."

"I know that. But I also know you didn't want to come. I know you're only doing this because Kandi badgered you."

"Do you now? Are you a mind reader and someone forgot to tell me?"

"Sam?"

"Seriously, how can you possibly know what's on my mind? We've done nothing but fight since…well for the last couple of years. There is no way you know me. Not even my reasons for coming tonight."

"Can't you just let me show my gratitude? I'm not trying to buy you. I just want to say thank you by telling you, even if we're fighting, if you ever need me, I'll be there for you."

"And if I happen to need a date, even a last minute date, you'll go? No questions asked?"

"Deal."

"And you'll pretend that we're a couple."

"Yes."

"Fawning included?"

"Yes."

"Wow this shindig must be very important to you. Tell me a little more about it."

"What are you doing, Sam? You know about this. You're the one who convinced me to go four years ago." She saw a flicker of something in his eyes before he began chewing on his lips again.

"Look, Rebe, it's been years since we were friends. Back then neither of us had to try, let alone try so hard to find things to talk about. Granted, we're no longer friends. But it shouldn't be this hard for us to talk. I'm trying to find a topic we can talk about without fighting. Just tell me as though I have never heard of this thing. I'm trying okay."

Trying? Was that what he called it? She'd play his game at least until the dance was over. "Okay, Sam, we'll do it your way. Do you know anything at all about my second career?"

When he arched a brow she continued. "Well, stranger, since you asked, I write romance and with doing that I have to go to events, conferences, workshops, signings, and things like that.

But this dinner tonight is the major event of the year. At least for the romance authors, and romance fans of Illinois. We started with just Chicago, but as more and more authors wanted to participate, it grew to encompass the entire state. Since the authors foot the bills, we have to limit the number of fans who can come. We have a strict sign up by, and space limited to—. Each year the number allowed to attend has increased. The more authors willing to pay, the more fans we can allow.

To keep it fair each paying author has a set number of fans she can allow. After that it's first come. It's a time for fantasy. All of the romance authors show up with their fantasy heroes. It's all done for the fans, to make them believe in love and romance, in heroes and heroines. It's to give them escape, and hopefully we'll all sell more books in the future."

"And your fantasy man, where do all of you find your hero?"

Rebe laughed. "Mostly we hire them. Our heroes are perfect with maybe a tiny flaw, maybe a small scar that will make him look more masculine. No real life man could ever fill the role of our perfect hero."

"And physical appearance?"

"Well, they're all over 6 feet, broad shouldered, a six pack, super rich and handsome."

"You're right. Most men do not have all of those attributes. And he also has to be rich?" he tisked. "Most of the male population is not over six feet. Why didn't you hire a model?"

For a moment Rebe cringed. *What the heck*, she thought and plunged right in not liking how what she was about to say would sound.

"I write interracial romance mostly, some paranormal and even women fiction. But my fan base is interracial, multicultural romance. Because of what I write, the guy I take with me to this event has to represent that."

"And…"

"They were all out of the type that I wanted."

"Do I even have to tell you how that sounds? We both know I don't fit your bill for a romance hero. That means that even though most of the times you won't even make eye contact with me, the fact that tonight you lowered yourself to allow me to take you, boils down to one crucial fact. You want me because I'm the other half of your little interracial couple. As a Black woman I would at least expect you to know better. If the situation were reversed I would catch hell for even thinking about doing what you're doing, let along acting on it."

Sam took in a deep breath. "And now what? You're going to show up with the frog prince and be drummed out of the club? Readers will stop buying your books. What? Rebe, you're a lawyer, does this in any way sound even the slightest bit like discrimination?"

Sam had a valid point. It was discrimination against short, fat, or not very attractive men. The fact that Sam wasn't any of those things wouldn't calm him down. And yes, he did also fit the bill for the other half of her interracial couple. Of course she'd never say it out loud, but the amount of pigments in his skin made him just the man she needed for tonight.

"Rebe, just admit it. The only reason you want me to take you to this event tonight is because I'm White. You want us to be the symbol of the couples you write about."

Sam was looking at her as though she'd lost her mind. Did he really think she'd admit to him that she was glad they would be seen as an interracial couple? Wasn't implying it enough?

Rebe shuddered for a moment as she remembered clearly attending an event at the Dolton library and the instant coldness of the crowd when another really well known interracial romance writer came into the room with her African American husband. Readers didn't want the writers to write fiction as they were doing. They wanted them to paint a picture of the lives they led. That was the dream they were selling. The women in the room had wanted to see the writer in an interracial relationship. But she wasn't about to get into a debate with Sam right now. She was nervous enough as it was. She had to give her speech and she didn't want to be any more anxious than she was. She decided to take a different route.

"I meant it earlier when I said you looked nice. And I meant it as a compliment not an indictment. And, Sam, it has nothing to do with… you know"

"You think I look nice. You said that with surprise, as though you didn't think I knew how to dress. But thank you."

Sam slowly allowed his gaze to roam over Rebe's entire body. She was waiting for him to comment on her. And he would have. But she was expecting it, and he was still annoyed that she'd waited until countdown to ask him to go. She could have asked him a week ago, or even the day before, but less than two hours. She deserved to stew and wonder.

"What happened to your boyfriend?" Sam asked instead. "He fit the description of your perfect hero and he also would have been the perfect companion for your interracial party. He's taller than I am, and blonde. And I assume blue eyes are really a seller considering that even Kandi, who barely tolerates Chase, has said more than once that he has beautiful, blue eyes. And even though I hate to admit it, women seem to find his looks appealing. Look at you. You go stupid gaga over him."

Sam had to make himself stop talking. There was no way he wanted Rebe to know he was the least interested in her relationship with Chase. Or that he thought the man wasn't good enough to even take her on a pretend date, let alone share her bed. He glanced toward her noticing she'd not answered his question. "Now look who's being quiet. What happened to Chase?"

"We broke up."

That he'd already known. He glanced at Rebe, a part of him wanted to feel sorry for her, but she'd made her own problems.

Women! What in the world was wrong with them looking at the external instead of the internal? Okay, if he were honest, men did the same. Sensing her sudden sadness he glanced at her again. He was aware how important this night was to her. It was time to lighten up on her, at least a bit.

"By the way, Rebe, you look very nice." He watched as her lips curved into a soft smile. She was pleased. He felt something happen round the vicinity of his heart, a tiny, microscopic crack. He found himself smiling, glad he'd done the right thing. Had she really not known how beautiful he thought she was? Had he never told her? He thought about it. He hadn't. It didn't matter now.

"Sam, is there anything about me that you like?"

Oh hell. Why was she asking him that? And especially when he could tell he was melting toward her and didn't want to. He pretended to think about it. But the things he liked about her required no thought. He loved her vivacious personality. Rebe had a smile that could light up the world. He was sure if she were allowed, she could stop wars with the brilliance of it. She was or rather she used to be sweet, caring, and so damn vulnerable that he wanted to protect her from ever hearing a harsh word, he wanted to protect her from pain. But Rebe was also strong and fiercely loyal. He thought about Jamie. She'd loved her brother so much she'd never seen he was flawed, just like everyone else.

Those were the qualities he thought about when he chose to think about Rebe, her inner beauty. Her outer beauty wasn't half bad either. He remembered the first time he'd seen her long toffee legs encased in tight short shorts. He'd gotten an instant erection. Then she'd turned around and he'd glimpsed her rear and had to turn away, but not before her brother had punched him in the arm and told him not to even think it. But he'd thought it. For over two years he'd thought it, every single time he'd looked into her eyes, or at her full lips begging to be kissed. They looked so delicious painted or natural. And her eyes regardless of her endless array or colored contacts, always seemed to be just on the verge of revealing a secret to him. She'd teased him mercilessly.

Sam sobered knowing it would be best not to think of the times the four of them had spent together. None of them with the exception of Rebe had dated much. All of them had for the most part been content to spend their time in their own little group. Friends to the end, or rather, it was supposed to be. No one could have anticipated their group would end with the worst tragedy they could imagine.

Nowadays the foursome was more of a twosome, with him and Kandi, or Rebe and Kandi. Rarely was it the three of them. And when it was, Sam was uncomfortable because he was unable to forget how it had been. And he could not make things go back to that time. For a mere second in time he finally admitted that he wanted that. No, it wouldn't be the same, because their foursome was no more. But they shouldn't be at such crossroads because of it either.

"Sam, is there nothing you like about me?"

The sadness in Rebe's voice permeated his senses. He smiled at her. "I like that you take your writing seriously enough that you'd date a frog." She laughed and hit him playfully, her movement making his heart clutch. It was with great effort that he didn't grab hold of her fingers and give them a squeeze.

By the time they'd reached the entrance to the hotel, Sam had already decided he would be everything Rebe needed in a hero tonight. He wouldn't make things any tougher for her. And he'd start by being a gentleman.

After parking he made a mad dash to the passenger side and opened the door for Rebe. She gave him a curious look as she gathered her shawl and threw it around her shoulders, then reached for her clutch purse. She stepped out, gave him another look accompanied by a smile. Then the unthinkable happened. Rebe reached for his hand as they walked toward the banquet hall. Her fingers were trembling. She hadn't been kidding, she was nervous. This was a big deal for her. The instinct that screamed out for Sam to protect her, rose suddenly. Like a fierce lion, he gazed around the room stalking out would be prey, anyone who'd be an enemy for Rebe. She was his main and only concern. "You okay?" he asked.

"I hate giving speeches. What if my throat closes up? What if I forget what I wanted to say? What if…"

"Didn't you write it down?"

"Yeah and I memorized it. I didn't want to read it because I had a dream of the papers falling to the floor then me crying. It was a mess."

Now Sam really was feeling sorry for Rebe. Stopping their entrance into the ballroom, he turned her around and cupped her face in his hands. Something he should have expected but hadn't counted on happened. He noticed the softness of her russet skin, the luscious shape of her full, red, strawberry scented lips, which were made for kissing, and her deep chocolate eyes, sans her contacts... And then damn it, he could feel himself begin to harden. He'd better get this over and done with as quickly as possible."

"Listen to me, Rebe. You're going to be great. Just look my way if you get nervous. I promise you will get through this."

"How can you make that promise? You're going to be on the dance floor and I'm going to be up there at the podium." Rebe pointed toward the podium. "I'll be alone."

"Just do it. Make sure you know exactly where I'm standing and together we'll get you through this. Now come on, let's do whatever it is we have to do. Sign in and get our badges then you can introduce me as the troll in tow. I'm sure you'll get a kick out of that." He saw a smile on her lips but the fear lingered in her eyes.

Rebe, Rebe, Rebe, Sam whispered in his mind. *Please don't cry or I'll be lost. You have to leave me something to keep the barrier in place.*

He gazed into her eyes and knew it was too late. He had sworn to never allow Rebe back into his heart and look how easily he'd broken that promise. The thought of her hurting was too much for him bear. The thought of him being the one to hurt her was never going to happen. If only he could, he knew he'd be much better off. With a sigh, Sam asked. "Are you ready for me to fawn?"

"Now is as good a time as any," Rebe answered him, wondering what on earth Sam had in mind. His hand slipped around her waist and he drew her close to his body. His touch felt familiar and too good. She couldn't resist turning her head toward him and cupping his cheek as he'd done to her. Then she kissed him lightly on the lips while trying not to remember the good times they'd shared in the past.

Her mind zeroed in on one particular moment. When she'd lived with Sam for two weeks she'd dared to come out of the shell of grief she'd built for herself to go looking for him. His apartment had been quiet and dark. She'd glanced at the clock wondering where he was at 3 am. She'd moved about his apartment as quietly as she could when she'd come upon him in the kitchen looking into the fridge. He was wearing dark blue boxers, the clingy kind and she'd stood for a moment staring in awe at his sculpted back. She'd been about to make her escape when he'd looked behind him, saw her, and smiled. "Couldn't sleep?" he'd asked. For a long moment their gazes locked and held and Rebe found herself breathing deeply. It took another moment before she could answer him. "I've gotten so use to having you next to me that I woke when you weren't there," she'd answered.

They'd stared at each other once again before Rebe turned and padded back to the room. A few seconds later Sam followed her with a tray of food, two glasses of juice and him in long pajama bottoms. They ate in a companionable silence then watched comedies until she'd drifted off to sleep

She didn't know why that particular imagine came to her when it did, but it had. She hadn't thought he'd looked sexy that night she's seen him in his underwear, or if she had, she hadn't registered it. Now she had the full image and darn it all. Yes, Sam was sexy, more than likely that was an image she'd never wanted to have of him. Too dangerous.

Kandi was right. Sam was a good guy. Suddenly she realized she was staring into his eyes, his beautiful eyes. For a guy who didn't even like her she'd have to give him major hero points. Maybe in her next book she'd make him a best friend, and find a really nice fictional girl to fix him up with. So she was about five inches taller than him while wearing heels, so what. This was one night. And he'd really saved her. "You're sweet, Sam."

"Thank you." Sam didn't want to hear anything in Rebe's voice that she wasn't saying, but somehow he was hearing it anyway, a sort of longing.

This was all supposed to be pretend, but it felt too real. When Rebe pressed her lips against his he'd wanted to use his tongue to force her lips apart and taste her hidden nectar. He groaned. Wanting Rebe would be way more trouble than he wanted to deal with even for one night. But he was supposed to be fawning right? She'd asked him to be the loving boyfriend in her life, to make the fans believe she belonged to him.

At that moment Sam heard a small sigh from Rebe and her lips parted. Somehow their positions had shifted; they were in perfect alignment to kiss. No thinking was involved. Rebe's eyes closed and she became all soft and pliable. She was asking him in a non-verbal way to kiss her, so he obliged, moving slowly over her lips for the texture before entering and tasting.

Sam explored Rebe's mouth as though he was taking in sips of air, and then he stilled his tongue as she began an exploration of her own. When he felt the probing of her tongue he almost stopped the kiss to enjoy her examination. The moment their mutual searching ended, the battle for dominance began with their tongues. He couldn't get enough of kissing her, which was why he finally ended the kiss. He wasn't the man Rebe wanted and when this dance was over she'd return to her real life. He couldn't allow her to think there was anything more to the kiss than him pretending.

He stared at her lips still thinking how sweet she tasted, but knowing it was time for them to at least partially return to their reality "Rebe, did I tell you it doesn't bother me that you're excessively tall?"

Excessively tall? Rebe's mouth opened but she couldn't find the words to rebuke Sam. She was not excessively tall. "I'm not. I'm five-ten. Isn't that being what you accused me of, a bit discriminatory?"

"Hmm. You're right. Besides, you say you're not enormously tall and I have to take your word. My mistake. You seem a lot taller, more like a giantess. Oh well, I'm only five-nine."

"You are not five-nine."

"In my stocking feet."

"I've known you for almost five years. What did you do, have a growth spurt? You've always been this little bitty thing." Rebe suddenly stepped out of the five inch killer stilettos and stood in front of Sam. He grinned and made a measurement with his fingers.

"Well I'll be," Rebe laughed. "You did grow. You're almost taller than me."

"You're a liar, Rebe. I'm taller than you after all. You're not that tall." He gave her a smile before adding one more thought. "You're a poser." She gave him a cheeky grin and held on to his shoulder as she stepped back into her stilettos.

"Now I'm taller than you," Rebe grinned.

She was teasing him and it was fun, just like in the days when they were friends, and on occasion more than friends. It felt good. It felt right. Sam stared at Rebe remembering how it had been.

"Of course I'm not surprised that you thought you were taller, or that you've always thought I was short. It was all in your mind. Heck, you even thought Jamie was short, and he was six three."

Sam stopped short remembering Rebe didn't like for anyone to mention her brother since his death. "I'm sorry, Rebe."

"Don't be. I have no problem talking about my brother with you, Sam. You two were friends. And you're right, I thought he was short. But you're shorter."

Sam studied Rebe for a moment wanting to make sure her mentioning Jamie was truly okay with her. Her eyes were sparking with mischief and her smile was melting a bit more of that ice his heart had been encased in for the past two years. He'd always enjoyed teasing her and being teased back. He didn't know why but for this instant his old Rebe was back and he intended to hold on to her as long as possible.

He watched as she strutted around in the stilettos smirking at him, her hands on her hips. He couldn't help but laugh. "I thought we just proved that in actuality I'm taller than you. I knew you wrote fiction, but I didn't know you actually believed it. Then again, being a lawyer I guess would account for that." He grinned and waited for her comeback.

"We did not prove any such thing. Like you said, I'm not just any fiction writer, I write romance and I can spin the story to my advantage. The heroine is the real star of the books. The hero is only there for window dressing, for someone to provide the heat, you know, a good kisser." Then she stopped, gave him a look that would scorch and smiled. "As I was saying, if you're only an inch shorter than I am, how the heck can you call me excessively tall?"

Sam shrugged. "Since I'm here to do your bidding, we'll play let's pretend, even in matters of heights. You're in charge. So here's my answer... I'm a man." Then he shrugged again and grinned at her.

He held his breath when the mischief disappeared from her eyes to be replaced with fear. "What's wrong, Rebe?"

"Sam, do you really think I look okay? You were glaring so much at me when I picked you up that you didn't look at me."

"Why are you so nervous? I've never seen you unsure about anything."

Rebe gave a short snort. "You've seen me much worse."

For a moment he stared at her knowing what she was talking about, surprised she'd mentioned it. For two years she'd behaved as if it had never happened. Another fracture could be felt around his heart. Damn it all to hell. She was killing him.

"You're right. I didn't give you a good look. Stand back a little." *You're always beautiful and you always look stunning*, he wanted to tell her.

Suddenly it was becoming hard to breath. He moved a couple of feet away and put his hand on his chin to pretend he was doing a critical analysis of her. He knew there was no need for the inspection but he did it because she was worried.

Rebe's dress was exquisite; it was a really soft blue fabric that clung to her curves. Her shoes were clear. He frowned; they were nice and so damn high that she probably did think she was taller than everyone else. But the sparkle at her earlobes was what caught his attention. She was wearing the diamond earrings he'd given her more than four years ago for her birthday.

His heart caught in his throat and he wondered if she even remembered who'd given them to her. It couldn't be that she'd deliberately worn them because of him. He took another moment to see she was wearing the diamond bracelet her brother had given her. He knew what it meant to her, she'd told him that when she was nervous, having something on given by someone who loved her, someone she loved, made her feel better.

Could that be her reason for the earrings? Did she love him? *Stop it* he wanted to scold himself. Rebe was getting nervous, biting her lips, and turning him on. He had to tell her how gorgeous she looked before she shattered him.

"Well, do I look okay?" Rebe asked.

Sucking in a breath, Sam released it in jerky movements. "You look spectacular. I love the color of your dress. It's different. What color is it?"

"Ice blue."

"Come on, let's go in. People are starting to stare at us." Sam held his hand out for her and when Rebe placed it in his; he felt a tingle and another slight crack. Darn it all to hell.

He'd thought he was in trouble with his hand around her waist, but the skin to skin contact of holding her hand in his was having a most disturbing effect on his body. He found himself rubbing his thumb across the back of her hand.

Stop it, he scolded himself, but didn't. And to his surprise Rebe didn't attempt to pull away. In fact, he felt her give his fingers a squeeze as she pulled him from group to group, introducing him to fans and writers alike. He saw her eyes light with pleasure when the women began quizzing him about when they'd met. He had a ready but true tale. He'd been bowled over, literally. He'd fallen over a stool and he laughed telling the women that was the moment he'd fallen for Rebe. He could tell one reader doubted him by the pursing of her mouth, so he waited for her to ask her question.

"So, Sam, can you tell us how you feel about your girlfriend writing romance and having to be around such hunky guys?"

"I love that Rebe uses her talents to entertain." His gaze connected with Rebe and she gave a slight nod. Gazing around at the group of women gathered around them, he could sense most wanted to believe that he and Rebe were a couple. But there was always an exception to everything. The one exception came in the form of a very well dressed, but catty woman. Her eyes held a challenge. He didn't have to be a psychic to know what her question would be about. Chase.

"Are you Chase's replacement, or do you not know about him?"

"I know Chase. And to answer your question, I'm not Chase's replacement. He was merely standing in for me, until Rebe came to her senses, and realized the worth of a true hero."

That did it. The women approved and so did Rebe. She kept looking at Sam as though she'd never seen him before. As though she'd not slept in his arms, in his bed, for two weeks.

Better not go there, he chided himself. The subject was taboo. And it was what had ruined their friendship. It was strange that she thought he hadn't known what was going on. He'd just allowed it to continue until it seemed they'd gone too far to turn back. Watching her now it was beginning to look as if the tide had turned.

This romance event was more fun than he'd thought it would be. And he'd imagined it as being plenty of fun. Hell, he'd imagined it for the four years she'd been going when she'd never taken his hints and invited him.

Being with Rebe, even as her friend, her pretend lover wasn't nearly as hard as he'd thought it would be. Matter of fact it was downright easy. Too easy he realized. The lines were becoming blurred. He needed to not do that. Tomorrow would be another day and Rebe would be back to making snide remarks. And he would be back to thinking her despicable. But Sam couldn't stop himself, Rebe was having a great time and so was he.

When the sound of the unadjusted mile screeched loudly he knew the round of speeches would begin. Rebe stood in front of him and it was only natural that his arms slid around her. It was even more natural that his lips found her neck and nibbled, planting soft kisses, feeling her shiver, and kissing her again.

Sam groaned when Rebe made no attempt to move, not even when the hardness of his body couldn't be ignored. It hadn't been planned, but it also wasn't something that was strange. It had been a long time since he'd been with anyone he realized. *It wasn't Rebe,* he tried to tell himself. His body's reaction would have happened if he'd been in that close a proximity to any woman. Yeah right, and chocolate cows produced chocolate milk, and strawberry…he laughed and nuzzled Rebe's neck again. She smelled so good. She always had.

He stood behind her, holding her, until it was her turn to go to the podium. Then she turned to him, gazed into his eyes and asked, "How about a kiss for luck?" Before Sam could answer, she'd laid one on him, a kiss that burned away several more inches of the ice he'd erected around his heart to keep Rebe out.

CHAPTER THREE

Breaking the kiss off, Rebe made her way to the podium, stumbling a tiny bit when she glanced back at Sam. What in the world was happening? The pads of Sam's fingers had ignited something deep within her. Heat pooled in her midsection and spiraled downward. *No,* she wanted to scream, not Sam. She'd worked so hard to never become attracted to him, to not allow her feelings for him to become more than friendship. With Sam there would be no turning back, no relationship where neither of their feelings mattered. Sam mattered to her. As much as she'd tried to make him believe otherwise she'd always known. With a groan she realized this was a bad idea coming here with him.

By the time it was her turn to go to the podium, she was darn near floating on air. Standing at the podium Rebe's eyes zeroed in on Sam. He was making silly faces, making her laugh. His touches and kisses to the back of her neck had more than calmed her down She'd have to perhaps give Sam a bigger role in her next book. The man could definitely kiss like a hero. Yazoo, yazoo. Even though it was a bad idea for anything to happen between them, she was glad he'd come with her. She was going to get through her speech.

A few minutes later, a round of applause, then the women standing on their feet cheering her gave Rebe a feeling she'd never had. Her eyes remained glued to the spot where Sam had been because now he was lost in a sea of screaming women. For one brief second she wondered if he'd ditched her. Suddenly he was there in front of her, grinning like the old friend she used to know.

"You were fantastic," Sam said. "I knew you would be." He leaned in and gave her a butterfly kiss on her cheek.

For one long moment Rebe just stared at Sam. Her cheek tingled where he'd kissed her, so did a few other body parts. "Are you still being in character, Sam?"

"You have no idea. Tonight I will be you hero. And when I'm in need, you're going to be my heroine."

Rebe needed something to say, to do, anything. "Have you noticed the decorations?" she asked and moved away as Sam gave her a knowing look.

"Of course I noticed. This place looks as though any second I'm going to walk upon a full-fledged orgy. What gives with all the hearts and the cut out cupids? And all the red, it's a bit sleazy. Sorry."

"You don't have to apologize. This room was specifically decorated to make the women feel hot and sexy. You know the intent is to be erotic."

"So this was purposefully trashy?'

"Stop it." Rebe laughed glad to be able to enjoy being with Sam.

During dinner he was the perfect companion, talking to the women around her, and the men, but keeping his focus on her. His manners were impeccable. Why, he'd make the perfect hero, except he wasn't perfect, was he? He was an artist, a starving artist by the looks of things and he wasn't the required height.

Okay, she'd admit it; Sam wasn't as short as she'd always thought. Egads, he was actually a wee bit taller than her. But still he wasn't tall enough to be a hero. *If only*, she thought. Hmm. But his shoulders were broad and his chest was perfect for her…and his lips.

Rebe found herself turning from her dinner in order to focus on Sam's lips, and found him smiling at her. Oh yes. She thought back to his lips, they were beautiful, and kissable, and his kisses were so delicious. And she wanted…stop that. *Oh no*, she groaned. She wanted more. A moment later she heard Sam's chuckle as though he could read her thoughts. Please no. She would die. She gazed into his eyes, his beautiful green eyes, with flecks of gold, but sometimes they looked brown, like hers.

Who said he should have blue eyes? His eyes were perfect and they went with his complexion. He was naturally tanned from spending so much time outdoors where Chase chose to use a tanning bed. And of late he'd positively fallen in love with spray tanning. She couldn't imagine Sam ever doing that, not even in the winter time when his skin was paler by quite a few shades and the contrast in their coloring was even more obvious, but in a good way.

Rebe had never been picky about the men she dated in real life. Race had never been a factor. Being African American her skin darkened in the summer just like everyone else,' and depending on how much time she spent in the sun she could be anywhere from golden tan to a creamy coco. And in the winter she'd return to caramel.

For whatever reason she was crushing on Sam she was

remembering things he'd said to her, not the mean things he'd said in the past two years, but the things he'd said before their riff that happened without even a fight, just a slow death of their friendship.

A ping of pain as she thought about her brother was replaced by a smile as she remembered that Sam had once told her she looked like buttery caramel as he'd sat watching her spray lotion on her body. She'd given him a quick look and he'd just as quickly looked away. Her brother had given her a look. Then he'd growled and had given Sam a hands off look.

Darn. She had to stop thinking of all the good times she'd had with Sam. *Think of your case*, she commanded, think of anything but Sam. Like magic the image of the man who was as different from Sam as day and night popped into her head complete with his megawatt, white bright smile. Oh crap. Why the heck was she thinking of Chase?

She wouldn't be much of a romance writer if she didn't know the answer to that one. Chase was her picture of a hero, the man she modeled her heroes after in her books. He was tall, very tall, ocean blue eyes, cornflower blonde hair and killer abs, great smile, great kisser, great in bed, and they definitely looked good together. So what was the difference here? Chase could also charm the room. She was truly puzzled. What made one man a hero on the outside, and another a hero on the inside? There had to be something. So what the heck was the difference in the two men?

Rebe gave another peek toward Sam and found him looking at her. *Ah, that was the difference.* Chase's attention never stayed on her. He'd never snuck glances at her when she wasn't looking. He'd never given her a different adoring look than he did any other woman.

And that was why Chase was perfect for her. She wasn't special to him. And he wasn't special to her. But Sam, now that was an entirely different matter. One she was very much aware of. Sam made her want to touch him, to… hmm… at least dance with him. At least she was glad when dinner was over and the dance music began. When Sam moved his chair back, he gave her a look biting on his lips as he did so, as though he were deep in thought. Then he issued an order, 'an order,' not a request. "Let's dance," he said.

There was a slight growl to his voice, all raspy and deep. When she held his gaze something dark and dangerous glittered in his eyes. Hmm, she thought, *Sam is a lot more than I thought.* But he didn't give her much time to think as he whisked her into his arms and they began the first dance, a nice slow ballad. His body had a good feel, strong and sturdy. She found herself wanting to just lay her head on his chest, but hey, she was too tall for that. A chuckle as though he could read her thoughts and a gentle hand guided her to where she wanted to be. But it felt awkward because she was towering over him.

"If you want to lay your head on my chest, you could just take the damn shoes off," Sam muttered.

That was all it took. Rebe's head popped up from his chest instantly. "Thank you, Sam. You made it so easy for me to go up there and give that speech. Give me a second." She stopped in the middle of the dance and ran toward their table with her heels clicking. Once there she opened her bag and took out her flats that she always carried for when she tired of walking in the stilettos. Then she raced back out to the floor to Sam and found her position, her head on his shoulder, her arms around his neck, his hand around her waist slowly caressing her. His laugher soft and sweet in her ear.

Without a doubt she was aware she'd utter the same words of thanks to him more than a dozen times through the night as Sam played the perfect---well almost perfect hero. She watched his interaction with the fans. They were fawning over him—over Sam. What the hell? And he was smiling at each of them as though they were the only woman in the room, being not only polite, but friendly.

The most amazing thing of all was that when Sam looked at her, even knowing it was pretense, he still took her breath away with his smoldering looks and wicked grin. Oh she'd make sure when she wrote his character she included those reactions.

When the night was nearly over she regretted it. Everything had gone perfectly. She'd signed a record number of books, more so than her fellow authors with the gorgeous hunks. And she was cognizant of the fact that it was because Sam had gone out of his way to charm the women. They'd bought her books because of him and she was grateful. Hey, a sale was a sale.

Walking out the door with her arm entwined in Sam's, Rebe stumbled a bit and he caught her to his chest and held her for a long moment. How she wanted to pretend that she'd had a bit too much to drink, but in truth she'd had nothing but soda and neither had Sam. Neither of them could blame their actions on alcohol. Butterflies were doing a dance in her belly. If wishes were true she'd definitely wish for the night not to end. She didn't want things to go back to the way they'd been between them for the past couple of years. Her fault, yes, but Sam had never demanded that she talk, so she hadn't. She'd assumed he wanted things between them not to develop into more, same as she'd wanted.

Arriving back at Sam's car, this time things were different. This time, he held the door open for her and waited until she was seated, then he gave her a smile and walked around the vehicle to the driver's side. Her body easily adjusted to the butter soft leather in his SUV. Turning toward Sam the moment he entered the car, she was aware something had changed between them. They were now at least on their way to being friends again. She owed him.

"Sam, about that debt I owe you. I just wanted to extend it and tell you if you ever need my legal services, I'm there. You really helped me tonight."

"Debt?"

"Yeah, remember if you ever find yourself in need of a date, I'll be there for you?"

"Right." He'd almost forgotten about that. They'd had so much fun he'd allowed himself to reminisce about how things had been for them before they lost....Sam glanced at Rebe as she buckled herself into the vehicle, then he took in a very deep breath and sighed as he allowed it to escape.

It was just like Rebe to remind him that the night had been only pretense. But it did seem that she at least wanted them to go back to being friends. He wasn't betting on her having a permanent change. He'd wait and see, give it a few weeks.

"Who came up with that after party chat with the authors?" he asked and waited for her answer, knowing it had been Rebe's idea.

"I did. I thought after giving people free drinks, we needed to sit around and drink coffee and soda and have after dinner munchies. The fans come to see and mingle with us, so it was a perfect solution to ensure no one walked out inebriated."

"That was good planning. Very much like the old Rebe."

"The old Rebe?"

"Yeah, the woman who used to be my friend. That woman I liked. I saw her again tonight." Why the hell did he say what he had? Damn it all, he'd have to cover that. The night was over. They had to return to what they'd been doing for the past two plus years. Rebe had become quiet. He was holding his breath, then she spoke.

"I kinda think I like that Rebe myself, Sam. I don't think it's going to be that easy to find her again though. Listen, do you mind pulling into Wal-Mart's parking lot? It's right up ahead about a half block."

"You want to go shopping now? I'm not sure if they're open or not."

She smiled, but didn't answer him. When he pulled into the lot she gave him a slow but steady gaze. "Before this night ends and we go back to hating each other—"

"I told you I don't hate you."

"Well, before we go back to whatever it is we do, would you mind kissing me again?"

Would he mind? Hell no. But he shouldn't. They shouldn't. The deal was over, the fawning had been for her fans, the kisses were okay there, but they wouldn't be here in the car, in a damn near empty parking lot. She was waiting and her look was…he couldn't be sure. He didn't trust Rebe's emotions at the moment. She was grateful to him for going, and for behaving and for…, *oh hell why don't you just kiss her and get it over with?*

"I'm not a toy, Rebe and neither are you. I did the fawning bit because I promised you I would. But I think it's time to end this pretense. We both know that the moment Chase tweaks his little finger at you; you're going to go running back to him. Hell, all he has to do is buy you some expensive trinket, a humongous bouquet of flowers…and oh yeah what was it he did about six months ago, hired a damn blimp and a skywriter to tell you he was sorry. If he was so sorry he wouldn't keep doing it. Damn, Rebe, don't you have any sense at all?"

"Sam, believe me I know who Chase is. I'm not going back to him. This was it, the last straw. I'm serious."

"I'm still not going to kiss you. Like I said, you can't tweak your little finger at me and get me to do your bidding. It's not going to work."

"Please, Sam." Rebe's eyes grew moist as she stared into Sam's gaze. When she heard his throaty exhale she leaned in even closer. "Please, Sam."

"You've had too much to drink. You don't know what you're doing." Sam wanted badly to give them both an out. But hell he wanted to kiss her like crazy and never stop kissing her. That was the problem, the real reason he didn't just do as she asked.

"You know I only had soda. I've very aware of what I'm asking you."

"Is this for just a kiss?"

"Would you like more?" Rebe pressed on, willing her mouth to shut up. This was like the fairytale balls she'd read about from her childhood days. And she was feeling like Cinderella. She had to kiss the prince while he was still a prince, before the clock struck the doomed hour and he turned back into a frog, and she turned back into the uncaring woman Sam believed her to be. She couldn't believe she was going to continue to beg him. But she was. "Please, Sam, just one more kiss before the fairytale ends."

Sam gently pressed his lips to Rebe's for all of two seconds, not taking her in his arms, not tasting her the way he wanted, the way she'd asked him to do. This was a hell of a lot safer. After the almost chaste kiss, he moved away. Their gazes locked then Rebe looked out the window on the passenger side and he put the car back in drive and continued toward home, inwardly cursing himself the entire way. But it didn't matter how he berated himself, Rebe was on the rebound. He didn't do rebounds, and especially not with Rebe. There was too much at stake to even contemplate that.

As he pulled into the parking lot of his building he got out, opened the door for Rebe then walked her to her car. "Don't think I'm stalking you or anything, but it's pretty late. I'd feel better if I trail you and make sure you get safely home. Okay?"

"Okay," Rebe answered. She started her engine wondering if Sam meant it when he'd said he was seeing her safely home, or if it were a ploy to try and come into her apartment. Not that she'd mind. After all, they'd shared a bunch of kisses and there was no mistaking that he'd become aroused several times during the evening. Well so had she, but he didn't need to know that.

She thought of her asking him to kiss her, she'd wanted him to do as he'd done throughout the night. Instead, he'd given her little more than a brotherly kiss on her lips when she'd been craving so much more. Heck, for what he'd done it definitely hadn't required him to pull into a parking lot.

For a long moment Rebe wondered what she'd do if Sam changed his mind and decided he wanted the kiss after all and maybe a bit more. What if he pulled into a space at her building? Would she let him up? Would she accept more kisses? And if she did would she let him into her bed. "Don't go there," she said aloud. She knew the reason why she couldn't go there with Sam. Only tonight, her defenses were down. He'd been so nice, and his kisses had stirred a yearning for things she'd given up on having. He could never be the man she accepted into her life. He meant too much to her for him to take that position. When she reached home Sam waited while she opened her door and went inside, then he blew his horn a couple of times, waved and took off. A warm feeling enveloped Rebe. When her landline instead of her cell phone rang she smiled. Sam was being Sir Galahad in overdrive.

"Hey."

"How was the party without me?"

'Oh, Chase, it's you. What do you want? If I'd known it was you calling I wouldn't have bothered answering.

"Then why did you?"

"I thought you were my date."

"Your date? You had a date tonight?"

"Yes. Does that surprise you? We're not together anymore, remember? I'm tired of your cheating."

"Come on, Rebe, you know it doesn't mean anything. I always find my way back to you, don't I?"

Mr. Hunk, every woman's idea picture in her head of the heroes Rebe wrote about, talk, dark and handsome, and yes, wealthy, very wealthy. But Chase knew and played on his assets. He was a dog, a womanizer, a skirt chaser. How many ways could she say it? He had the external hero qualities, just not the internal. If she were a witch she'd merge his external with Sam's internal and create the perfect man, the perfect hero.

"Look, Chase, I meant it when I said I was done with you. Finito. Got it?"

"Have I told you how sorry I am?'

"You mean sorry you got caught."

"That too. But I am sorry. I have a surprise for you."

"No, surprises. No flowers, no blimp and no skywriting a tired apology is going to make me take you back."

"How about being second chair with me on the Alton case?"

The word no was on the tip of her tongue and that was definitely what she knew she should tell him. She'd been working with Chase on the case, but she was only doing research. She wanted badly what Chase was dangling in front of her face. She thought of Sam telling her she would take Chase back the moment he dangled the right bait in front of her face. Darn him anyway. She heard Chase chuckling.

"I'll let you give the opening remarks, Chase said and laughed."

"How about the closing ones?"

"Rebe, now you're being greedy."

"Forget it then. If this is how you plan to make it up to me, this is what I want." Chase was thinking it over and so was she. She was weak and superficial. *Sam it's your fault* she whispered in her mind. *If you were here with me now, I wouldn't be tempted by Chase.*

"Okay, it's a deal. So we're back together?"

"Not as a couple, only as business partners. And, Chase, I want this agreement in writing."

"Sure. How's the research coming?"

"I've had a few distractions, like a cheating boyfriend."

"Ouch," Chase chuckled.

"I was going to work on it when I get up."

"Instead of waiting until then, how about I come over tonight and we work on it together."

Right. There was no way he was getting in her bed tonight. But ooh she wanted the bait.

"I'm not your booty call. You can come in the morning and help me with the research.

With a sigh, Rebe settled down on the couch to talk to Chase. How many times had they broken up? Too many to count. And why on earth did she always take him back? She wasn't in love with him, and he wasn't in love with her, but they did look damn good together. She loved being seen on his arm and vice versa. And ...*you're shallow and superficial.* Her nose crinkled in disgust.

One pretend date with Sam had her ready to analyze her behavior. Who in the world wanted to look into their own motives that closely? No one. That was not the stuff fantasies were made of. And she was in the fantasy business. It was the perfect accompaniment to being involved with the law.

Sam this is all your fault. I was contented with what I was doing at the firm. You're the one who pushed me into wanting more. Now I like it.

CHAPTER FOUR

Sunday morning Rebe returned to the real world. She had a case she needed to work on. Off with the writer hat and back on with the one that paid the bills. She smiled when she thought of the previous night with Sam. It had been fun. Not to mention she'd had very erotic dreams that involved a lot more kissing with Sam and a lot more of things they'd never done. Her skin still tingled with the things he'd done to her in her dreams. Enough of that. Sam had made it plain he was done with the kisses when the party ended. She'd turned out to be Cinderella after all and her carriage had been merely a pumpkin. There was no prince coming to rescues her, frog or otherwise.

Now it was time to concentrate on work. Chase was on his way over to help her with the case. Deciding to put on a pot of coffee, Rebe tried to remember if Chase had ever gone out of his way for her. She shrugged what man really went out of his way? Then her thoughts turned once again to Sam and the way he'd anticipated her needs, bringing her something to drink while she was signing, helping to get her sales, leading her from the dance floor when she'd become tired, and following her home to make sure she was safe. Yes, she owed him and if he ever asked her to repay the favor, she'd make sure she did.

It was a good thing her bell rang at that moment because the way in which Rebe was hoping Sam would ask for repayment was X rated.

Chase came in with a smile as bright as the sunshine streaming through the windows. His cheating forgotten, at least by him. Before she could even think to say a word he'd swooped her into his arms and was ravishing her mouth, turning her legs to jelly. The man totally knew what to do with his tongue. When she began moaning in spite of her plan to show no emotions, she knew the reason Chase was so gifted with his tongue. He used it a little too often on too many women. That thought gave her the incentive to push away.

"You must really think I'm easy if all you have to do is come in here and kiss me, and it's as though nothing happened."

Chase grinned. "You know I don't mean anything by it. We've

been together a long time, more than two years. We always get back together."

"I know. Aren't you getting tired of that?" Rebe watched while Chase gave her a curious look and plopped into a chair.

"You said you had a date last night. Are you saying you hired an escort for the dance?"

"No, of course not. I went with Sam."

"You're serious; you're talking Sam, Kandi's friend right?"

"Yes, but he used to be my friend also."

"He can't stand you."

"I know, he told me that last night."

"So why did he go with you?"

"I'm sure Kandi begged him. But in return for his cooperation, I promised him a couple of favors."

"What kind of favors?"

"What I promised Sam is none of your concern,"

"Oh baby, I'm so sorry to have ruined your evening. I called you quite a few times. I was assuming you were making me sweat it out by not answering either of your phones. Actually, when you told me last night you'd had a date I thought you were lying to make me jealous. What time did you return home? As soon as your speech was over I'm guessing. I'm sure you weren't just getting home when you finally decided to answer your phone."

"Then you'd guess wrong. Sam and I had fun together. By the time the evening was over, I think he may have gone from not being able to stand me, to being able to tolerate me."

They both laughed and for some strange reason Rebe felt a slight niggle of disloyalty. She'd had fun with Sam. Why did she have to pretend otherwise? And why for Chase? Why didn't she attempt to make him jealous of Sam instead? Easy answer. there was no way Chase would ever be jealous of Sam. Chase was way too confident, too arrogant, too shallow and superficial. There she had it, the reason they remained together was because basically they were the same.

"Oh God," Rebe groaned covering her face with both hands. "Noooooooooooo."

"What is wrong with you?"

Glancing up, she saw Chase had a horrified frown on his handsome face. She shook her head and smiled, though there was nothing to smile about. "I just realized the reason the two of us get back together so often. We're alike."

"And what's wrong with that?"

"We're both shallow."

"We're both out for fun, and we're aware of it. There is nothing wrong with that. I guess Sam laid into you last night, and made you feel bad about yourself. Don't let him. Remember it's your fault you had to settle for him. I told you I'd take you to the dance."

"I didn't want you to go. You only wanted to be around a bunch of fawning women."

"Of course. I love being around women."

"Do you think you will ever want a serious relationship?"

"You're my serious relationship."

Was he completely crazy? Shallow was one thing, being...what the heck was he, if he thought being with her while he slept around was anything close to a serious relationship. "We're both insane, Chase. One day I'm going to meet the man of my dreams, and things are going to change."

"Please don't tell me, you're getting hung up on Sam."

This time she wasn't going to let it go. It just wouldn't be right. "I'm not hung up on Sam. But neither am I hung up on you. We work well together professionally. I would like your help on the research and I do want to work the case with you, giving the opening and closing arguments."

"You are aware it was second chair I offered you, right?"

"Yes, but after negotiations you capitulated and agreed to my terms and guess what? I wrote up a contract. I've already signed. I just need your signature."

"I'm going to give you a bit of advice for free, Rebe. Please don't paint yourself into a corner. Like you said, you need my help. You caught me kissing another woman. Big deal."

"And feeling her up."

"Did you see that?"

"Yes, how could I not? Your hand was buried to the elbow underneath her skirt, which was so darn tight; I'm surprised you didn't split the thing."

"I'm pretty good at not damaging a woman's clothing."

"Do you truly think that's funny? You're despicable."

"It was a joke. Rebe. I thought we were good. I apologized for my behavior. I'm sorry, truly I am. I can't seem to help myself with the cheating. But it's always you that I return to. You are my shelter in the midst of a storm."

"I'm the only woman who doesn't care that you fight me for mirror time. Your ego is so huge any woman with you will be relegated to the back. You're good for one thing and one thing only." She thought about that. "Okay, you're so damn big, that I feel safe with you. And—"

"And you can get favors at work. I am your ticket into that partnership you've been wanting."

"Like that's going to happen anytime soon."

"Yes, but when it does, and if we're still together, I will buy it for you. My gift."

"And your price is me staying with you and ignoring your penchant for other women. No thanks. I don't want it that badly."

"Rebe, be reasonable. We're good together. I like what we have and so do you. Don't give up on us. Come on."

He moved toward her, touching her, his hand moving to her breasts, tweaking her nipples, making her swallow.

"Can't we at least continue going out? You know we have fun when we're together."

Rebe was so weak. And so not behaving like a heroine. Then again a heroine only existed on paper. A real woman was flesh and blood, with needs. Perhaps if she negotiated for better terms. She'd readily admit that Chase was fun. And she did like going out with him. Right now he needed to stop caressing her, so she could think.

"Okay, okay, on occasion we can go out. But, I will not be having an intimate relationship with you."

There, that should redeem her in the minds of fantasy readers. Then again, no one would ever be able to please every single reader, every single time. So, considering she wasn't a heroine, the only person she needed to please was herself. To be honest she wasn't even concerned about pleasing Chase. This was, for once, all about her.

But what did her hero do? He laughed at her, he didn't give her a pitying look, nor did he fall down on bended knee and propose. And the words, 'I'll never look at another woman again,' didn't fall from his lips. Not that she would have believed him, even if he'd uttered the words. Okay girl, get a grip. Chase is who you have been saying you wanted for over two years. He's Gorgeous and he…well, he more than get the job done. Stop it. *No sex. No sex.* She'd buy herself a toy or two to scratch the itch. She didn't need to have Chase, not the cheating two timing Chase. But the Chase who was tons of fun wouldn't be a bad compromise.

When Chase laughed as though he could read her mind, it annoyed her. "Let's get to work." She went for the files and the contract she'd drawn up for him to sign. When she returned Chase was contently sipping coffee. Rebe arched a brow in his direction as she glanced toward the counter, then the table. "Did you pour me a cup?"

"No, I assumed you'd get it when you returned. I would have waited for you to get mine, but the attitude you're giving me, I didn't think you would."

Rebe stared ahead at the wall and envisioned herself banging her head into her beige wall. What the heck had she done with the last two plus years of her life? Chase grinned at her and she swallowed. Was it shallow to keep coming back to the bed of a man who took her to heaven and back, who knew her body inside and out, who could make her scream with pleasure. Yes. It was beyond shallow, it was degrading. She swallowed again. And so much fun that she wasn't ready to give it up.

"Come on, Rebe, forgive me."

She was dead. As crazy as it might be, she liked Chase's cocky, arrogant attitude. She liked him. She really did. He didn't demand much from her…and she also liked that. He was moving toward her, and she watched him move gracefully, not falling over himself, not tripping, not like Sam. Chase rather pounced like a lion and he was heating her up as usual with nothing but a smile. Then he decided to take it up a notch and began running his fingers up and down her body, cupping her behind, then he pulled her closer to him. Reaching for her hand he placed it directly over his erection.

Oh crap, Chase was ready to make love. As many times as they'd made love, she knew his body as well as he knew hers. His steel like hardness was no joke. And the wetness in her panties was also no joke. Maybe a quickie, just to take the edge off. Her mind flitted to Sam and how he'd resisted giving her one last kiss. She'd be like Sam, she'd resist. Then Chase cupped her mound and rubbed her between her thighs, and she groaned.

How long could she go without giving into the needs of her body?

Again she thought of Sam. And with his face in her mind she slowly moved away, albeit she moved away panting, but still she moved away. Did Chase get angry? No way. He didn't believe he'd have to wait that long before she caved, and more than likely he was right. He pulled her close again and this time she wondered if she'd have the ability to resist if he began feeling her up again. She sighed and waited for his next move like a lamb being led to slaughter. Then he ruined the seduction by talking.

"Rebe, how about some toast to go with the coffee. I didn't eat. I had thought you would make breakfast for us."

"Seriously?"

"I am here to do you a favor."

Staring at Chase, Rebe couldn't believe him. Even a narcissistic prick should have his limit. "You offered. I didn't ask for your help."

"But you needed my help."

In disbelief Rebe adjusted her stare to a glare and a frown, hoping her facial expressions would get through the thick wall of male in front of her. He only grinned at her. What an egotistical MAN.

"Chase, you offered because you were attempting to apologize for being a two timing worm. Now you want me to make breakfast." In disgust she lifted his hands from her body and moved out of his reach.

"What? I was planning on making it worth your while. You feed me now and satisfy my craving for food, and I'll satisfy every craving you have later." Chase grinned. "Promise."

"Sign this first." She'd expected him to quibble on it, but he didn't. He took the papers from her hand looked them over briefly then signed and handed them back to her. If he'd given her papers to sign she would have gone over them with a magnifying glass, then she would have had another lawyer look them over, just in case.

Rebe shook her head, sighed, went to the fridge, cracked four eggs, added cheese and a little milk, then popped bread in the toaster while she scrambled the eggs. When she was done she dished the food up, putting most of it on Chase's plate. He eyed her, winked then dug in. He was almost done before he looked up again. Apparently he recognized that she was still annoyed.

"Don't look so put out about making me breakfast. I'll take you out for lunch after we're finished working…and after that we can come back and have dessert."

"Apparently you didn't hear me. I said no sex."

"I heard you. I just don't believe you."

With a smirk Chase returned to shoveling the remainder of the food into his mouth. For a moment Rebe watched thinking, whoever Chase was sleeping with apparently didn't cook. Very interesting.

A few hours later the research was over and Rebe was in a much better mood. Admittedly, she would not have finished so quickly if Chase had not helped her with the research. She was also thankful he was going to be her partner on this case. To put it more accurately, she was his. She'd only been going to court for less than a year. Most of her cases at the firm were mere paperwork. If something needed to go to court one of the other lawyers handled it. It had been okay by her.

In fact since she'd begun her secret career she relished the free time. But Sam had said something to her a year or so ago, something about her being complacent, allowing others to move ahead while she lagged behind. Now she was busier than she wanted to be. With a start she realized she'd changed several things in her life in the years she'd known Sam. *Why?* she wondered. Why did Sam's constants jab get her to moving, when even her father telling her practically the same thing had no effect?

Sam had been the one to get her to go to her very first romance gala. When she'd complained that she wanted to keep her real life as a lawyer separate from the writing, he'd given her such a look of disappointment that she'd been forced to defend herself. She could still remember their conversation word for word.

"What if I meet someone there that I know... a client?"

'So what?" he'd come back.

"What if...?"

"Would you little a little cheese to go with that whine? Come on, Rebe, what's the real reason you don't want to go. Do you perhaps think you're better than your readers? They're good enough to buy your books, but not good enough to socialize with."

"You know that's not the reason."

"Then tell me what is."

Rebe could picture them now, the foursome as they'd been then, sitting in Kandi's kitchen fighting as usual. When she'd looked around the room, first at her brother, then Kandi before her gaze fastened and stayed on Sam. And she took in a breath and quietly said, "The four of us spend so much time together that I haven't had a chance to meet any men. I don't have a date, okay."

Sam had given her a look that she'd gotten but chosen to ignore. She'd turned her attention to Jamie and he'd told her in no uncertain terms to forget her harebrained scheme, that he'd never accompany her to a dance and pretend to be her boyfriend. And when she'd dared to glance in Sam's direction Jamie had said an emphatic, 'hell no.' She'd had no one left to ask but Kandi. Even that had taken a ton of promises and her pleading with her friend to go with her before she'd agree. What the heck was wrong with her that on one wanted to go to the dance with her?

The next year they'd had the same conversation almost word for word and when Sam had arched a brow in her direction, she'd once again admitted she didn't have a date. She shook her head at him. "I'm sorry, Sam. I need someone who will wow."

Kandi had given her a look. And her brother had called her name indicating she was being beyond rude. Well, it had been partially his fault. He'd told her more than a dozen times to keep her hands off of Sam. He'd been off limits from the moment they'd met.

"Rebe, I'm serious," Jamie scolded. "Don't you dare give Sam any ideas. I don't want the two of you dating."

"Why?" she'd asked.

"Because Sam is my best friend, and you my sister collect men as trophies, then toss them aside when you're done. Sam cannot be tossed aside, so hands off. Understand?"

"Hands off of Sam. I understand." She'd consented. But she'd wondered why Sam was making himself available if he too wanted her to keep her hands off of him. Why was he ignoring Jamie's edict not to start up anything with her. It was as if he didn't care what her brother thought. An involuntary groan came from Rebe and she wanted to stop remembering. .

Even now she could still picture the look on Sam's face when she'd told him she needed a man who would wow. Sam had swallowed not saying a word. She'd felt badly, but Sam had a way of making her feel vulnerable. He was always there when she needed him, always giving it to her straight. She realized she'd come to depend on him in more ways than one and she couldn't allow that to continue, or develop into more. Despite Jamie's warning there was something about Sam that Rebe didn't like. He reminded her too much of her brother, always watching out for her. He gave her a feeling of safety and she wasn't looking for safety.

Knowing she'd hurt Sam's feelings she's rushed to explain. "I'm thinking of asking this lawyer at my firm. His name's Chase and he looks like the heroes I write about. I'm sorry, Sam, but all of the authors bring these model type guys."

"Of course they do," he'd said. "It's perfect. Superficial people seeking out other superficial people."

With that remark he'd given a bitter chuckle and left the apartment. Despite Kandi and Jamie trying to tell her to go and apologize, she hadn't, she couldn't. It was too late, the damage had been done. She'd ticked him off and he was angry. It was better to allow things to cool down. Besides, she'd invited Chase to go with her. And she'd done her best to ignore the hurt she sensed in Sam.

"Rebe, what's going on? You're too quiet, and nothing good happens when you're quiet," Chase asked bringing her out of her reverie.

A lump rose in her throat. She'd known she should have never begun comparing Chase and Sam, never thought about how she'd gotten together with Chase in the first place. Like Chase had said, no good would come from that.

Looking across the room at Chase, Rebe winced. She'd never told Sam, 'thank you' for all he'd done for her. For being her rock when her brother died. For giving her refuge. The thing of it was she really liked him, in actuality she more than liked Sam.

But there was one huge problem with Sam that had not died with her brother. Sam still made her vulnerable. He'd torn down her walls and wouldn't accept pretense from her. He made her raw and she didn't like it. She'd been reduced to nothing the two weeks she'd lain in his arms, in his bed. She'd not wanted another living soul to see her in that condition, not her parents and not her lifelong best friend.

Sam was her safety net and that frightened her. A perfect 360 was what she'd chosen to do with him when she'd left his bed. She'd decided in order to be around him, she had no choice but to become what he was always calling her. Shallow.

A shallow woman didn't have to worry about doing the right thing. She didn't have to worry about hurting the feelings of the people who meant the most to her. A shallow woman didn't have to become close enough to anyone to allow herself to become vulnerable. Sam frightened Rebe. Her reactions to him frightened her more.

As for Chase, he didn't make her feel safe and secure. And he definitely didn't make her feel vulnerable. He made her scream out in pleasure. He made her angry. But vulnerable, raw, those weren't the emotions Chase brought out in her. Would she ever lie in his bed, in his arms, and cry. And not have sex? No way. But Chase was a good fit for the life she'd chosen.

Rebe took in a deep breath and released it. Then she turned her full attention to Chase. "We're good. I was just thinking about things that will never happen."

"And you forgive me."

"I don't know if forgive is the right word, Chase. I accept you." And having said that Rebe moved into his arms and plastered her lips against his.

The more sun that streamed through the windows of his apartment, the better Sam was feeling. He didn't want to think his feelings had anything to do with Rebe, but he'd been unable to stop thinking of her. He'd had a perpetual hard on since he'd trailed her home. As crazy as it was he'd dreamt of her, and the dream had been very explicit. They'd done a lot more than share kisses and touches.

As he thought of her taste and her teasing, Sam couldn't help but smile. As he'd drunk his morning coffee he'd continued to think of her, wondering why on earth he'd agreed to go with her last night. Then he thought of the remark she'd made about him being a frog prince and he laughed out loud.

There were so many things he didn't like about Rebe. Heaven knows she had more than enough faults. So why hadn't he just told her to go to hell? Going to the window, he looked out. He remembered that besides the fragments of her that he'd seen so often through the past two years, there was a different Rebe, the one who showed her kindness and vulnerable side. He'd witnessed many acts of kindness from her. But those acts hadn't provoked him to say yes when every atom in his body was screaming, 'NO'.

It was Rebe. Sam remembered when their little group had been unbreakable. It was the Rebe he'd seen when her brother died shortly after being involved in a tragic accident. Sam had held Rebe in his arms as she'd sobbed. It was the only time he'd seen her broken.

After the funeral she'd taken a leave of absent from work and from her life, asking him if she could stay with him for a little while. She'd not wanted to be with her parents, or with her best friend, Kandi who lived across the hall. Rebe wanted him.

When he'd taken his pillow to move to the couch she had looked at him, her brown eyes bright with tears and said, "Please don't leave me, Sam. Lie down with me." If she'd worn one of her many colored contacts perhaps he wouldn't have been so moved, but she hadn't and he'd imagined he could see straight through to her soul. She needed him and there was no way in hell he wouldn't be there for her. So he hadn't questioned her when she'd asked him to sleep beside her. He'd merely stared at her, then her voice whispered to him soft, and pain filled.

"I need you, Sam. Please lie down in the bed next to me."

And that was what he'd done. He could have offered her Jamie's bedroom. Or he could have slept in the room. But neither one of them had wanted to do that. For two weeks Rebe had lain in his bed, in his arms, and grieved. And when the two weeks were over, she'd gotten up from his bed and told him she was ready to return to her life. She hadn't spoken another word, not a thank you, not a hug. Nothing. Just her getting up and leaving him with an ache in his heart.

When Rebe left, the temperature of the room changed. She'd stolen the warmth from the room, and from him. He worried about her, and each time he'd called to ask if she was okay, her answers became colder. When he'd see her, she'd look through him as though he didn't exist, as though they weren't friends, had never been friends. And then the day came when she'd turned into the woman he couldn't tolerate being around. It felt good knowing a tiny spark of his old friend still remained.

A sudden urge to actually talk with Kandi about Rebe came over Sam. She'd been bugging him since early this morning, but he'd told her to go away. Now he went across the hall and pounded on her door, when she answered he grinned. "Are you busy?" Sam asked.

"What do you have in mind?"

"I thought we could grab a bite and talk."

"About last night?"

"Yes." Sam grinned and waited for Kandi to throw on a coat. And just like that the two of them walked the block and a half to their favorite neighborhood restaurant. A few moments after they'd been seated and had given their order they were reminiscing over Sam's details of the party. He'd had fun and admitted it.

"Sam, are you catching feelings for Rebe?"

"No, of course not. The idea of the two of us …I'd strangle her within a week. But I am glad I went. She promised to take care of legal work for me." He started to tell Kandi, Rebe had also promised him a date, but kept quiet on the subject. "I am glad that she's finally dumped Chase. I hope this time it's for good. She deserves so much better."

"I think she knows that. Did you really have a good time?"

For a moment Sam stared at Kandi. Ignoring her question he allowed his gaze to move over the restaurant décor thinking they could use a few of his paintings to liven the place up.

"You're avoiding the question."

His hands were moving and his face was doing strange things. Sam could only image that he had a goofy look on his face. He found to his amazement he had to work his throat muscles in order to answer.

"It's been a long time since Rebe and I have had fun. It made me remember the good times the four of us shared. I didn't know until last night how much I've missed those times."

"I've missed them too. Rebe hasn't been the same since Jamie died. I don't know if she ever will."

"I know. That's one of the reasons I haven't cut her out of my life completely."

"Right. You still didn't say if you had fun last night. Did you?"

"I did. She called me a frog prince. But she was teasing, I think," he laughed. "And I was teasing her. At the beginning of the evening we took several snipes at each other. But as the evening progressed we were bantering and saying things that made the other laugh, nothing mean. I'm glad I went with her. I think there might be hope for her."

No sooner had the words left Sam's mouth; he was wishing he could take them back. He lifted his eyes and swallowed as he stared at the couple coming toward them. Something happened to him deep inside, a remembrance, a ping that summoned up sadness. For a moment he thought he was mistaken, but there was no way in the world he'd ever not know Rebe.

He glanced once more around the restaurant hoping that he'd been thrown off with his critique and his talking with Kandi about Rebe. Perhaps he'd interwoven the two. A sigh escaped him bringing the pain he was feeling to the surface. His mouth opened but he found himself once again unable to speak. He was going to make a snide comment to Kandi, to show her that he didn't care that just after a few hours of being with him; Rebe was right back with Chase. But he suddenly found himself unable to say a single thing, nothing, not one dratted word.

"What's wrong, Sam?"

When Sam refused to answer Kandi glanced behind her to see what had affected Sam to the point where he could only stare at her. She couldn't prevent the long groan that escaped. Rebe with Chase. She should have known. She said a quick prayer that the couple would not see them, not move toward them, but knew it wasn't going to happen.

Kandi watched as Chase slid his arm around Rebe and looked down into her face. They both laughed as though he'd told her the funniest joke in the world. When Rebe looked away for a moment her gaze landed on Kandi before blinking. She saw her friend pause when she glanced at Sam. Kandi groaned again and wondered why Rebe had chosen this particular restaurant. Why hadn't she gone someplace else? It wasn't as though she didn't know that she and Sam frequented the place. They all had back when they'd been the merry foursome.

For a moment it felt as though they were in some kind of alternate reality. Rebe was staring at them and Sam was too quiet, staring at Rebe. Kandi didn't want to but she had to ask him. "Sam, are you okay?"

"Of course I am."

"We can leave before they decide to join us?"

Sam glared at Kandi as he tried in vain to tear his eyes from Rebe. Since he couldn't he closed them and began a mental count.

"Sam, seriously, we don't have to stay."

In order to glare at Kandi he had to open his eyes, so he did. But he refused to answer her ridiculous question. What the hell? He wasn't leaving. There was nothing between him and Rebe. So why did he find himself biting his lips as Rebe made her way toward them? For a moment she looked almost apologetic, and then he noticed some kind of a change come over her, something in her eyes that said a transformation had been made, from caring friend to ditz. *Damn*

"Hi guys, do you mind if we join you?" Rebe asked with a half-smile.

Did they mind? Her? Maybe not so much. Chase— yes, they minded. Sam couldn't sit there with his eyes closed in order not to look at Rebe and Chase, so he took a drink of his water and refused to answer, to meet Rebe's gaze. He noticed Kandi had also not answered.

But did that prevent Rebe and Chase from sitting with them? Of course not. Why would they care if their mere presence bothered anyone? They were shallow, beautiful people, who thought nothing of another's feelings. To top it off, Chase was watching him with a stupid smirk on his face, alerting Sam to the fact that as always the man would say something so asinine that Sam would want to leave or deck him. Too bad he was a mature adult, and couldn't just go around decking the men Rebe wanted to date.

"Hey, Sam. How's it going? Rebe told me you went with her to her little shindig last night. I know that's so not your scene. If she hadn't been so darn stubborn, you wouldn't have had to go through that. I wanted to take her. In fact I begged to take her. I even called Kandi to plead my case. I owe you one. Thank you for looking out for my girl."

Should he have been surprised? The answer in his head was a resounding no. But hey, who could help the way their thoughts went. "Your girl? I thought the two of you had broken up."

"We had. But Rebe can't stay angry with me."

"Perhaps she should try harder," Sam said through gritted teeth. "Did you make up after she returned from the dance?"

Sam wanted to stop questioning Chase, but since he didn't mind answering the questions, Sam was going to get the truth. He didn't think Rebe was capable of giving it.

"I called her. What am I saying? I've been calling her constantly for the past week, cell, landline, she's been refusing to answer. I've even gone to her apartment several times and banged on her door. She wouldn't answer. And you would think working in the same office she'd have no choice but to talk to me right? Wrong. She wouldn't talk to me at work. It was downright embarrassing. Rebe can be cold when she wants."

"Tell me about it."

"Excuse me?"

Sam sighed. "Okay, so if she hasn't been talking to you, how did you end up here with her now?"

"She answered the phone without checking the caller ID. She said she thought it was you calling. Then she told me you'd taken her to the event. After a few nasty comments on her part and a thousand more apologies from me, she agreed to accept my help on this case we're working on. There's a ton of research and Rebe is no fool. Two lawyers working on this is a lot easier than her doing the research alone. So we made plans for this morning. I went over, we worked."

Chase gave a smirk that had Sam wanting to deck him. His look was meant to indicate they'd done a whole lot more. That was total disrespect. How in the world Rebe put up with the guy was a mystery. "If you had so much work to do, why are you here?" Sam tapped on the table with the tines of his fork, knowing his voice sounded sharp and angry.

"We finished. I told you, the two of us doing the research for the case we're on made the work go a lot faster."

"I meant, why are you here, in this particular restaurant, in my neighborhood? There are plenty of restaurants by Rebe. Why didn't you go there?"

"Are you upset about something, Sam? I knew you lived near here and I wanted to talk to you about an idea I had, something that I think you might be interested in."

While Chase's words hung in the air, Sam had a horrible thought. "Were you planning on coming to my apartment?"

With a smile Chase answered. "Yes, I wanted to see your face when I told you of my idea. I also wanted to thank you for standing in for me, for taking Rebe to the dance. It's a very important event for her."

"You don't owe me any thanks. I didn't do it for you."

"Of course I owe you my thanks. I'll bet you couldn't wait to get out of there."

"You'd bet wrong."

"Really. Then I guess the women kept you so busy that you didn't have to even dance with Rebe. I know how she annoys the hell out of you."

Count to three, don't go off on him, Sam thought. "Chase, how would you know that Rebe annoys me? Do you know that you annoy me even more?" Sam glared at Chase angered because Chase didn't even have the decency to be insulted. He just laughed and continued his spiel.

"Seriously, Sam, I know firsthand how crazy those women can get. I'll bet you were thanking God for them keeping you from Rebe."

Was Chase really serious? Sam brought his eyes upward and glanced in Rebe's direction, holding her gaze for a long moment. What the heck was Rebe doing with Chase?

"Listen, I'm not sure what your experience was, but I thought the women were great." Sam stopped for a moment, glared at Chase and shook his head at Rebe before he continued. "As for Rebe, I went as her date. Why on earth would I even think of ditching her? I enjoyed her company. She's a beautiful woman who has a wicked sense of humor and intelligent conversation."

Chase glanced at Rebe and smiled at her. Sam followed suit, but glared. Shaking his head he firmly closed his eyes and took in several hard breaths. He wanted to rescue Rebe and deck Chase. When he opened his eyes the first thing he noticed was the pleading gaze Rebe was fixing on him. He wanted to ignore her pleas. Rebe deserved to be respected by the man who accompanied her. He found himself unable to not voice his opinion.

"Rebe deserves so much more than she's received from her boyfriends."

"Whatever," Chase said waving away the innuendo, not caring that Sam was talking about him not respecting Rebe. "Our relationship is not one-way. As I said, Rebe and I have been working all morning on one of her cases that she needed my help with. It's a lucky thing for her that she's dating one of the partners."

The plea in Rebe's eyes deepened but Sam decided to ignore it. What the heck? Where was his Rebe? Why was she pretending to be this mindless robot? Didn't she even mind that Chase was being disrespectful to her in front of her friends? Hell, he did.

Sam brought his attention back to Chase. "So, did your family buy that partnership for you, Chase?" Sam asked, not even wishing he could take back the words. But Chase's answer did surprise him

"Of course they did. I'd have to work my ass off for years to earn it. They fast tracked it for me."

A kick to his shin from Kandi stopped Sam from saying the obvious, Chase hadn't earned the partnership. Why bother? Chase didn't care and apparently neither did Rebe. Sam took a slow sip of his water trying to calm the burn inside his chest, wanting to leave, but not wanting to give Chase the satisfaction, and not wanting Rebe to think he'd thought last night was anything but him doing her a favor. Finally he turned his attention to Rebe.

"What did Chase use this time to get you back? Was it another blimp? Or was it jewelry?"

"Rebe's going to be second chair on this high profile case I'm trying, the one she was doing the research for," Chase offered. "I had to think of something really big this time. She's giving the opening and closing remarks. Can you believe she even made me sign a contract?"

"Of course I can believe she'd make you sign a contract. You aren't exactly known for keeping your word about things. The only thing that puzzles me is how easily you were able to negotiate a price." Sam's gaze swung from Chase to Rebe

"A price? What kind of person do you think I am, Sam?" Rebe asked angrily.

"As the saying goes, what kind of person you are has already been established. It appears Chase had to only negotiate on the right price."

The look on Rebe's face made Sam cringe. He shouldn't have spoken to her like that, no matter what Chase had said or what offer of his she'd accepted. It was her life. He watched as the tears formed in her eyes. With everything in him, Sam wanted to tell her how sorry he was for saying the things he had, but he was fighting against it. Rebe deserved so much more than what she was settling for.

Taking another sip of water Sam was aware what was fueling his frustration. One night of being in Rebe's company had made him forget that she'd changed in the past two years from being his friend to being involved with Chase. With a sigh he acknowledged what was at the root of his irritation and decided to deal with it head on. He'd forget about the kisses he'd shared with Rebe, the softness of her skin, his perpetual hard on which as he thought of it had been sent scurrying into submission.

Who the hell could maintain even a semi-erection when Chase

was around spouting such nonsense? The only thing Sam had now was a headache. If he didn't leave soon, he couldn't be held accountable for what he might do.

When thirty minutes later Chase was still talking about the case he was working on with Rebe, Sam had had enough. Standing, he took out several bills and handed them to Kandi. "I'll see you back at the apartment."

He'd decided not to give any lame ass excuse that he had something to do, though he did. The urge to puke wasn't imagined. When Chase stood Sam made his getaway before he'd have to be even ruder, and refuse to shake hands. The only good thing that came out of this was that he and Kandi lived within walking distance of the restaurant or he would have felt guilty leaving her. He shrugged. Okay, so he wouldn't have left. He would have stayed and listened to Chase ramble on.

"Sam, hold on. I forgot to tell you something. I have an idea you might be interested in," Chase called after him.

Like he'd ever be interested in any idea Chase had. Sam kept walking toward the door and took in several good breaths of the crisp air, sighing as he walked back to his apartment. The image of kissing Rebe refused to go away. Damn it all to hell.

Chase turned from where he'd been yelling at Sam to face Kandi and Rebe. "Darn, I should have told him sooner. Kandi, give Sam back his money when you see him. I'll take care of lunch." Chase smiled.

Rebe had been mentally absent for the past uncomfortable half hour or so that they'd joined Sam and Kandi. She was secretly glad Sam had finally left. The look he'd given her made her cringe. And his comment that she could be bought for the right price rankled her more than she wanted it to. She was feeling guilty, as though she'd made him a promise the night before. Had she? She didn't think so. She'd said she wasn't taking Chase back no matter what he dangled before her face, but an opportunity to open and close on a big case. She'd be crazy to turn that down. Right? She glanced up then down quickly. Kandi was staring at her with a smirk on her face when she looked at Rebe.

Rebe was aware of what Kandi was thinking of her and of Chase. *Please don't make a big deal out of Chase's buying lunch,* she wanted to say, but didn't, not with words anyway. She did it with her eyes and by biting her lips, hoping Kandi would take the hint and just accept the lunch. Besides, what was the big deal? Chase wasn't a bad guy and he wasn't all bad. He was trying to be nice. He wanted to treat, and he had the money. What was so bad about that?

Yet, Kandi was shaking her head as though Rebe had betrayed not only her, but Sam. it wasn't as though she'd been on a real date with Sam. It was no one's business if she'd decided to take Chase back. Her friend shook her head and turned toward Chase alerting Rebe to the fact that Kandi was not going to just allow Chase to treat.

"No thanks, Chase. Sam was treating me," Kandi insisted. She held out the bills Sam had given her for Chase's inspection.

"Kandi, he wants to treat both of you. Please, just allow him to do this. It's no big deal," Rebe insisted.

"Sam wanted to treat me. It would be rude of me to…"

Just let him do this, Rebe tried to convey to Kandi, again without words.

"Kandi," Chase interrupted. "I owe Sam. I want to do this for him for taking Rebe to her event. Seriously. He doesn't have to pay and neither do you. I support the arts, and a starving artist like Sam needs all the help he can get."

Now this time even Rebe groaned. "Chase, stop."

"You two are making me forget my surprise for Sam. I would have told him myself if he hadn't rushed out of here. I have the perfect way to repay him. The firm wants a mural done of all the partners. Why don't you ask Sam if he wants the job?"

"He's probably busy," Rebe interjected.

"Please, it's obvious the guy can use the money. Hell, no artist makes it big until they die." Chase laughed. "Then it's too late to enjoy it. Just tell him about the job, Kandi, and tell him, he doesn't have to thank me. I already know he'll appreciate it."

Rebe groaned out loud and rolled her eyes. "I'm sorry," she said to Kandi. "Chase is actually trying to be nice in his own way." When Kandi stood to leave Rebe had also had enough. There were now two people besides her that were wondering what in the world she was doing with Chase. Her friends, people she cared about, loved, she didn't want them thinking she was crazy for dating Chase.

She knew very well what she was doing with him and it had nothing to do with his being a partner, well almost nothing. Besides, if they'd not already been dating when he'd made, or rather bought into the partnership, their relationship wouldn't have been allowed. But he'd negotiated her into their contract.

Rebe grimaced, not really liking that she'd been bargained over, not liking the connotation, but deciding to choose to think that Chase cared enough for her that he didn't want them to have to hide the fact that they were dating.

There was no denying some people at the office thought of both of them as arm candy for the other. Neither of them had done a thing to dispel the talk. Neither of them had cared enough about the opinions of others. But Rebe cared what Kandi thought of her. As for Sam, his opinion of her had always mattered more than she'd ever wanted to admit.

CHAPTER FIVE

"I'll take the job." Sam laughed at the indignant look on Kandi's face.

"Why on earth would you take the job? You can't stand Chase. My God, his arrogance knows no bounds. By the way, he paid for lunch. Here's your money."

For a moment Sam stared at the bills in Kandi's outstretched hand before accepting them. "That was very generous of Chase."

"Listen, I know you have something you're planning on doing to Chase. Let me in on it."

"Why in the world would you think I'd have a devious plan? That was what you were thinking. Admit it."

"Yes, that was exactly what I was thinking." Walking around Sam's cluttered apartment Kandi stopped in front of a canvas he was working on. "Are you doing another painting of Rebe?"

"Why would you think that? There's not even the hint of a person on the canvas."

"There are certain colors you use when you're angry, hurt or disappointed; the same as there are different colors you use when you're happy." She waved her hand at the canvas. Only Rebe has brought out those colors from your brushes and only when you're truly upset with her. That's why I know you have a plan to teach her and Chase a lesson by accepting his offer to paint his office mural."

"You know an awfully lot about me."

"You're my friend. And besides that, I'm very observant."

"Did you happen to observe that Rebe wouldn't step foot into my apartment last night? She hasn't crossed the threshold since the moment she…well, went back to work." He stared at Kandi grateful that the words at the tip of his tongue had not come out. He didn't want Kandi to know he'd taken it personally, or that he felt as though Rebe had left him. Those feeling he would keep buried.

"I noticed.'

"Why do you believe I have a devious plan?"

"Because you took the job knowing Chase will now believe you're in his debt."

"I actually don't care about that. Speaking of owing someone, remember I told you Rebe's promise. I think it's time to see if she meant it."

"One day, and you're calling in your marker?"

"Yes, longer than that and Rebe might just renege. I think I'll have her write up a contract to protect me from any partner that doesn't like the way I portray them. You know, I want artistic license."

"You're going to make Chase look awful."

"Probably."

Sam laughed aware that wasn't the only reason he'd taken the job. He wanted to get a better look into Rebe at her work environment see which persona she used. If there was really nothing worth saving about her, he'd give up and leave her to her own devises. But he wasn't ready to do that until he knew for sure. He laughed again. This should be fun.

After receiving calls from both Sam and Kandi, Rebe had decided it was best to go and see them and clean up the mess Chase had made. Besides she was having dinner with Chase later. It had taken some convincing to get him not to accompany her. For some strange reason it didn't bother him that Kandi and Sam hated him. He found it amusing. She didn't. Allowing him to accompany her would be like lighting the powder keg. Since she didn't like running, she doubted she'd have time to duck for cover when the dynamite was ignited. So she'd bribed Chase with the possibility of them returning to their previous physical relationship in return for him waiting for her at her apartment. She had to see what was up with her friends.

Within a few minutes after being briefed by Kandi that Sam was going to take Chase up on his offer to paint the mural for the law firm, Rebe sat flabbergasted, stunned temporarily into silence.

"What is he up to?" Rebe frowned considering it. She'd not for one moment believed Sam would accept Chase's offer. If there was one person in the world Sam thought was more shallow than her, or one person who he absolutely couldn't stand, it was Chase. He was Sam's nemesis if ever there was one. And the laughter in Kandi's eyes as she talked about Sam's interest in the project just made her know it wasn't what it was supposed to be. Something about the whole thing stunk.

"What's he planning on doing?" she continued to question Kandi hoping she'd give up the info. But she wouldn't, not even the promise of the diamond earrings she'd been drooling over. Nothing worked.

"He'll be here in about an hour. He's working on a painting, but said he'd take a break and come over and talk to you. Rebe, I was wondering why we're not having this conversation in Sam's apartment."

"There's no reason."

"Of course there is. Is it because it was also Jamie's apartment? Or is there another reason that only involves Sam? You didn't have a problem with it being your brother's apartment when you barricaded yourself in there with Sam for two weeks. But since you left his apartment things have never been the same. Are you ever going to tell me what you and Sam did in there all alone for two weeks?"

"Let it go."

"But we're friends. Heck we're best friends."

"I know that. Listen, I'm going to call Sam and see if I can hurry him along." Rebe took out her phone and punched in Sam's number hoping her diversion would prevent her friend from further prying. She saw a veil of hurt cross Kandi's eyes, but it couldn't be helped. Rebe wasn't ready to talk about those two weeks she'd lived with Sam.

"Sam. Can't you drop whatever it is you're doing and come on over?" Rebe kept her fingers crossed hoping for once Sam wouldn't become combative.

"Be patient, Rebe. I'm working. As soon as I can take a break I'll be there."

When he clicked the phone off there was nothing to be done but sit and wait. When Sam finally came over with paint on his hands having not even bothered to clean up, Rebe groaned inwardly and gave him a look. And he gave her a grin and held his hands out to her.

"I'm an artist, Rebe. I could care less about anyone knowing what I do for a living."

"Are you earning a living with your paintings?"

"You know, Rebe, I'm not sure if what you just asked is rude or not. Sometimes, I think you just don't think before you speak. Yes, I make my living painting, either on the easels, or the house painting I do. I've very good at my job."

"I didn't mean anything by it. Do you think we can possibly call a truce? I thought we were headed in that direction. If you're going to take that job at my firm, I think it will work better if you don't make a habit of snapping at me."

"And?"

"And what do you have in mind for Chase? What are you planning on doing to him?"

"I plan to paint his portrait in oil, same as I will all the other partners."

"You don't plan to do anything weird?"

"That depends on what you mean by weird. Do you ever write anything that I would consider weird?" Sam cocked his head to the side. "Has the pretty heroine in one of your novels ever had a happy ever after with the frog prince?"

"Nope, never," Rebe answered softly. When Sam looked as though he was going to say more she turned away. They would do better at snapping than getting serious.

"By the way. I wanted to collect on one of those favors you promised me." Sam waited until Rebe turned back to face him. "I can tell by the look on your face, you're wondering which one, right? I need your legal expertise. I want you to draw up an iron clad contract for the mural. I don't want to be harassed by your firm if they don't find everything to their liking. And I want to be paid three fourths of my money before I start the painting. I want the balance to be given to you, at the same time I receive my funds. You will relinquish the balance to me on the day I unveil the mural."

"Why are you putting so many strings on how you're paid?"

"I've heard lawyers are notorious for paying their bills."

"Sam, you should be grateful Chase recommended you for the job. You're behaving as though you're in great demand. What gives? Are you afraid to take the job? Afraid it might be too much for you to handle. Are you worried that Chase will have the last laugh?"

Sam pursed his lips and smiled at Rebe. She deserved to be taught a lesson about judging people, and on her assumptions. She'd judged him harshly without anything to back up her reasoning. He wondered if she'd keep her promise.'

"You promised if I needed legal help you'd be there for me, no questions asked. Am I now your client?"

"Are you going to make me regret this?"

"Only if you renege."

"I need to get some help on the contract, okay. If you want it iron clad I think it would be best for me to bring in someone with a bit more experience. And don't worry, since this is part of the favor I promised you, I'll pay the cost for the assist."

"You don't have to do that."

"I'm aware of that. I could probably get it done for free, but I think I'll negotiate a cash price." Rebe gave Sam a look waiting for him to take back the comment he'd made about her and Chase. He didn't.

"Don't ask Chase, anyone else, but him." Sam stared at Rebe aware of the remark that hung between them. She would have to prove to him that what he'd said wasn't true.

"Believe me, I had no plans on it. In fact I'm going to get someone from a different firm. Which make me wonder why you didn't get a different attorney."

"Lawyers cost money. You're free. At least for this transaction."

Rebe's mouth opened in a gasp "Sam, that wasn't necessary"

"You're right it wasn't. I shouldn't have said that."

"That's not the same as saying you're sorry."

"Rebe, do you have any idea why I say the things to you that I do?"

"Some."

"Tell your boyfriend I'll agree to paint the mural, and I'll be there to talk over details next week."

"Sam, you didn't give me an amount to negotiate."

"Oh that. There will be no negotiations. This is my price." He gave a slip of paper with the figure on it to Rebe and waited for her mouth to open and for her to give him a look of incredulity.

"Sam, you're crazy. The firm is not going to pay you this much, nowhere near this. You're an unknown. Come on, get real, and be grateful for a paying job."

"Just worry about the contract." He then handed her another sheet of paper with his personal clauses. "Those are also not negotiable. Do you think you can have the contract ready by next week when I go in to meet with the senior partners?"

"That's not how this is generally done. Most people don't meet the senior partners."

"I'm not most people."

"Sam, please."

"I know what I'm doing?"

"Please don't allow your dislike of Chase to cost you what can turn out to be your big break."

"Are you worried about me?"

"You're my friend."

"Am I?'

"You used to be. I'd love nothing better than for us to recapture what we've lost.

With a long and exaggerated sigh Sam stared at Rebe until she dropped her gaze. He'd also like nothing better than to return to where they'd been before her brother died.

"Okay, Sam. I made you a promise and I intend to keep it. I am your lawyer and I will do everything in my power to make sure the contract is exactly what you want. I'll let the partners know you want to meet with them and I'll arrange an appointment." She smiled then stuck out her hand to Sam. "Congratulations."

With all the intuitiveness she possessed Rebe was fully aware that the last person that should have been painting the office mural was Sam. And the very last person who should have offered him the job was Chase. She wanted to warn Chase that perhaps he should make nice with Sam. Then again, in a perverse way she wanted to see exactly what it was Sam had in mind to do.

CHAPTER SIX

The flurry of activity at the firm had been crazy for the past three weeks. There was no other way to describe it. Sam has swooped in with his sketch pads and taken over. He'd insisted on unlimited access to each of the partners, during important meetings, while they wined and dine the big wigs, even during meetings with clients. There was no way Rebe had thought the partners would agree to that. Of course the meetings Sam attended were with the clients' permission.

Another unexpected perk that had been agreed to was that Sam would accompany whichever lawyer he chose out to sociable events, including lunches and dinners. And he would be given carte blanche for himself and a dining companion.

Suffice it to say, Rebe had been Sam's dining companion. For three weeks they'd both eaten on the company's dime. Sam had also insisted on having a table in close proximity to the partner he was tailing, in order to better observe them. He'd even managed to wangle concert tickets and an excursion on one of the gambling boats in Illinois. Even for those he'd insisted on being allowed to take a date. Her. Chase of course had been semi-livid because he'd not been invited to either event by the senior partners.

To Rebe's surprise Sam was taking the job seriously, using a small notepad to jot down drawings, of a hand reaching for the check, or a glass of wine, a genuine smile, a handshake. He'd made a believer out of her. She almost believed he deserved the over inflated sum she'd gotten for him to do the mural. She'd expected the partners to want to haggle on the price, but not Sam. And he'd been right. Instead of haggling, the partners seemed honored that he was willing to do the mural, as though he was a famous artist known by them. When she'd mentioned it to Sam he'd given her a quizzical look and said, "I guess they don't see all of my warts. " It didn't look as though he had any plans to let her frog prince remark go.

With most of the things Sam had demanded Rebe had merely laughed them off, pleased to have been on the receiving end of being his date and having the company pay for it. That is she hadn't minded as long as they were tailing the senior partners. She'd forgotten he could intrude on any of the partners. With his focus firmly fixated now on Chase it was a bit uncomfortable. Rebe wondered how Sam was even aware of the business meeting they had with a client. Somehow he had a spy in the office feeding him info on the partners' appointments.

She was more than a little annoyed because at the moment while she was preparing for her date with Chase, Sam had taken things a bit too far. He was more than being intrusive, he was downright attempting to sabotage the evening with Chase. Perhaps she should have warned Sam to be at his best behavior. It wasn't just a date with Chase, or just a dinner. It was an important business meeting.

Chase was trying to woo a new client for the firm and she was to play his arm candy with a legal brain. Sam had insisted he come to her apartment and watch her dress for dinner. Never before had she worried so much about the way she would dress. There was one rule: Dress to impress. Tasteful and elegant, but there always had to be understated sex appeal that worked to her advantage, pouty lips made even more so with fire engine red lipstick, a tiny bit of expensive perfume, or a skirt with a discreet slit that would ride up just the right amount when she was seated. Sam was watching as she dressed, insisting it would help him capture Chase's inner spirit with a better understanding since she was his woman. The way he said the words rankled her, made her feel dirty. Chase had only laughed at her, telling her that she should play along if it would help Sam paint a better picture of him.

So here they were, Chase critiquing her looks and making suggestion, wanting more sex appeal and Sam frowning and writing notes.

"Chase, how far do you expect Rebe to go with these would be clients of yours?" Sam had lowered his notebook and was staring at Chase.

Rebe's head snapped around and she glared at Sam, but still she waited for Chase's answer.

Turning from studying Rebe to glare at Sam, Chase asked, "What are you suggesting, Sam?

"I mean it looks like you're her pimp and you're getting her ready to make a sale. Why do you even need Rebe along? She's a lawyer same as you."

"And that's why I need her. She's a lawyer. Besides that, she's bright, beautiful, and female. The men I'm courting like to look at

beautiful women while they eat. They like to imagine they have a
chance with her, even if they don't."

"You could hire a hooker. Or you could take one of the other
women from the office that you're always flirting with."

Rebe's face flamed and she glared at Sam. But if she'd expected
Chase to say something that would make either of them look better
she was wrong. The instant Chase opened his mouth she was aware
he would make matters worse.

"Did you not hear me say I need a lawyer? And guess what, Sam?
I'm a partner. Rebe wants to make partner one day, and with my help
she will. We have a very good arrangement, it's not one sided. If
there's a male client who's a bit too aggressive I always put him in his
place. Or if he bats for the other team then I'm there for her. If the
client we're trying to woo happens to be female, then I'm the one
trying to look sexy. We look out for each other."

"Could either of you possibly be more…?"

"Brilliant?" Chase suggested.

"Conniving, deceitful, egoistical, shallow, and arrogant. That's the
list I'm going for, but keep deluding yourself. You two really are
Barbie and Ken aren't you?"

"Well yes, but we're Barbie and Ken with law degrees."

Glaring at both Sam and Chase, Rebe closed her eyes and
groaned. *Kill me now; please someone put me out of my misery.* Did Chase
miss the part that Sam was insulting them? That he thought they
were pandering? She took a tissue and swiped away some of the
bright red lipstick.

"No babe. Don't listen to Sam. What does he know about what a
man of power wants, or what looks good on a beautiful woman? I
would like to see his choice of a date."

"You've seen her," Sam tossed back. "Just imagine Rebe without
all of the war paint, the glitz and glamour and the willingness to be a
man's arm candy." He watched as Chase picked up the lipstick tube
and handed it to Rebe to reapply.

Staring for a long moment at Rebe as she held the lipstick
between her fingers Sam sighed. "Look you two; I think I'll take my
own car. I'll meet you at the restaurant."

Rebe waited until she was sure Sam had left, in fact she glanced
out the window to be sure, and when she saw him getting into his
SUV she turned toward Chase. Tilting her head she stared up at him

and waited for him to say something that would make her feel better about the two of them and their insane relationship.

"What has gotten into Sam?" Chase began his rant. "You'd think he'd be more grateful to me for getting him this job, but he's being awfully critical of me. If the other partners hadn't told me that his method works and speaks so highly of him, I would have gotten him fired. How the hell they even know him is a mystery."

"You can't get Sam fired, not without paying him in full. It's in his contract. Besides you're right, all of the senior partners love him."

"He's a strange man, more than a little weird. He's always saying things that I'm not sure if he's just being Sam, or if he's been serious. What the heck do you see in him anyway? I can't even believe you're friends."

When Rebe thought of Sam, she smiled. She appreciated his brutal honesty. Sam pushed her to be her best. He'd done that for the past five years and she'd never realized it until now. She could tell Chase without a doubt that Sam wasn't kidding with him.

"Are you going to answer me, Rebe?"

"Yeah, then I want you to answer a question for me. Sam is a great friend, loyal, protective and wanting the best for those he cares about."

"I take that to mean he now cares about you and that he doesn't think I'm the best for you. Since when did he care for you, since that stupid dance?"

"I think he's cared for me for a very long time."

"But he dislikes you almost as much as he dislikes me."

"Yeah, but I think he still has hope for me. You, not so much." Rebe chuckled then turned serious. "Chase, how far would you want me to go to help you reel in a client?" There was a strange gleam in Chase's eyes that made her wonder if he'd actually tell her.

"Don't listen to Sam. We're a team and we help each other out. There's nothing wrong with making the most of your assets, Rebe. You're a valuable asset." Chase paused, "And I'm an even more valuable asset to you. Now since I know where your pretty little mind is going, I'll answer the question. Do I want you to sleep with any of the clients to get more business for our firm? Hell no. I want you to myself."

To prove it Chase took Rebe in his arms and kissed her until he could feel her resistance melting. Then he righted her. "Do you think

I want anyone else tasting you? Do you think I'm that low? After dinner tonight I think maybe it's time we had a reminder of just how good we are together."

"I said no more sex." Rebe attempted to make her words have that no nonsense quality, but her voice was soft and wispy and without power. A shiver claimed her as Chase ran his fingers over her curves, the look in his eyes hungry and pleading. She wanted him and wasn't sure how long she'd continue to hold out.

"It's been too long, Rebe. How about we wait and see what happens?"

"Do you have condoms?" Rebe asked, "Just in case." Chase laughed and she reapplied her lipstick

Sam sat across from Kandi, scowling as he drew bold black lines in his sketch pad. His annoyance had risen from the moment Rebe walked into the restaurant with Chase. One look at her and he was able to tell she'd reapplied the lipstick she'd blotted off. It was such a little thing but the disappointment in her filled his chest and saddened him. He was trying to tell himself it was her life. He wanted to forgive her for failing herself, her brother and him. He wanted so much more for her. For the moment the only thing he could do was glare at her.

When the clients Rebe and Chase were meeting joined them, Sam watched intently from the table next to them. It annoyed him that Rebe was laughing prettily as though she were really enjoying herself. Cringing inwardly he knew he wanted it to not be true. He didn't want her to enjoy being with Chase, or cozying up to men for the sake of getting a client for her firm.

Toying with the appetizer on his plate Sam made an attempt at conversation with Kandi. He tried to keep his gaze from the table across from them, tried not to hear the conversation, the flirting, the suggestive innuendos. He didn't hear a single word that sounded like business. He was aware that he was watching them intently. He was also aware he was frowning. But when Kandi snapped her fingers beneath his nose he realized he'd been ignoring her.

"Sam, why don't you admit you have a thing for Rebe and perhaps later you can tell her?"

"I do not have a thing for her, so drop it. I'm here to sketch Chase."

"Sure you are. Why are you so angry? And why are you looking as though you'd like to kill someone?"

"I don't like the way that guy is looking at Rebe."

"You're not her boyfriend, Sam."

"I beg to differ. I'm a boy and I'm her friend."

"If you'd concentrate on talking to me you wouldn't have time to notice what's going on at Rebe's table."

Kandi's voice was so sharp that Sam was taken aback. Didn't she see what was happening at Rebe's table? Didn't she care? "Kandi, I'm sorry. I'm not trying to ignore you, but I can't help but to be worried about Rebe. Why is she laughing as though she's enjoying herself?"

"Maybe she is."

"She can't be. I'm going over there and put a stop to the way that guy is looking at her."

"Sam, don't you dare. Rebe is an adult. She told you this is just a business dinner, leave her alone. She doesn't need to be rescued."

Turning his eyes away from Rebe, Sam tried, he really did. But it was her laughter that drew him back. Irritation flared as he turned to see Rebe's potential client began to take even more liberties by allowing his eyes to roam all over Rebe's body. Sam wanted to leave the table and deck the man. Chase however was smiling. Rebe had a half-assed smile pasted on her lips. She was behaving like an android. He was right to have called her a Barbie, she was behaving like one.

Rebe's gaze met his and she wet her lips with her tongue. He noticed her shoulder sagged and she gave him another look, this time pleading with her eyes for him to behave. He wouldn't. He had no plans on sitting there while she was used as a closer in a business deal. One glance in Kandi's direction and he knew she was getting angry, and not with Chase or the men who were ogling her best friend. Or even with Rebe herself. No, she was getting angry with him, apparently the only person who had sense enough to see what was going on.

"Sam, for the last time, would you please stop glaring at Rebe? You knew she was going to be here with Chase. And you knew she was going to help him bring in a new client to the firm. You didn't tell me that you were going to try and ruin the evening for her. If you had, I wouldn't have come," Kandi scolded.

Sam had gotten himself so worked up that he was beyond listening to reason. He did what any man in….well, what any friend would do. He went to Rebe's rescue. He stood in front of her looking deeply into her eyes, then he held his hand out to her. He was surprised when she took it and stood.

Now what? he wondered. He was the frog prince in her mind. What was the frog prince supposed to do in these situations? She was waiting for him to speak. Chase and the clients were frowning at the interruption and Sam was standing there making everyone himself included, uncomfortable. He glanced at his own table and saw Kandi shaking her head at him using her finger to beckon him back to their table.

Not just yet. He'd not done what he came for. The princess needed to be rescued. The villain needed to know she had a knight willing to fight for her honor sitting just a few feet away. In that instant Sam knew exactly what he was going to do. He used the palm of his hand to cup Rebe's face and gently kissed her. When she squirmed his arms encircled her and he took the kiss to a new level, one filled with passion. When he broke off the kiss, he looked toward the client who'd been eyeing Rebe. And then he glared at Chase.

"I'll be sitting just over there if you need me." He glanced again toward the client. "I'm Sam," he said and moved away

Kandi laughed. "And you don't have feelings for Rebe?"

"Shut up," Sam growled low. "That was a huge mistake. I had no plans on kissing her, none whatsoever. I don't even know why I went over there. But I didn't like the way the guy was looking at her. And I definitely didn't like that all Chase was doing was smiling. Why in hell does she go along with this nonsense? Does she really want to make partner that way?"

"I didn't know Rebe wanted to make partner." Kandi glanced at the other table. "She never mentioned it to me and she tells me everything, well almost everything, because surely something happened between the two of you when you took her to her event."

"Chase said it, that Rebe wanted to make partner. Rebe didn't correct him." He'd decided not to mention anything that had happened between him and Rebe when he'd taken her to her event. "Rebe is not..."

"Not who you thought she was? Yes, she is. She just doesn't want to be the person you think she is. But she is that person, Sam. Don't give up on her."

Glaring toward the table next to them Sam wasn't surprised to see Chase giving him a, 'what the F' look with both arms opened wide. The client, same thing, without the open arms. And Rebe, she looked petrified, like a deer caught in the crosshairs. If he could have thought of a better clique he would have. That was the look Rebe was wearing and as far as he cared a clique was one because of a reason. *Damn*, he thought, he shouldn't have kissed her like that. But realization dawned. She'd kissed him back. He glanced at Kandi and broke out in a smile.

"The last thing I plan to do is give up on Rebe. I think she needs me in her life."

"And you?"

"This isn't about me."

"Right. You kissed Rebe the way every woman would want a man to kiss her, with such gentle passion. And it didn't mean anything to you? Sam, you're a terrible liar."

Sam sighed and gave up trying to convince Kandi that he was not interested in Rebe. "Rebe has way more imperfections than I'd like to deal with. I just don't want her to sell herself short. She needs to know she's so much more than arm candy."

He glanced again at Rebe's table. "She can't want to make partner so badly." The pretense was shattering. He was fuming, being bad company, but unable to prevent himself from glaring at the group of people seated across from them.

When Chase moved his chair to return Sam's scowl, Sam laughed and told Kandi to order the most expensive items on the menu. When the waitress returned to their table he ordered them a bottle of champagne and included full meals for both of them to take home. This would be a night he'd make sure he dined in style.

When Rebe looked down and didn't look back up Sam swallowed. He owed her an apology. Taking out his phone he texted her. When her gaze went to her small clutch purse that was in front of her on the table he could tell she knew it was him. He gave her a nod and what he hoped was a pleading look. His text simply said, 'I'm sorry.' He watched as her hand slipped inside the clutch and she viewed his message. Tears filled Rebe's eyes and she rushed from the table. When he rose to follow her, Kandi put her hand over his.

"You've done enough, my friend. Let me go after her."

Kandi ran into the bathroom two steps behind Rebe. She grabbed her friend before she could disappear into a stall. "Okay, Rebe, spill it. What the heck is going on with you and Sam? For the past two years you've been sniping at each other, ever since Jamie had his accident, and you stayed locked away in Sam's apartment for two weeks, not even allowing me to come over, not talking my calls. What did Sam do to you?"

With tears in her eyes Rebe came as close to telling her friend the truth as she'd planned. "All of this is my fault. I never thanked him for those two weeks. Sam was a good friend to me, and I shouldn't have treated him so shabbily. And no, we didn't make love. It was nothing like that. He allowed me to just be, to wallow in misery, to grieve my brother."

"And you're angry with him because of that?"

"I can't be what he wants. I don't want to be. I was totally raw with Sam, completely vulnerable. Losing Jamie was so hard. It still hurts. I...I...I." but she couldn't finish.

"And you never want to go through that again. You don't want to love anyone as much as you loved your brother and then lose them. Rebe, you're in love with Sam, aren't you? I knew it."

"Please, Kandi, don't say that to him. I can't be in love with him. I think it works better for us for him to think I'm totally superficial and shallow, to be so disgusted with me that he can barely stand to be in the room with me. It has to be like that. Promise me you won't say anything."

"Rebe, this is crazy. I'm sure Sam is in love with you too."

"Please. Let it be. Don't tell him. You're my friend, my lifelong, childhood, best friend. You can't tell him. Promise."

"Rebe, I promise but this is a promise I hate giving." Kandi gazed into Rebe's tear-filled eyes and when Rebe's head dropped to her shoulder and she shuddered in agony, Kandi knew it was wrong to not tell Sam. Rebe loved him. But she'd promised. Sam would have to break down Rebe's defense. Only the two of them would be able to work this out no matter what she wished for them.

Sam tried tapping his fingers on the table to release the pent up anger as he waited for Rebe and Kandi to return. The thing of it was he wasn't quite sure who he was most angry with. Rebe for being with Chase, himself for not haven't had the courage to tell her what had been in his heart for almost five years, or Chase for treating her the way he did, cheating on her and now the pandering. Instead of his anger leaving it had increased to a new level. The culprit was Chase. Sam absolutely refused to allow Chase to continue to use Rebe in the manner he was. He couldn't do anything about Rebe's bad taste, but he sure could make sure Chase learned to respect her. Without taking a moment to think it over Sam headed once again to the other table.

"Chase, I need to speak to you for a moment. Excuse us," he said to the clients and waited while Chase decided if he would get up. If he didn't Sam would forcefully help him up.

"Sure, Sam. I think it's time the two of us had a little talk," Chase said and rose from his seat to follow Sam.

When they'd walked away from the table Sam ignored the fact that Chase was getting ready to make a little speech and spoke instead.

"You will never ever treat Rebe like she's your dumb ass side kick, or your arm piece. Not ever again. Do you hear me? You will not be pimping her out."

For a couple of seconds Chase could only stare at Sam in a dumbfounded manner. *What the heck was going on,* he wondered.

"This is a business meeting. Are you crazy? We both told you before we left Rebe's apartment that this is how it goes. Get your mind out of the gutter, Sam. The only thing we've been discussing is business."

"I know what I saw. Your client was salivating, looking Rebe over as though she were on the menu. That is not going to happen, Chase."

"I never planned for it to happen. Listen up, will you? Rebe and I have worked this out between us. It's none of your business."

"Try it again and you will know first-hand whether or not it is my business."

"Are you threatening me?"

"I'm not exactly sure what you'd call it in legal terms, but I will kick your ass."

"I can fire you, you know."

"Like I give a shit. I'll tell you what, Chase, why don't you do that first thing in the morning? Go to the senior partners and tell them you want me fired. Let's see if your family's money can buy that for you. But as far as Rebe goes, she's off limits to you and your slimy friends."

"She's my girlfriend. What are you talking about off limit?"

"You've disrespected her for the last time. Now let me know how it goes trying to get me fired." He glanced behind Chase's back and saw Rebe and Kandi returning. "Rebe's coming back. I expect you to put your client in his place if he gets fresh with her, understand?" Sam waited a moment, with his jaw clenched for Chase to comply.

"This isn't over, Sam. You've over played your hand."

"Whatever. It's time for us to return to our respective tables." And Sam did just that, returning a couple of seconds after Kandi. He didn't want to look in her eyes and put it off for as long as possible. Lifting his eyes he grinned. "Go ahead."

"What in the world were you talking to Chase about? He looks plenty pissed."

"Rebe, what else?"

"And?'

"And it's between the two of us. Is Rebe okay?"

"I don't think a kiss is going to make her freak out. But perhaps the two of you need to talk about what's been going on between you for the last couple of years. You're taking casualties because the two of you can't admit what's going on. You're in love with her and have been for a very long time. Deny it. I don't care, and I didn't say that you like her. Anyone with two eyes can see that most of the time you can't stand Rebe. But being in love with her, and liking her, are two different things."

"But…I'm not."

"Save it, Sam. I'm ready to get the hell out of here. I've had more than enough drama for tonight. And our being here is making Rebe crazy."

"Sorry, Kandi, I can't leave until Rebe does. She used to be my friend. Jamie was my friend and he'd want me to stay here to make sure his sister is okay."

"Exactly what do you think is going to happen?'

"Haven't you been watching? That guy wants to sleep with her."

"You must have a very poor opinion of Rebe if you think she'd allow that to happen. Seriously, Sam, get a grip. I know you can't stand Chase. I know he's a jerk and that Rebe deserves better. But she's a big girl and she can take care of herself. Besides, I don't think even Chase is low enough to actually want something like that to go down."

"You don't like him either. Why are you defending him?'

"I'm not defending him. But I don't think he's capable of what you're accusing him of. And even if he were, Rebe wouldn't go along with it. She's not going to like that you think she needs rescuing."

"I want to make sure she's safe."

"Sam."

"What? Jamie would want me to look out for her."

"Is that why you're acting crazy, like a man possessed?"

Sam refused to answer that. Yes, he was aware he was being irrational. Yes, he knew Kandi was angry with him and wanted to leave. And yes, he knew he'd embarrassed the hell out of Rebe and even Chase. But leave her. No. It wasn't going to happen. He couldn't make excuses for why, he just knew he'd leave when they did. Taking his sketch pad he began to furiously sketch the occupants at the other table. When he stopped, he glanced at Kandi's frowning face and sketched her too.

An hour later he watched as the clients shook hands with Chase, then Rebe, and left the table. While standing with the clients Chase scowled at Sam. When he and Rebe left Sam sighed and gazed for a moment at Rebe's retreating back before bringing his gaze to rest on Kandi.

"I'm aware I'm saying this a lot tonight, but I really am sorry. I had to make sure Rebe didn't leave the restaurant with the client. Thank you for coming with me."

"Did Chase take care of our bill?'

"Yeah."

"In that case I want dessert. And I want you to pay for it, you big jerk." Kandi reached across the table and gently caressed Sam's face. Be glad that I love you, Sam. Think about what I said and talk to Rebe."

CHAPTER SEVEN

For two days Sam had not talked to Rebe. Every time they'd passed each other at the law firm she glanced away and walked past him. This was getting ridiculous, it was affecting his creativity. He found himself for the first time in his life unable to paint, unable to draw, unable to even sketch. It was time a cease fire was declared. He supposed in a way he'd started it, so it would be up to him to wave the white flag.

Heading toward Rebe's cubicle, Sam noticed her walking toward him then hurrying to walk away from him once again. He had to sprint to catch up with her. Touching Rebe's arm he moved in front of her and held her gaze.

"Can I talk to you, Rebe?"

"I think I've heard everything you have to say. You're going to criticize me. Then you're going to feel bad about it and apologize."

"Please, Rebe. Can I come over to your apartment later? "

"Does it even occur to you that Chase might be coming over?"

Rolling his eyes, Sam snorted. "Give me an hour of your time okay. I think the least you can do is listen to me."

Groaning loudly, Rebe glanced around the room then back at Sam. She'd known Sam's working at the firm in any capacity was a bad idea. But she'd thought it was a bad idea because his portrait of Chase would more than likely be awful. She'd never thought it would extend into her private life. Heck, she wasn't a partner, she wasn't even on the track to make junior partner. Why was it necessary for him to invade her private life in order to paint a mural of the partners of the firm? It wasn't. But somehow Sam had gone behind her back and talked the bosses' into issuing an edict demanding everyone cooperate with the artist.

Who knew that edict would allow Sam to butt into every aspect of her life? And who knew that she'd given him a legal right to do so. Now Chase was ticked with Sam and with her. He'd tried his best to get Sam fired. He'd actually gone overboard and was behaving as a whining child might. The senior partners had told him in no uncertain terms that Sam was doing the mural and Chase was to cooperate, and that was that. To say that was strange was more than curious.

Who the heck was Sam to the partners? And why would the senior partners take his side over a partner with enough money to buy into the firm? Something was going on. It was time she attempted to find out just what that something was. Besides, it was well past time the two of them cleared the air between them before their little private war took on any more casualties.

Her gaze fastened on Sam she studied him for a count of five before giving him her answer. "Sure, come on over. I should be home around six."

"Would you like me to pick up dinner?"

Rebe was angry with Sam, and he was not too pleased with her. So it amazed her that in the face of all of that, he was still thoughtful. "That would be great," she answered at last. "Anything will do."

Sam had a look in his eyes like he was going to kiss her again. God help her. She wanted him to kiss her. In spite of the fact that Chase's kisses made her melt, Sam's kissed had taken over her world, and something inside of her had screamed out in recognition. She'd heard it loud and clear. "Yes," the voice said, "He's the one." Ignoring that she knew the voice was right; Rebe left Sam standing in the hall as she walked toward the conference room

By the time Sam was ringing her bell, Rebe had showered and changed and had made ice tea for them. She wondered for a moment what he'd bring then knew exactly what it would be, a chicken salad for her and cheese fries. She'd never acknowledged that Sam knew what she liked to eat or drink, but he did. Every single day for two weeks he'd made her favorite foods, had found her favorite movies and stayed in his bed with her to watch them. He'd not allowed anyone to bother her. In fact the phone had not rung, the doorbell only a couple of times and only once had he not been there when he'd gone to her apartment to pack a bag for her. He'd treated her like fine crystal or like a woman he loved. She'd known even back then how he felt about her. And she'd known how she felt about him, just not the depth. It was only when she'd returned home that she realized the depth of their feelings and she'd backed away. Now it was time to talk about it, time for her to finally thank him.

A second latter she opened the door. "Hey, Sam," she said and moved away. Stepping back into her apartment Rebe observed Sam, his movements as he made his way to the kitchen. He fit her, and he fit into her life. She just wasn't ready for what he represented. She continued watching while he placed the bags of food on the table then turned slowly to face her as though he was aware she was watching him. She might as well be the one to start.

"Sam, you're right that we need to talk. It's way overdue. I'm sorry I never thanked you for taking care of me." Annoyance spread across Sam's face and Rebe paused.

"Do you think the past years have been because I wanted a thank you?"

There was hurt in his voice. She wanted to look away at anything, the beige walls, the candles on the table and the vase of daises. Her tongue slipped between her lips and she moistened them with the tip of her tongue. "Sam, I don't know what you want from me."

"Nothing that you aren't willing to give. We were friends before Jamie died. Later we became enemies without us ever having a fight. I know something about being with me spooked you the two weeks you stayed in my apartment. I've wanted to tell you I was sorry if I'd done something that frightened you. I just wish that you'd told me what it was, or that you'd tell me now. I have no idea." His lids fluttered and he turned and made a move as if to return to the kitchen.

Again Rebe had the thought; *she'd done Sam a disservice.* She'd had no idea he'd thought he'd done something wrong. "Sam, let's leave the food for a little while okay. Let's sit in the living room and get comfortable."

Taking the short walk from the kitchen to the living room, she couldn't help but notice how different her apartment was from his. Her apartment was neat and almost sterile. But it was also, pretty, chic and classic while Sam's was messy with paintings covering every wall and stacked in every corner. His place reeked with life, with pictures of his family and hers, pictures of their foursome, pictures of Jamie. His apartment held memories of those she'd loved and lost. It gave her another reason for not wanting to spend time in Sam's apartment. It was strange that she was thinking about that now, but the fact was that instead of following her Sam was poised in front of her blank beige wall and he was studying it, letting her know he wanted to put a painting on that wall and probably all of them. She'd love maybe something small but perhaps flowers. She no longer wanted to display family portraits. She watched Sam and wondered just how long one could study a blank wall, even an artist. Finally he turned toward her and smiled as though embarrassed to have been caught in the act.

"Rebe, would you like for me to make your apartment more cheerful? I can give you some paintings. In fact I'll do something special for you, whatever you'd like. And I'll give your walls colors that will make you weep with joy."

"We'll see." Rebe wasn't sure how much of the kind of joy Sam was referring to that she might want in her home. "Come on, Sam. You asked to talk and you were right. We need to." She held her hand toward the sofa indicating he should sit.

She sat in the huge overstuffed rocker recliner and pulled her legs beneath her. Sam gave her a look then moved to the sofa. She marveled that he was in-tuned to her, had always been, about most things. She was in the chair to create a barrier between them and he was aware of it. It seemed the only thing he'd ever gotten wrong was the reason they'd stopped being friends. He blamed himself and she had to set that straight pronto.

"Sam, you need to let me get through this okay. I know you're aware of my relationship with my family. We were always extremely close. Home was a place where I knew I would be safe. I was loved and I loved them in return. As for Jamie, I loved my brother the most. He was my hero, my everything. I went to him for advice about boys, school, life. Jamie was my heart, my safe place."

Rebe felt tears coming and didn't want to be stopped by crying. She took in a deep breath, sucking in her lips, biting down softly. "Jamie not being here….his dying devastated my parents, but destroyed me. I hadn't known how important you were to me until that time. We were friends and I valued our friendship."

"If you valued our friendship so much, why did you allow it to turn into what it did?"

"You weren't supposed to speak, remember? Besides, I was about to get to that.

"Sorry,

Rebe frowned at Sam then held up her hand for him to be quiet. "This is what you didn't know. For me what we had was a bit more than friendship. But I never knew you were also my safe place. I don't think I could have been there for my parents without you. I was so lost. Then the two weeks after the funeral I became aware of the depths of my feelings for you. I knew after maybe the third night that I should leave your home. If I had I think we would have never become enemies."

Sam was staring at her. She could tell he wanted to ask questions, but she needed to get it all out. "When I finally left your apartment, I had to force myself to leave you. I didn't want to. I wanted to remain in your bed, in your arms, in your home, and never see another person. I didn't want to return to work, and I didn't want to talk to people. I didn't want to talk to my parents because I couldn't help them. They'd lost a son and then I took away their only remaining child. I didn't want to see their faces, didn't want to see our home. I could only live if I just allowed myself to exist in the world. No strong connections. No safe havens. No you."

"Rebe, are you saying what I think you're saying?"

"Probably. Go ahead and ask. I'll be honest with you tonight. Tomorrow, I'm not so sure."

"I didn't know you hadn't seen your parents."

"I talk to them everyday, sometimes two or three times a day.

"It's been nearly three years, Rebe. Have you really not been home to see your parents?"

"No."

"But I thought you went every Christmas."

She licked her lips and stared at him.

"Where have you been going?"

"I've been holding up in my apartment."

"All this time you've been pretending to leave town. You've spent the holidays alone. You allowed your parents to spend the holiday alone. Rebe, why?"

"I couldn't."

"If I had known I would have stayed in town with you. I wouldn't have allowed you to spend the holidays alone."

"And that's why I didn't tell you. If you even brought up the holiday I started a fight. She laughed softly. "You probably don't remember."

"Not specifically. It seems anything I said or did pissed you off. I can barely remember when we didn't fight in the last two…almost three years."

"I know. I'm sorry.

"But what about Kandi? Didn't she know you weren't going home?"

"She knew. I told her I couldn't. She's been trying to get me to go home. I haven't told her why. Sam, Kandi isn't my safe haven. You are. And I know you're thinking I'm a coward, that I'm selfish and that my parents need me. I know all of this but…."

"You're pushing away all the people who truly love you, all the people you love." Sam blinked. "Rebe, are you in love with me?"

"I wouldn't mind being in love with you, Sam. But it's more than that. It's…you. I—"

"You're worried I'll die."

She didn't answer.

"We're all going to die."

"I know that. But I don't have to feel it so deeply. It doesn't have to destroy me."

"And you think if you aren't around the people you love, and something happens to them you'll be protected?" Sam frowned at her trying to understand her logic

"You can't be my everything, Sam. I can't depend on you. I can't give you my heart. Recently I've been thinking about the way you've manipulated me to keep living, to move on, to get back out in the world." She gave a snort.

"I didn't know at the time that you were doing it, but I recently figured it out. You've done something for me my own parents haven't been able to do and that's to make me care about living. It was because of you that I'm looking to do more with my law degree, that I allowed myself to become more involved with the writing. What you think about me matters…way too much. I don't want us to continue being enemies, but I don't want to be more with you. You make me weak. And I need to be strong."

"My kiss was that bad huh?"

"No, the opposite. I know you're the one, Sam. I know it with everything that's inside of me. But I chose not to avail myself of you. Besides, you still hate me, don't you?"

Sam lightly scratched his chin as he stared at Rebe. She'd dropped a bombshell on him. Right now she was weak. He could tell if he pushed they'd move past their play of animosity and she'd blame her loving him on him. She wouldn't enjoy a moment of it.

Did he hate her? Hell no. He'd loved her for years, so in a way he'd been hiding also. But for different reasons. He'd read her books and all of her heroes looked like Chase. It was apparent they were modeled after him or men who resembled him. But the characteristics she'd given to the heroes were not what Chase possessed. While Sam stared at Rebe he smiled, knowing she'd combined him and Chase for her hero. *What did he say?*

"I don't hate you. I just hate the way you behave at times. I'm disappointed in you and the way you've allowed Chase to use you."

"I know you're disappointed."

"And you don't care.'

"Wrong. I do. Which is part of the reason I'm having this conversation with you. I know who Chase is. He's fun and I like being with him most times. But I also know he's not the one. If something happened to him, I would grieve, but after some time passed, I'd wake up and my life would return to normal."

"And if I died?"

"I'm not going there with you."

"Rebe, you have to go and visit your parents. If we could get back to being friends, I'll go with you."

"You going with me would be the only way I could go. You're right as usual. It's time for me to go home. Are you sure you're going to be okay with going with me?"

"It depends. I still have a couple of questions I'd like to ask you."

"Ask."

"So, you're not in love with Chase?"

"No."

"And you have any plans to be in love with me?"

"Are you in love with me, Sam?"

"Like you said, you're an old friend of mine who has gone astray. My goal is to help you get back on the right path."

"I will find my own path. For now Chase is someone I want to be with me on my journey."

"Then I guess I have no choice but to be okay with whatever decisions you plan to make concerning your life."

"Did you threaten Chase?"

"Did he tell you that?"

"No, but I saw the two of you together and the way he behaved afterwards. He kept glancing at you. He wasn't himself. You know that contract you have with the firm doesn't give you license to mock

Chase with your painting."

"You're worried about him?"

"I'm not sure."

"My painting will depict him exactly as I see him."

"Oh God. I hope you never do another drawing of me. I've heard that you think I have way too many imperfections for you to ever love me."

Sam grinned at Rebe. It was a loaded question she'd asked him. She wanted to hear that he loved her while she had no intentions of returning his love. He laughed instead.

"Call your parents, do it now. Tell them we'll drive down in a couple of weeks, a couple of months, or whenever you want. Just make it soon, okay. You can even ask Kandi if she wants to come. I think that might make it easier for you to be with me."

"I don't want to end up in your bed for another two weeks. There would be nothing of me left."

"I promise that won't happen. You'll remain whole. Now let's eat." Sam walked into Rebe's kitchen took out two plates and scooped out the food putting her plate in the microwave to warm her cheese fries, then his own.

Rebe watched Sam. The things he did were so automatic. He was the epitome of the perfect hero, only he wasn't the one she wrote about physically. He was an inch shorter than her and husky. Rebe smiled to herself. *Alright already, he wasn't shorter than her.* She'd been proven wrong on that score. He wore his hair long and uncombed most of the time, and he wore unattractive glasses. He was generally covered in paint splatters and was often clumsy; or rather he used to be.

Hmm, what had happened with that? She tried to remember the last time she'd seen Sam stumble over something and she remembered perfectly. It had been the day before she'd received the news about her brother. She reminisced how it had been the last time their foursome was just that. Sam had stumbled over something or other and the rest of them had laughed. She'd teased him, hugging him as she told him he should take out accident insurance before he found himself in big trouble.

The next day when she'd needed him, Sam had not stumbled once. She tried to think of a time, but couldn't because he hadn't. Nope, not a single time. What had changed in twenty-four hours where he'd become her safe haven and he'd become rock solid? She looked at Sam as he made his way back to her with the plates in his hands. It was in his eyes, in his touch, in his scolding of her. The thing between them was love.

"Are we friends again?" she asked.

"Yes, but don't ask me to change the way I'm going to do my painting. That's personal. I'd never try to get you to change your writing, not even to redo your version of what makes a man heroic. I believe we feel the same about our art."

Sam put the plates down and stared at Rebe. It felt different and odd for them to be moving to another phase of their relationship. They'd been friends, Frenemies, and now what? Friends again? He thought of the kiss a few nights before, how soft Rebe's skin felt. But he'd known that already.

Once what he'd only imagined he now knew as fact. Rebe's mouth had fit his perfectly. She tasted like warn sunshine and life bursting with energy. He'd forgotten while he was kissing her exactly where he was. Kissing Rebe in front of her boyfriend had not even been a consideration. She'd been Sam's for that moment. Now they would move to trying to pretend neither of them had felt the things they'd felt. The urge to kiss her once more before they began this impossibly hard journey caused him to smile.

"You want to kiss me again don't you?"

"Well, what if we only imagined what we felt?"

"It wasn't my imagination."

"I'm not sure about my feelings. It was a bizarre night. Things could have gotten a bit mixed up," Sam said. He walked closer to her. "We should at least be sure, don't you think?"

Sam gazed into Rebe's eyes deciding to just go for it. He kissed her gently at first, just barely tasting her lips, wanting to remember everything about this kiss in case she was foolish enough to let go of what they could have.

Over and over he tasted her lips with his tongue before entering her mouth. The electrical zap was wholly unexpected as he went deeper. Hearing her low moan in the back of her throat he plundered her mouth as though he was a marauding pirate of old. Sam could do nothing about the instant erection, it came with the territory. He continued kissing Rebe until the need for air prevented it.

Rebe was trembling when he slowly pulled away, a look of

surprise on her face, her nipples erect and standing at attention. "So what do you think?" he asked.

"I think we'd better finish eating, and then you'd better go."

"Not even a movie?"

"Not on your life."

"Is this really the way you want this to be?"

"It's how it has to be, Sam. I never doubted we'd be good together. That doesn't mean I'm going to change my mind. And just so you know, it's not out of vanity. Actually I like you just as you are—all your imperfections and nagging ways. You make me want to be much better than I am. But I don't know if I want the lofty goals you have in mind for me."

"Are you hoping to marry Chase?"

"Don't worry. I'm not fooling myself that I have a future of marriage, babies, and happily ever after with Chase. I do want to clear something else up with you though. There is one of your perceptions of me that I don't want you to have. I'm not with Chase because I'm trying to make partner. I'm with him because I like him. He's fun, and most of the time we're good together. Chase is easy breezy. And easy breezy is about all I can handle. Truly, even though I know I sound like it, I'm not an airhead. I'm just looking after myself the way that I believe is best. Chase is best for me."

Sam dropped his fork and stared at Rebe. Did she really believe the line of garbage she'd just given him? Chase better for her. Like hell he was. But he had no intentions of trying to convince her that Chase was not only, not the best thing for her, he was out and out bad for her. Did he have any idea who the best man for her was? Of course he did. But he had no use for a woman he'd have to coerce to be with him.

In spite of everything, Sam would be Rebe's friend. As far as their immediate future, his plans were to do his best to at least get her over the silly notion of not being around the people she loved. To think she'd not seen her parents in years because of nonsense. He would have read the riot act to her if she'd not told him of her reason. Now how could he? He sighed. When Rebe finally decided to love a man with all that was in her it was going to be a sight to behold. Even if he wasn't that man, he wanted that kind of happiness for her.

Feeling her staring at him, Sam lifted his eyes to find Rebe's gaze fixed firmly on him. Her eyes were two huge pools of sadness that pulled him from his seat and to her side.

Running the pads of his fingers slowly down the sides of Rebe's face, Sam sighed and hugged her close to his body. He felt her shiver. Or had the shiver been his? He wasn't certain. But he did know holding her as he was doing was putting them both in a place Rebe said she didn't want to be. His mission had always been to protect her. So, it was up to him to back off. Taking in a deep breath he held it and moved away. Only then did he allow the breath to escape.

Safely back on the couch he picked up his plate and silently ate. When he was done he waited for Rebe to be finished, then took the plates to the kitchen and placed them in the sink. Then he turned toward Rebe. "I think you're right. I think I'd better go."

CHAPTER EIGHT

Three weeks had passed since Rebe and Sam had cleared the air between them. She had to admit things were much better at work and at home. Not having the tension between them was a welcome. Being able to spend time with Kandi and Sam without fighting was beginning to feel like old times. She needed them in her life. More importantly, she wanted them in her life. For no particular reason she was feeling cheerful.

Walking into the office the excitement was contagious. Rebe didn't have to wonder who was bringing the excitement. Since Sam had started working on the yet to be started mural the women had flocked to him, so had the men. It was as though he had this thing about him that attracted people, this certain aura. She'd noticed the women had begun dressing in a variety of pastels. Flowers of all sorts were appearing on the desks in the office as if by magic. She didn't have to ask to know that the reason their office now reassembled a painting of a beautiful summer day. Sam. He seemed to have that effect on people, a way of bringing joy and sunshine wherever he went was but many of his attributes.

Following the incessant chatter and the oohs and ahhs, she walked into the hall where Sam would paint the mural, a place he'd said when he began the actual painting of the partners, no one would be allowed. He'd deliberately chosen a wall where the foot traffic could be halted. She stopped and stared, first at Sam, then the wall. Sam of course had paint splatters on his body even in his hair and on his glasses. For a moment she wandered if he did it deliberately considering there was not a drop of paint on the floor. Then she looked at the wall, and gasped, he'd painted it a silvery blue, the same color of the dress she'd worn to the dance. Ice blue. She didn't even have to ask to know that Sam had mixed the colors. She'd thought he'd be backing away from the praise of so many people. But he wasn't. He stood to the side, his eyes on her as though it was only one opinion that mattered. Hers.

"Sam, it's beautiful." Rebe stared again at the wall then back at him. I love the color. It reminds me of a night of fun," she teased. "This wall looks too beautiful to put a mural on it."

Sam laughed. "That's the point. The mural will need to be showcased so painting the wall was necessary. And ice blue has now become my favorite color, with the exception perhaps of chocolate brown, the same color of your eyes." He took a look at her purple outfit and purple contacts then laughed.

Rebe was relieved she didn't have to answer Sam's flirty, teasing banter. The noise of the staff brought out the partners, including Chase.

"What's all the fuss about?" Chase asked. "It's just a wall with a coat of paint."

All eyes except hers turned in Chase's direction. Rebe knew why Chase didn't have praise for what Sam had done. One glance at the office staff and she was aware he should have said nothing.

"You have got to be kidding. The man is a genius," one voice rang out.

"Then maybe he can come to your house and paint your walls," Chase hissed.

"You've just made things ten times worse, Rebe thought as she glanced at Chase and shook her head discreetly in disapproval. Her gaze met Sam's and she saw the look in his eyes. He'd removed his glasses and was staring at Chase. There was a confident challenge in the way he looked. *Please Chase,* she wanted to warn him. *Let this one go.* Mr. Newton turned slowly toward Chase, and Rebe's heart sank. She could feel a reprimand and felt sorry for Chase.

"Chase, apparently you don't know a thing about art," Mr. Newton, one of the senior partners scolded. "Sam is an artist, a great artist. You should be pleased that he accepted this job. You should be proud he will be painting you. It's an honor."

Rebe wondered about the praise from Mr. Newton. She turned toward Sam who had a serene smile on his lips.

"Don't worry about it," Sam said looking at Mr. Newton. "I am an artist and I work with all elements of paint. As for Chase thinking I should be painting houses, I do house painting as well. I'm very proud of the homes I've transformed… now if you approve of the color I've chosen, it's time for all of you to leave me to my work. By the way I'm having a door installed here in a couple of hours. I will have the only access."

When Mr. Newton turned to look at him, Sam smiled the most beautiful smile Rebe had ever seen. "It's in my contract," Sam said.

"Don't worry, when I'm done, you'll never know a door was ever installed."

Had Sam always been this powerful, confident man that was standing calmly before her, telling the partners he was having a door installed to deny them access, and boldly lying that the clause was in his contract? It wasn't. She knew that for a fact, she'd not written it in. She caught the slight quiver as Sam's lips curled into a smile. He was counting on the fact that the bosses wouldn't remember, nor would they pull out a copy of the contract to verify. By the time anyone thought to do it the door would be up and Sam would have his privacy. They wouldn't force him to take it down. Rebe laughed. Score one for Sam

By the end of the day everyone in the office had gone to check-out the newly installed door. She could hear soft music coming from behind the door and put her hand on the knob just to test if Sam had left it open. She should have known. It was locked. When she took a second look she saw it had a keypad entry and then something that required more, possibly a hand print. Rolling her eyes Rebe crossed her fingers that her eccentric artist friend didn't lose the job for over spending. Putting up an inexpensive door was one thing, but high tech? What in the world was Sam thinking? She turned away at the same moment the door opened and Sam stepped out complete with even more paint splatters.

"Did you want to take a peek?" he asked.

Of course she did. Rebe was as curious as everyone else, but she wondered what Chase would say, or her bosses if Sam allowed her to see the progress and not them.

"Forget it," Sam said. "I forgot you're too into what others think of you."

With that Sam closed the door. Or rather he slammed it and returned to whatever it was he was doing. She heard male laughter and turned.

"Did you really think Sam cared any more for you than he does the rest of us?" Chase asked. "He's not going to let you see it. You're lucky this moment you're not a partner. I know he's going to do something awful to my portrait. I want to see the contract you drew up for him."

"No."

"Why not?"

"Because it's none of your business, and he's my client."

"I'm a partner."

"A junior partner. Besides, I don't answer to you."

"I'm telling you now, if your client makes a mockery of me, I'm going to sue his ass for every dime he'll ever make."

"It won't stand up in court." Rebe smiled at Chase. "Sam has a very good lawyer and an even better contract."

"But he still wouldn't let you look at his progress, so you can't be that good a lawyer."

Rebe turned ready to tell him that Sam had offered to allow her a look, but she'd taken a moment too long to say yes, because she'd worried about it hurting his feelings. After all Chase was her boyfriend and she should think about his feelings, right? But she didn't say any of that to Chase? No. She lied.

"Yeah, I guess I'll see Sam's work when the rest of the office does. It's better that way."

"Who gave him permission to install that kind of lock? And why in the world did he think he needed such high tech security? I mean it's just a painting."

"He takes his work seriously. He doesn't want it seen until its ready. I can understand and respect that."

"You're just kissing up."

"Maybe if you'd kiss up you wouldn't have to worry so much about how he's going to make you look."

"I still want to see Sam's contract. I'm a partner and I have a right to know. Plus, I was the one who got him the damn job."

"You're a junior partner, Chase. You do not have a right to see it. If you think so, go talk to Mr. Newton, and ask to see his copy."

Rebe walked away making sure to walk extra hard so the click of her heels sounding on the marble floor could be heard. Chase was being a jerk and he was annoying her.

"Rebe," Chase called, "Are we still on for dinner tonight?"

"I don't think so." She didn't turn around, but she heard the slight click from Sam's door and smiled. *So, he was listening.*

Several hours later Rebe was home relaxing with a glass of lemon seltzer. She wasn't a bit surprised when her bell rang. Shouldn't her hero come to apologize? Shouldn't he know exactly what she needed, and bring dinner to her?

Smiling, Rebe opened the door and stood back so Sam could enter carrying his bags of food with the delicious smells wafting toward her.

"You don't look too surprised to see me," Sam grinned

"Why should I be? Now that I've had some time to think about it, I've realized a few things about you. You've been looking out for me for years, haven't you? Even when you didn't like me you've been there."

"Let's get something straight," Sam said making his way to the kitchen and putting the food on the table. "There have been many times I've wanted to strangle you. To pound some sense into you, times that I have absolutely not been able to stand you. But there has never been a moment I didn't care about you, or your well-being. Do you think I would have given a fig about finally going to your event if I didn't care?"

"Finally?"

"Sorry, that slipped."

"I was mean about that, wasn't I?"

Sam rolled his eyes. "Okay, I know we've decided to try not being enemies, but if you're going to look at me like I'm a stray puppy in need of your sympathy, then we can go back to being enemies. I get it. You needed a hunk and when the hunk cheated once again and Kandi refused to go, you took me. Or rather I took you. It's over and done with." His jaw clenched and he walked down the hall to her bathroom.

"Let me wash some of this paint off, then we can eat."

"Sam, tell me something, you're a professional. Why do you get so much paint on yourself when you work?"

He laughed. "Because it's expected. People want to believe they're getting their money's worth. And if they see an artist, or even when I'm painting someone's home, if they see a splotch of paint, then they're relieved they didn't have to do the job. And they're thankful that I'm the one doing it. So of course they're more than happy to pay me."

Rebe had never thought of that. "Do you really paint houses?' she asked.

"Not so much anymore, but I have. Sometimes I need a larger canvas to work on and a house suits my needs." He glanced around her apartment. "You could do with a fresh coat of paint. I was serious when I asked if you'd like for me to paint your apartment for you."

"When will you find the time?"

"When I'm done with the mural."

Rebe didn't answer. She just stared at Sam as she remembered his last visit. She could barely concentrate on what he was saying because she wanted Sam to kiss her again.

"Rebe, did you really think I was so inept that I couldn't paint without spilling paint? You definitely don't know very much about me do you?"

"Well....maybe a bit more than you think."

"You think I'm a clumsy oaf. Don't deny it. Kandi told me."

"Kandi talks too much. She's supposed to be my best friend."

"And she is, but she still told me. I will admit the first time I met you, I tripped over a footstool because I was staring at you."

"It was more than once."

"Okay, maybe twice, but that doesn't mean I trip every day. Think about it, Rebe. When was the last time you witnessed me tripping? You've judged me on so many levels. You met me while you were wearing six inch stilettos and looked down your nose at me and called me short. I was taking steroids for an infection, and had gained a few pounds, and you called me fat. But you never noticed that after the treatment had ceased the weight went away, or that after you'd kicked off your shoes you didn't tower over me. You saw me for the first time and your image stuck.

"Listen, I have to know, do you really and truly believe in the fantasy kind of romance that a guy finds the perfect girl or vice versus, no flaws, just wham and cupid shoots an arrow straight to the heart? Sometimes the things you say I do lose patience with you. I project the image my clients want to see. I'm their fantasy artist, a bit chaotic, messy, long hair, paint splotches, glasses, a bit forgetful and socially awkward. There are so many things you do not know about me. I dare you to find five things you don't know about me. Your search will take time and you're not to ask Kandi if you accept my challenge."

"Doesn't a challenge work two ways? What will I have to give up if I lose? And what will I get if I win?"

Sam smiled. *You'll get me,* he wanted to say, but instead said. "I'll take you to one of the fancy places you like to eat and I'll even wear a suit with not a bit of paint on it. I might even think of getting my hair trimmed and taking off the glasses."

"You don't really need the glasses?"

"No, and that one is for free." He handed the glasses over to her.

"All these years, I never knew."

"Jamie and Kandi knew."

"Was I always such a bad friend?"

"You have been a lot of things to me. If you'd always been a bad friend, I don't think I'd care so much about you."

"You care about me, Sam?'

"I plead the fifth. Now back to what we were discussing. I forgot to add, you're not to do an internet search on me. You will have to become a bit more creative."

"Sam, why do you want me to do this? It's not as though we're going to be dating."

"Because we're friends, Rebe, and friends should be a bit more interested in the lives of their friends than you are. Say for instant, if I was on a ventilator, do you know if I'd want you to pull the plug, or allow me to continue living until a cure for whatever I had was found?"

"That's crazy?"

"Really? I know what you'd want. You'd want to be never be put on life support. You have faith that God is in charge of your life and if it's your time, it's your time. Besides, you'd never want anyone to visit you with a tube down your throat, not your parents, not Kandi and not me."

"Wow your opinion of me is really low."

"But am I right?"

Rebe didn't want to answer but Sam laughed and hit her playfully, loosening her tongue. "That's not entirely a true assessment, Sam. I'd never object to your seeing me in any condition, with tubes, down my throat, weak and crying, your having to hold me up in the shower and bathe me, your feeding me, refusing to leave my side. Your…lov…" Rebe stopped smiled at Sam and continued. "I meant your caring about me. You're right that I wouldn't want anyone else to see me in that condition, but you, I'd never refuse you, Sam." He reached out his hand to her and gave her fingers a little squeeze.

With tears in her eyes, Rebe asked, "Seriously, am I really that vain?"

"More than you were two years ago. I personally think dating Chase has had a very bad side effect for you. You're becoming more like him. The two of you are just beautiful clones."

"Wow."

"Come on, Rebe. Lighten up, don't get upset. You can easily prove me wrong by taking the challenge. Prove to me that you really want to be friends." He arched a brow. "Think of it like this, what would one of your fictional heroines do?"

"You'll have to give me a moment to think about it," Rebe laughed, tilting her head and eyeing him. Sam was baiting her, but she'd decided to take the bait. In fact it would be fun to find out more about Sam. And she did like a challenge. It had nothing to do with the fact that after he'd kissed her in front of Chase, she'd begun to see him in a different light. He wasn't quite as short. And he wasn't quite as un-wow as she'd always thought. In fact Sam was kinda wow.

More than likely Sam has always been kinda wow. She'd just failed to notice it. But she'd seen the way the women at the firm had fawned over him. She'd begun to notice the things they'd said, the things Kandi had been telling her for years. Sam had the most beautiful eyes. And when he smiled they lit up. And the way he held her...mercy.

"So, tell me, Sam, how I am going to find out things if I don't use the internet?"

Sam laughed. "My God, this is beyond stupid. We've known each other for almost five years. I know everything about you, Rebe. Try getting to know me, talking to me, asking me."

He stopped for a moment to take her hands and peered deep into her eyes, wanting so much to touch her, to run his hands over her body, to make love to her in the worst way. He had a feeling in this moment she might agree. But he wasn't going for a moment. He'd made a decision. Rebe deserved a real life hero. That part didn't belong to Chase, not even if he tried would he be able to be what Rebe truly deserved in her life.

"Sam, come on, you're tying my hand."

"Rebe, we weren't born with internet. You're smart, you'll think of something. Besides, this conversation is becoming more ridiculous by the second."

"Did you just call me ridiculous?"

"No, I said our conversation is ridiculous. You've been shutting me out for so long I'm afraid this thing with you may not be an act. You're a lawyer…a very good one. You're used to finding the tiniest detail. And you're a writer, you're also very analytical. Put the skills you have to work. Become a friend—my friend. Deal?"

Rebe's concentration had been on Sam's lips, his eyes. She barely heard his words. But when he stuck out his hand, she took it. And when he laughed so did she. She'd just fallen down the rabbit hole and was about to chase after the frog.

CHAPTER NINE

After listening to Rebe rant about her deal with Sam for over an hour, Kandi laughed. Rebe couldn't see what was happening, or at least she wasn't admitting to it. But the idea that Rebe was devoting so much time to learning about Sam was hysterical. She'd known the man for almost five years. Heck, she'd slept with him for two solid weeks, not in the biblical sense. Didn't that tell her all she needed to know?

And Sam, her poor friend who'd gone from loving Rebe to loathing her, was now back to loving her. She wondered what game he was playing. Rebe had belter look out. Sam didn't do anything halfheartedly or without purpose. And he only invested huge amounts of time in the people and things he cared about. But would either of them admit their feelings for the other was changing? Nooo... Kandi knew both of them very well, and she saw it in their eyes, and the way their glances followed the other.

"Kandi, you're not looking at me," Rebe complained. What are you thinking about?"

"You and Sam. I'm wondering why you don't ask him about himself."

"He wouldn't tell me."

"Probably because you put little thought in the way you were asking him. He's not a client that you're getting facts from. He's your friend. And under the right circumstances, I'm betting he'll tell you whatever you want to know. How do you think couples find out about each other? They ask."

"We're not a couple."

"No, you're not. But you can take this challenge on as such. What would you do if Sam were a man you could be interested in? A date, Rebe, try asking him for a date."

"I have a boyfriend you know. Chase."

"Right."

"Well, it's too bad that you and Sam don't like Chase. We're back together and that's that."

"So what if you're back together? Chase thinks nothing of dating other people. He's so much as told you that the two of you are not exclusive."

Kandi had a point, Rebe thought. Besides, having dinner with Sam wouldn't be exactly like dating, and Chase wouldn't get jealous of him, though he had begun acting differently since Sam had started work on the mural.

"You know you might have something there. I think I'll make dinner for Sam and get him to loosen his tongue."

"And just how are you planning to achieve your goal? What trap are you planning to use?"

Like a kid, Rebe rubbed the palms of her hand together in glee. "Why, I'm only going to use just a little wine or as much as it takes. It all depends on Sam."

"Sam doesn't really like wine."

Rebe stared at Kandi and laughed. "You're right, he doesn't." She ran all the times through her mind that she'd seen Sam drink. *Beer. Sam liked beer.* She smiled. "Of course he doesn't like wine. Sam drinks beer. How could I have forgotten that?" She ignored the smirk on Kandi's face. "I'll give him a couple of beers... or three or four, and then I'll pump him for information."

Kandi shook her head.

"What's wrong with my plan?" Rebe asked.

"I'm wondering why you always take the more complicated way toward your goal. For God sake, just remember who you're trying to get information on. It's Sam, Rebe. And he's right. He knows everything about you, as do I. You should be ashamed you've never taken more interest in him, even as a friend."

Rebe felt a bit offended. It was one thing when Sam called her out on being a bad friend. But when Kandi her lifelong bestie called her out, it hurt. "You don't think I've been a good friend to you?"

"If I'm being honest, no you haven't. Not since Jamie died."

Immediate tears filled Rebe's eyes. "I'm sorry Kandi. I know I've been a bad friend and a bad daughter. I'm thinking about changing that. Sam said he'd go home with me to see my parents. I think I'll take him up on that." She neglected to invite Kandi to go on the trip with them. Instead she hugged her friend close and made a promise to do a better job at being a friend.

Dreaming about Sam had been one thing. Waking up with him still on her mind was another. She had to get to the place where they could continue their friendship without the sexual tension. And yes, she was admitting to that on both of their parts. After much thought Rebe agreed with Kandi's assessment of her reckless behavior regarding Sam. She'd come up with a plan to become a better friend and admittedly she wanted to win the deal she'd made with him. How hard could it be to find out five things about Sam that she didn't know?

Getting dressed for work she devised ways of finding out tidbits of information about him. Considering that her relationship with Chase wasn't about being faithful, at least on his part, she'd decided it was okay to make dinner for a man who wasn't her boyfriend. Applying her lipstick Rebe studied her face in the mirror. She was dressing for Sam, not Chase. With that in mind she blotted off the fire engine red and applied lip gloss instead. Another glance and she popped out the hazel contacts.

Hmm. If she was writing a story and placed herself in the role of the heroine would she be allowed to want another man? To dress according to his wishes. What if the true hero turned out to be Sam? What about the romance rules that everyone attempted to convince others didn't really exist?

Taking a look around her bedroom at the white walls and white bedding that covered her dark and sturdy oak bed she decided to see the room through Sam's eyes. Her walls were bare, not a single picture anywhere. Her apartment had not always been so colorless. She had dozens of framed pictures, just not out on display. She'd taken them down after Jamie died. The thought of looking at her brother's smiling face, or the faces of her parents had racked her with grief. She'd been unable to embrace life until she'd put the pictures away and created a colorless existence for herself.

A few moments of musing and Rebe wondered if she were that heroine she was writing about would she appear as a sympathetic character or a complete nut job? Readers weren't very forgiving of a heroine who behaved in a manner they deemed inappropriate. It was funny that in most if not all romance stories there was a kernel of truth, of real life, but those few kernels weren't allowed to flit as freely as the writer might want across the pages. How could even a fictional hero or heroine ever measure up to the expected demands of romance readers? Heck, it was darn near impossible to do, more so if the writer had a rebellious streak.

With a smile Rebe's thoughts returned to Sam. She wondered if he'd be sympathetic to her plight or find she was a bit nuts. Laughing at her reflection that stared back at her, she was aware she already knew what Sam would think. Would that count as one of the five things she had to find out about him? She doubted it.

Walking slowly through each room of her apartment she came to a decision. Sam was right. She needed color back in her life. She was going to take him up on his offer to repaint her apartment. And she was going to ask him to do a couple of paintings for her walls, something with lot of colors, flowers for sure, just no people. She still wasn't ready to look at Sam's painting of the people she loved. He was very good and his paintings looked too real. She wondered why he hadn't become famous yet. He was that good. Shaking her head at having made a decision she walked to the kitchen to grab her mug of coffee to take with her.

Later at work Rebe knocked on the locked door of Sam's little sanctuary. "I wondered if you'd like to come for dinner tonight." She'd expected an enthusiastic yes. What she got was…

"I'm sorry, Rebe. I have a date tonight, perhaps some other time."

Before she could stop herself, Rebe was blinking rapidly, backing away from the door. A date. Did Sam have a girlfriend? If so, that would make him as bad as Chase for kissing her when he was involved with someone. She didn't believe in poaching other women's men. She'd have to find out. Hold it. Wait. Why would she have to find out? She wasn't interested in Sam.

Once outside the door Rebe turned to take another look at Sam's closed door, and when she turned back around she bumped into a hard male body, Chase. "Sorry," she said as Chase's arm slid around her to steady her. He grinned and she smiled in return.

"I was just looking for you. There's going to be a party at the Oakton Club tonight. Are you up for going?"

"I was looking to stay in."

"I really wanted to go, but if you're not up for it, we can stay in. You make dinner and I'll bring dessert."

"Dessert you buy from the store, Chase. You will not be the dessert."

Taking Rebe by the arm, Chase guided her toward the empty break room. "How much longer are we going to play the celibate couple?"

Rebe gave him a look but didn't answer.

With a sigh Chase stood looking at Rebe for a moment. "What would you like for dinner?"

"I don't care."

"Rebe?" Chase stared at her for a moment. "Okay, since you don't care, how about, steak, baked potato, and salad?"

"You pick up the steak, and the potatoes and a salad from olive garden. My cupboards are bare." She waited for Chase to acquiesce. It took him a beat too long, but he finally did, tilting his head a bit.

"Rebe, is something wrong?"

"No, why?"

"It's just that. Well…you never ask me to go to the market."

"Hmm. Perhaps that's the problem; you think a food fairy stocks my cupboard."

"Rebe, I take you out to dinner at least two to three times a week. I always pay. I didn't know that you resented making us a meal on occasion."

The thing of it was that she didn't mind. What she minded was that he expected it. And he never offered to bring anything but himself, or a bottle or wine which come to think of it, she wasn't that keen about drinking wine either. It had just become something of a habit, her having a glass with him. An image of Sam ringing her bell and bringing food came to her. Rebe blinked trying to get rid of it, knowing what was happening. She was comparing the men, dangerous territory, very dangerous.

She shortened the distance between them and gave Chase a quick kiss. "I'm sorry. I'm in a bad mood and taking it out on you."

"So you'll cook?"

"As long as you bring the food."

"And the celibacy?"

"It has been awhile hasn't it? I'll think about it."

Sam stood for a long moment looking at the almost finished mural knowing he should have been done with it at least six weeks prior. He was deliberately taking his time in order to observe Rebe at work and around Chase. Taking in a deep breath the floral scent of her perfume filled him and had him wondering why he'd not accepted her invitation, wondering why he'd lied about having a date. He opened the door to call to her, not that he planned to tell her he'd cancel the date for her. That would never do. But he had thought to invite her out the next night.

When he spotted Rebe standing in the hall with Chase grinning down at her, and his arms around her waist, Sam fumed. *That didn't take very long for her to find a replacement did it?* He stared at the image of Chase he was working on. Reason dictated he wait until he wasn't in such a foul mood, but his hand picked up the brush and his fingers closed around it. Before he could stop himself he was adding to the mural, painting with abandon.

Yes, just what Chase's image need. He'd have to buy a can of glitter to ensure the idea of the ornate glittered mirror stood out. He laughed because he was enjoying himself so much that he would have done Chase's portrait for free. Well almost for free. His work was sought after and brought in big bucks and had for the past four years. Did Rebe know that? Of course she didn't. Not even Kandi was aware of that part of his life, but the senior partners in the law firm were and had agreed in a private meeting he'd had with them to keep his identity a secret.

Something deep inside of him had wanted Rebe to know. Disappointment had swirled inside him that Rebe had never questioned his contract, or wondered why the partners didn't object to any of his outrageous demands. He shook his head. Because Rebe thought her friend Sam couldn't possible fill the shoes of her fictional heroes. She didn't think he'd be able to wine and dine her as Chase did.

Why in the world did he even give a woman so fickle a second thought? Rebe's idea of a man she wanted was something much different from Sam. And he had no plans on ever telling her the truth until she wanted him for himself. With a laugh, he added a more ornate touch to the mirror. This was the man she thought she wanted, taller than her, handsome to a fault and wealthy. Just wait until she saw his image on canvas.

By the time Chase rang her bell Rebe was feeling more and more annoyed. She'd not been able to keep her thoughts from Sam, wondering about his date, if it were serious. She couldn't help wondering why he hadn't asked her to go out another night.

"I brought the steaks and fixing as ordered," Chase said wrapping her in his arms and kissing her so passionately that he almost made her forget Sam, almost made her forget she was annoyed with him. Suddenly she found herself wanting more from Chase. Exactly what, she wasn't sure.

"Can you cook?"

"Why?" Chase asked with suspicion in his eyes.

"Because I thought it would be nice if you'd cook for me for a change."

"Seriously?"

"Yes."

"Why?"

"Sam would." *Darn it.* The words popped out before she'd had a chance to even think them.

"So, this is about Sam?" Chase released her and stormed away. "Rebe, we've been good together. Why are you letting that little pipsqueak bother us and the way we do things? Come on now, be sensible. Why are you worrying about what he thinks of you?"

"Well…because it's kind of true. You and I are a bit superficial. I don't want to be, not any more anyway."

"And my making dinner for you will make me less superficial?"

"Yes."

"What about me bringing dinner?"

"That you'd even expect points for this make you less…well…less heroic." She couldn't help but notice the eye roll. He did it right there in front of her, for goodness sake.

"Okay, Rebe. Let's say I go along with this new project of yours. Are we going to go back to our regular relationship? I mean having sex. I'm too damn old and too used to your body to go celibate for long."

"Not that you have anyway." Chase was staring at her.

"Okay, let's say for a moment that I'm going to agree with you, that perhaps I've been a bad boyfriend and you do deserve better. And I'm only being hypothetical, mind you. But let's say I agree. What if we make a pact to…"

"You can't even say it. What is it you're asking me? Are you suddenly wanting a committed relationship?"

"To be honest, I thought we were already committed to each other in our own way. But yes, I'm asking if you'd like to give a committed relationship a try."

"You mean one on one? You and me? No more women for you?"

"And no men for you. That includes Sam."

"Tell me something, Chase. Are you doing this because of Sam? Are you jealous of him?" Rebe laughed in disbelief.

"Are you serious? There is no way in hell I'd ever be jealous of that little pipsqueak. None."

"Why do you keep calling Sam a pipsqueak? He's not that short, not really."

"He's a lot shorter than I am."

"That's true, but I'm still wondering if this is not about your wanting to best Sam. After all, just a few months ago, you told me you didn't want, or that you couldn't be in a totally committed relationship. Which by the way, I've always conducted myself as though that was what we were in. I've never once cheated on you. Now you want to do the same, play by the same rules that I've been playing by."

"Do you want to be in a committed relationship with me, Rebe?"

Chase was looking a bit irritated and that alone irritated her. She'd wanted what he was asking for over a year now. "How about giving me a few days to think it over?"

"A few days?" He walked back toward her. "I don't believe this. We're working on being together for almost three years, and you want to blow what we have for what? Sam, an unkempt artist. I know the other women in the office are acting foolish over him, but you. You're a lawyer, respected. Sam obviously isn't making any money. Look at him. He can't afford to date you, Rebe."

"Do you know how you sound?"

"Unfortunately I do. But right now I don't care. Like I said, I think we're actually good together. I thought we always were. We definitely have fun together and we're good in bed, we match. We both love sex and that's a big plus. But if you're wanting more I'm going to do my best to give it to you. Perhaps I should be thanking Sam for opening my eyes."

"Perhaps you should," Rebe whispered. But that was all she was able to say because Chase was kissing her and wiping away all of her objections and good intentions about not having sex. It had been a long time and he did know how to make love to her body.

Rebe sighed when Chase lifted her in his arms and allowed her head to drift to his shoulder ignoring the voice that said it was a big mistake. Even if Sam wasn't on her mind, Chase was stepping up for the wrong reason.

Why was it that women didn't listen to the things that were going on outside of the bedroom? Sure Chase made her knees weak but then again so did Sam. Rebe screamed silently inside the safety of her head. *Sam, go away from my head, please.* He wouldn't because he'd niggled his way under her skin. And now she wanted to know exactly who he was with and what he was doing at the moment.

"Rebe, are you with me? I'm kissing you and you're not here with me. Come on babe, what are you thinking about? I hope it's me."

"It's us. Chase, I'm hoping you're meaning what you're saying and not just doing it for now."

"Hush, Rebe," Chase said and kissed her, laying her on the bed and undressing her before she had time to have another thought.

Hours later and well sated Rebe stretched beside Chase and watched the self-satisfied grin appear on his face. "Don't say anything cocky," she warned. "Or we're back to square one."

"I wasn't going to say anything…well anything other than you make me feel like I'm in heaven when I'm inside of you. I enjoy making love to you, Rebe."

Sweet words, perhaps sincere. She wanted to believe them. She had to believe them, she was just about to commit to a happy, committed relationship that included sex. She would not be inviting Sam over to make dinner for him. She would not be accepting dates with him, or asking him out on dates. She groaned. And then wondered why you were given the things you'd prayed for long after you'd stopped praying and wasn't even sure you wanted them anymore.

"Sam, would you please stop pacing? It's not my fault that you didn't accept Rebe's invitation." Kandi complained.

"I know that. But did she really have to walk away with that Ken doll less than a few seconds after asking me?"

"You said no."

Sam tilted his head. "Kandi, are you not listening to me?"

"Apparently not, it seems you got what you wanted, for Rebe to take an interest in you as a friend, and then you turned it down. You can keep telling me all you want that you're not into Rebe, that it's all about protecting her, being a friend to her, honoring Jamie. Sam, my friend, I know you're not being completely honest."

"You don't expect me to tell Rebe that I have feelings for her above and beyond friendship do you? She already thinks all she has to do is crook her little finger at me, and I'll come running. I refuse to be at her beck and call."

"I don't blame you. But Rebe is not going to make the first move, we both know that. Besides, the relationship she has with Chase seems to be really strong in an odd sort of way"

"I don't get it. How can she keep taking him back after he cheats on her over and over again? I mean seriously, does either of us think he's changed? Does she?"

"I doubt it. But you know how her relationship with Chase is. They're volatile together. They fight, he cheats, and they break up then get back together."

Sam turned toward Kandi and glared, but his thoughts were on Chase. Blowing out several hard breaths he closed his eyes. Calming down was what was needed. "Does she love him?"

"I have no idea. But she is… well…she does like certain things about him. She's pretty happy in that department."

"What are you talking about?"

"She doesn't have to fake it with Chase, not even a little bit."

"That's disgusting."

Laughing Kandi covered her face with her hand. "It is not. Why do you men want to have sex with us, but want us to pretend we don't enjoy it? Believe me, a lot of the time women have to fake it."

"Why?"

"Think about it. If a woman is with a man who's not getting the job done but is determined to keep on until he does, I mean heck you have to fake it out of self-preservation. Or you're going to have a very bad burn in an area you don't want. It's harder than you might think for a woman to find a man who can give her the big 'O' and one who can do it over and over again is a real treasure. Sometimes I can see Rebe's point in sticking with Chase. I like sex. She loves sex and so does Chase."

"But you should have sex with a person you have an emotional connection with. Do you have any idea how long it's been for me?"

"I'd say going on five years. I have never seen you with a woman. Rebe was actually beginning to think you were gay. She thought that was why you'd turned all bitchy toward her, and why you were hating on Chase."

Sam was stunned to the point of disbelief. He'd never known, never suspected that Rebe had had thoughts that he was gay. For several seconds he simply stared at Kandi before he could ask her the question that was uppermost in his mind.

"Did she think because I didn't touch her when she spent all those nights in my bed I was gay?"

"No, at least I don't think so. To be honest she got tears in her eyes when I asked about it. All she would say was, you were much too good for her, and for me not to ask her anything else about what the two of you had, or had not done. She was serious, so I didn't ask, though now I wish I had pressed her. What happened between the two of you, Sam?"

"Do you think you can get me to tell you something you've already said Rebe didn't want you to know?"

"It was worth a try."

For a long moment Sam allowed himself to think about the time he'd spent with Rebe. He sighed wondering as he always did, what the hell had happened to change their friendship. Kandi was giving him one of her patented puppy dog looks. The last thing in the world he wanted was for her to start feeling sorry for him. It was time to take the conversation from Chase and talk about anything else.

"Kandi, I talked to Rebe, and she told me she hasn't been home since Jamie's funeral. What are your thoughts on her not having seen her parents face to face in the last two years?"

"That's not exactly true. She Skypes' with them."

"That's not the same thing and you know it."

"Jamie's death has been really rough on her."

"And on them."

Leaning closer to Sam, Kandi couldn't help but ask, "Sam, have you been in touch with Rebe's parents?"

"Yes." Sam studied the look on Kandi's face. "It's not what you think. I sent them a couple of cards and called to check on them. Then I started emailing them once in a while, sending them poems, things I thought would help them. With Jamie not here, I kinda got in the habit of making sure they were okay."

"Have you visited them?"

"And if I had, what would be wrong with that?"

"Did they ask you to spy on Rebe?"

"No, they'd ask if I saw her, or if she were okay. And I told them that they didn't have to worry about her, that she was hurting. I told them you and I were helping her through it. I never knew she wasn't going to see them. They never told me and I had no reason to ask. Rebe wasn't our main topic, just general conversation. As for my reassuring them of her well-being, it wasn't a lie and it wasn't invasive."

"But I don't think Rebe would like it if she knew."

"Like she'd bother to find out. Take that stupid challenge for instance, something I would have never done if I hadn't realized after all the years we've known each other that Rebe knows practically nothing about me. If she wanted to know about me, besides asking me, she could have talked with her parents for more than a few seconds at a time and the conversation more than likely would have gotten to the point that I keep in contact. So, it's not my fault if she doesn't know I've been checking on her parents. It's hers."

"You're just making excuses, Sam. You know that Rebe will be ticked if she thinks you've been spying on her. You're trying to make justifications."

"I am not. I gave her a challenge to find out things about me she doesn't know. Well, that's one of them. And I for one don't care if she gets angry about it."

"Would you like for me to call her?"

Glancing at his watch Sam sighed. "It's after midnight. What excuse would you use?"

"Please! Rebe and I have been best friends, and have lived next door to each other since our mothers gave birth to us. We do not stand on ceremony. We don't have a respectful time to call."

"And if she tells you Chase is there, what is that going to accomplish? I'll just play out this hand with her and see what will happen."

"How much longer do you have with that mural?"

"A week or so."

"Are you stretching it out?"

Sam couldn't help but grin. "Let's say I keep painting horns and having to get rid of them. But I'm not doing it deliberately. It would appear I have no control over my muse."

Kandi laughed and reached for two more beers. "Sam, why didn't you ever fall for me?"

For the space of a breath Sam was stunned. The question Kandi asked of him was the last think he'd ever expected. Pulling in a breath he decided to mix humor with truth. "Haven't you ever read those romance books Rebe writes? The hero always falls for the woman who doesn't want him, the stubborn, nasty shrew. And the good friend...well he loves her like a friend, and would never ever do anything to jeopardize that friendship."

"Does that mean you've never even gotten an erection around me? I mean I've pranced around in front of you nearly nude."

Once again Sam laughed. But this time he was aware Kandi was teasing him. "Sorry, Sis. Have you gotten aroused around me?"

"Nope."

"Then we're even."

"I know. But a woman doesn't want to be even. We want to be wanted."

"You are. As my friend."

Kandi studied Sam for several seconds before laughing again. "You've surprised me. I didn't know you've read Rebe's books."

"Another thing she doesn't know about me and something you will never tell her."

"Man, you've got it bad."

With a sigh Sam shook his head. "Please don't tell her."

"I promise you, I won't. At least not until after the wedding."

They laughed and clinked bottles. When Sam finished his beer he made his way across the hall to his own apartment.

Rebe woke to the growl of her stomach and a slight headache. They hadn't gotten around to having dinner, now she needed caffeine. When her hand touched the opposite side of the bed she woke fully. Chase had left. *When?* She wondered and sighed. Taking in a breath she sniffed caffeine, then meat. What the heck was going on?"

"Good morning sleepy head."

She must still be sleeping and no doubt dreaming. Chase was standing by the bed holding her favorite mug with steaming coffee.

"For me?" she asked.

"Of course."

"But you never..."

"I was never committed before."

Rebe didn't want to admit it, but she was getting the warm fuzzes around her heart. Heck, how could that happen after nearly three years? And to a man who had cheated on her no less than a dozen times. What would that be, every couple of months or so? Still, she couldn't help the warm feeling, around her heart and she smiled at him. "I smell food. Are you cooking?"

"Yes. I'm broiling the steaks. The potatoes I diced, and I'm scrambling eggs. I'm going to serve you breakfast in bed. Now drink your coffee."

Chase walked away and Rebe took a sip of the coffee. She'd not expected it, but it was good. The whole breakfast in bed was even better. If she was awarding points, Chase would have a ton right now. Licking her lips with the tip of her tongue she acknowledged the doubts that were swirling in her mind. Was this what she wanted? Was this real? How long would it last?

Then she thought of Sam and the way she'd felt when he kissed her. *He's the one*, the words whispered again through her mind. But Chase was the man she'd been with for years. He was the one she could be in a relationship with and not become lost in him. He wasn't her safe haven. Rebe glanced up sensing Chase staring at her. His gaze lingered on her and she sighed. "What's wrong?"

"You looked so beautiful. What were you thinking about?"

"Chase, I…you're being so wonderful."

"Good boyfriend material?"

"Yeah, I think so."

"And the commitment?"

"I still want the few days."

"You don't trust me?"

"I don't want to set myself up for a fall. I'm not trying to start a fight, but Chase you're a serial cheater. There is no getting around that fact. I'd be a bigger fool than I am already for repeatedly taking you back. At least before, I had no real expectations. A commitment will change that. I want time to think all of this over. I want to be sure we both understand what the changes in our status will mean.

"I know what it means, Rebe. I'll be faithful to you."

"I think you'll more than likely try."

"I can be faithful. You've never wanted or expected more from me. Maybe it's time you should. Maybe all of my cheating—"

"If you dare attempt to lay the blame for your cheating at my doorstep, it's over right now, no getting back together, no commitment."

"I'm sorry. It's just that I know how good we are together. I know we can be even better if we put in the effort. I want us to try."

"I didn't say no to a commitment. I'm just trying to give us both time to know if that's what we really want. Listen, Chase, this will work for you as well. Before last night, it was months since we'd made love. I don't want this to be after glow. If you change your mind in the next few days I won't be upset. I promise." Rebe was surprised when Chase merely smiled at her.

"It's what I want. You're what I want. I guess I'll just have to prove that to you," Chase said and went back to the kitchen to check on breakfast.

By midafternoon Chase had proved to Rebe several times that he wanted her. She'd never doubted he wanted her in bed. They'd always been good together and until recently she'd not required much more. It was Sam, with his disapproval of her that had made her question things.

What the heck was wrong with being shallow, if it was what she wanted? Darn it, and darn Sam for making her wonder. Once again he'd gotten under her skin and was having an effect on her. Heck, she'd even called her parents and promised she'd be home soon for a visit. Now she wondered if she agreed to a true commitment with Chase if Sam would still go with her to visit her parents. Perhaps she should discuss what Chase expected from her in terms of a commitment. With him watching her, there was no time like the present to ask.

"Chase, today has been wonderful. I've been thinking over what you asked me. But I have a couple of questions I'd like to ask you first. Since Sam kinda got you to make this turn around, we need to be clear on a couple of things concerning him. He's my friend and I'm not going to stop being friends with him."

"I don't care about your friendship, but I do care about your kissing him."

"He kissed me."

"You didn't stop him."

Rebe blew out a breath. "You're right."

"Rebe, I'm not doing this because of Sam. But he has made me realize that if I don't want to lose you I need to change the way I've been treating you. I need to treat you as though you matter to me.

You do matter, Rebe." Bringing Rebe into his arms Chase kissed her long, hard and deep, "Say yes, Rebe," he pleaded caressing her body, then burrowing his head in her chest and pulling her taut nipple into his mouth.

"Yes, Rebe murmured and surrendered to Chase's lovemaking, moaning in satisfaction.

Kandi and Sam sat in Sam's apartment sharing a pizza. Sam had not given in to Kandi's demands for him to call Rebe. Nor had he allowed her to do it on his behave. A man had to have some pride. He was beginning to get a headache from Kandi's constant badgering.

"So what are you going to do, Sam, keep your feelings bottled up and wait until Rebe's walking down the aisle to marry Chase?" Kandi asked.

"He's never going to marry her. Chase is not in love with Rebe."

"You know this how?"

"Don't you know it?" Sam replied.

"Yes, but I'm wondering how you have access to this information."

"Kandi come on. I can see. I hear him flirting with the women at the law firm. Besides that, no man alive who's in love with a woman, would use her in the manner he uses Rebe. I'd never treat her like that."

"I know," Kandi sighed. "Sam, come on, don't you think it's about time you told Rebe how you feel?"

"She's not ready to hear it. Moreover, I don't enjoy her rejections. To keep trying with her will give me a complex." He grinned. "But that doesn't mean I don't have a plan. The last thing Rebe needs is Chase. And I'll be damned if I don't do everything in my power to put a nail in that relationship."

"For her own good, right?' Kandi laughed.

"Of course."

"So, what's your devious plan?"

"Tomorrow I'll invite her to lunch as a friend. We'll see where it goes from there.

CHAPTER TEN

Sam had put as much thought into how to make Rebe see Chase was not the man for her, as he put into any new piece of art he was making. Rebe was important to him. She was his friend whether or not she'd ever be more. And for that reason alone he had no intentions of seeing her walking into certain danger and not doing everything in his power to protect her.

The very next day at the firm he decided to put his plan into motion. He'd been semi stalking Rebe all day just waiting until she wasn't being shadowed by Chase. At last he had his chance. He'd watched as Chase had taken a client into his office, then he'd darted across the hall the moment he spotted Rebe.

"Hey, Rebe, wait up," Sam called her name wondering if she'd been trying to flee from him. He laughed to himself. Why would she? They hadn't fought in days. And if she was upset that he'd not accepted her invitation he was about to remedy that.

He decided to continue as though Rebe wasn't displaying a weird and stank attitude. "I'm going to of my special places for lunch. I was wondering if you'd like to come with me." She gave him a funny look, one he was unable to decipher. "My treat," he added to make it clear. But the vibe he was getting from Rebe was really strange, she was looking away. "What's wrong, Rebe?"

"I'm having lunch with Chase. Well, I think I am anyway."

"You think you are? What's going on? You don't have plans, but you're using Chase as an excuse? Are you mad at me about last week?"

"No, but things changed this weekend. Chase and I are now in a committed relationship."

"If that's true you should be committed," Sam said too low for Rebe to hear him clearly.

"Excuse me?"

"I take it to mean your new commitment with Chase implies the two of us can no longer be friends?" He knew he was smirking and didn't care. To complete the look he added air quotes ignoring Rebe frowning at him.

"Of course we're still friends. Did you really think I'd allow Chase to dictate who my friends are? You say you know me so well, then you should know I wouldn't let go of you, ever."

"Rebe?"

"Your friendship, Sam. I'll never let go of your friendship. That's not what I want."

"If it's not, then tell me please, why you're making up excuses to not have lunch with a friend?"

"You don't think that little stunt you pulled by kissing me in front of Chase might have something to do with that? Chase and I talked…for days about redefining our relationship. And yes, he would definitely like for you to be gone from my life." Rebe stopped and smiled. "But that's not going to happen."

"Then why can't you just accept my innocent invitation?"

"You and I have to discuss boundaries. I have to check with—"

Rubbish. Sam refused to stand in front of Rebe and listen to her spout anymore nonsense. "Forget I asked."

Turning on his heel Sam headed back to his little enclave. He heard the click of Rebe's heel's behind him and tried to calm himself. After all, they were only friends with a few shared kisses. He couldn't help but wonder if he'd had dinner with her if she'd suddenly be in a committed relationship with a man she'd been dating for over two years. What kind of nonsense was that? Why now was the subject of commitment just coming into play? Why didn't Rebe see it as truly arsine and drop kick Chase out of her life?

Using his keypad as quickly as he could Sam rushed through the door. In his attempt to slam the door in Rebe's face, only quick reflex on his part saved her from having the door hit her. "Go away, Rebe. You're the most annoying, weakest woman I've ever had the misfortune of knowing."

He quickly pulled on the cord that would drop the drape shielding his work from Rebe. No one but no one was going to see the mural before he was done. And especially not Rebe. She'd want him to make changes and he wasn't going to. He was relieved that she'd barley noted what he'd done. She was angry that he'd called her weak and annoying.

"That is so not true, Sam," Rebe came back. "You think I'm weak, but I'm strong for not going after the thing that would make me weak."

Sam stared at Rebe in frustration. He saw Chase looking toward them and closed the door. "Am I the thing you want, that will make you weak?" She didn't answer, but her eyes filled with tears. "You're a silly woman, Rebe."

Before he could talk himself out of it his fingers were caressing her jaw and his head was lowering, his eyes fixed on a specific destination. Then he captured her lips, kissing, licking, holding her tightly. He never wanted to let her go, but this was her choice. Ending the kiss with a small sigh he held her gaze and finally allowed the voice outside his door to penetrate. He laughed at the indignation he heard in Chase's voice demanding he open the door.

"Do I open it?" Sam asked.

"Give me a moment."

Shaking his head slowly he rubbed his finger across her lips. "You look guilty as hell."

"I promised Chase that I'd stop kissing you."

"Technically, I kissed you."

"And I kissed you back."

"Why?"

Rebe shrugged her shoulder. "I wanted to. Pointing at a spot on Sam's lips she shrugged her shoulder. "Sorry about that, you need to wipe it off." When he was done, she turned and opened the door for Chase. She could see some of the staff looking in their direction and cautioned Chase to keep his voice down.

Stepping into Sam's domain Chase glared from Sam to Rebe. "Rebe, did you inform Sam that we're no longer casually dating, but that we're in a committed relationship. And with a committed relationship there will be no more kissing of other men?"

"And other women, Chase?" Sam asked. "Will you be allowed to continue kissing other women, ogling them, sleeping with them? Will your new strategy give you the rights to use Rebe for a bargaining chip?"

Chase's face turned red and he glanced at Rebe. "That's over. I made Rebe a promise to be a better boyfriend."

In disbelief that he was even having this conversation, Sam scowled, the urge to shake Rebe and Chase strong. "And how exactly do you plan to do that?" he asked instead of giving into his natural inclination to just slug the guy. He found it odd that in his entire life Chase had been the only person to bring out such a violent reaction from him.

Chase moved to stand directly in front of Sam in order to allow his height to intimidate. "Do you really want to know how I'll be a better boyfriend, Sam? Every time I make a move, I'll ask myself, how would Sam handle this. And I'll be as dull as I can possibly be, except maybe in one area that I'm sure Rebe doesn't have a problem with. As for you, Sam, I would strongly urge you to stop kissing her. I've been behaving in a civilized manner because I'd more than likely be seen as a bully if I just let you have it. You're really too little for me to just hit without the worst kind of provocation. But honestly, Sam, you have me to the point where I really want to clean your clock."

Seriously was this really happening? Could Chase possibly believe that because he was a couple of inches taller...? Okay make that more like four. Still, Chase's height had nothing to do with it. For his information Sam had also been behaving in a civilized manner. And he wasn't worried about messing up his model looks face. That would be Chase's department. Sam stared at Chase a moment before shifting his gaze toward Rebe. He was truly speechless.

"We're together. You lost, Sam." Ignoring Sam, Chase turned to Rebe. "Listen, I understand you're nervous about us, I do. I've made mistakes. But we've invested time in each other. Shouldn't we give ourselves a chance? We made a commitment to each other. It's not going to work if both of us are not in this 100%. I can't blame Sam for trying to poison your mind against me. He's your friend and he believes you deserve better than what I've given you in the past. So do I. That's why I'm doing my best to change. But there is something more, Rebe. I'm a man and I know it's not all about friendship with Sam. A friend doesn't continually put his friend in a compromising position."

Sam needed to leave or at the very least he needed to get Rebe and Chase out. He tried not to look at Rebe, but he couldn't help it. She had that stupid, dreamy look, girls tended to get around guys like Chase.

What the hell? He hoped Rebe wouldn't buy that bull. A sudden urge to laugh out loud overtook him at some of the things that had come from Chase's mouth. For him to even think that it was Sam constantly putting Rebe in a compromising position when it was Chase who wanted her to go with him while he wined and dined the clients. Perhaps Rebe thought it was because Chase was grooming her. Anyone with eyes and ears knew it was because he needed her legal expertise. He'd bought his partnership, now Sam wondered if he didn't buy his law degree. Didn't Rebe see that?"

"Compromising position," Sam said with a snort after having finally found his voice. "That would be you, Chase."

"Kissing, Sam, I mean kissing. A friend would not constantly attempt to kiss his friend, knowing she was with another man." Chase took Rebe's hand and pulled her to him leaving Sam staring after them. Sam laughed low.

Then Chase's head lowered toward Rebe and he cupped her face. He gazed into her eyes and Sam thought, *aw crap*, Rebe was falling for it. Before Chase could kiss Rebe, Sam opened the door and pushed them both out.

Rebe blinked in surprise. She glanced toward the closed door then toward Chase. "That was some declaration you just made."

"And that was some reaction from a man who's only supposed to be your friend. Rebe, do you really think it's a good idea to continue your friendship with Sam?"

"I already told you my friendship with Sam is non-negotiable."

"Why?"

"He's important to me. He's been there for me when you haven't." *And if this commitment with us doesn't pan out,* she wanted to add but didn't. It was wrong on so many levels to play this close to the fire. She was playing with Sam's emotions. She wasn't sure how much of Chase's emotions were involved, but she knew what she was doing wouldn't be good for his ego. It wouldn't be good for any man's ego. The thought made her wonder if what she was going for was perhaps a bit of payback for all the times Chase had cheated on her.

Tilting her head Rebe looked up into Chase's eyes wondering why she wasn't worried about his emotions. Something heavy filled her stomach and instant anxiety pushed down like anvils on both shoulders. She wasn't in love with Chase. And he wasn't in love with her. She knew that now more than ever. She wanted to cry. How the heck had she gotten here? She wrote fantasy, not lived it. "Chase."

"I know what you're going to say, Rebe. Don't say it, not yet. We haven't given us a chance. Don't you think we both owe it to ourselves to give it a real shot? If you think I can't hack it, or even if you can't," he smiled, "we can always end it later. But I'm seriously pulling for us. You're wrong about me, and so is Sam."

Rebe thought about it, never once had Chase said he loved her, never once had she said it to him. But still she wondered if they could make a go of it.

"What's wrong, Rebe?"

"Nothing. I'm just worried about Sam."

"Why worry about Sam? You're not committed to him, you're committed to me."

"I'm not sure. But for some reason I am worried about him, not that he'll do anything crazy. I mean, Sam is sensible and solid. But he was laughing at both of us and there was this something in his eyes."

"We're not going to worry about Sam. By the way I have a lunch meeting so I won't be able to have lunch with you. I'll see you later tonight though."

When Chase walked away Rebe stared after him until a feeling made her glance backwards towards Sam's door. Thank God the door was closed. Too bad she hadn't accepted Sam's invitation. She'd wanted to talk to him anyway. Now it was too late to accept. The macho display by her boyfriend, her committed boyfriend had definitely put a nail in that idea.

"What an idiot," Sam laughed to himself. After that little stunt of Chase's there was no way in hell he would leave Rebe to him. So, she was looking for a hero, a man to rescue her., hmm actually she'd said the exact opposite. She wanted a man who looked like a hero. He wondered what Rebe would do when she saw her hero with a slightly different look. Grabbing a brush he dabbed it in a bit of oil paint from his easel and laughed the entire time he was putting the finishing touches on his mural. It was time for him to stop dragging this out.

Pulling out his cell he texted Rebe. **Let the senior partner know that day after tomorrow I will unveil the mural. I want my check cut and ready for me**. He pushed send then immediately turned his phone off. He didn't want any possible word from Rebe to change a single thing about the way he'd depicted any of the partners. With a glance at the mural he suddenly remembered the lessons of right and wrong and karma. Painting furiously Sam cleared his mind of doubts. He had to hurry and finished before an attack of conscience made him change his mind.

The day of the unveiling and Rebe was as anxious as a mother hen. Every bone in her body warned that Chase was not going to fare well in Sam's painting. It would probably have been better if they'd both been a bit nicer to Sam.

While she didn't want to choose a side she knew she should show a united front and side with Chase. That was what commitment was all about. Right? Then she ran into Sam and the look he gave her, made her shiver. Heat yeah, but there was downright challenge in his gaze. Oh crap, she knew what was coming. If she could run home and hide under the covers she would. Thank God Sam wasn't doing her portrait. For now all Rebe could do was watch.

Taking a look around the space that had once only been a long, wide hallway; she marveled at Sam's use of space and marveled even more that he had a table laden with food and drinks. When had he done all of this and who in the world was fitting the bill? As soon as she thought it she remembered a clause Sam had had her insert in his contract. The company was footing the bill. She hoped Sam milked this for all it was worth because she didn't see how her bosses would ever employ him again. Sam walked over to her and handed her a cup. She took a sip and brought her gaze up to meet his. "Champagne?"

"Only for the two of us."

At that moment all of the senior partners gathered in Sam's domain. "No champagne for the partners?" Rebe whispered.

"None of this. This is special, just for the two of us. And I bought it. The rest…well the rest the company is paying for."

With a flourish Sam grinned at the assembled body and yanked the cover away from the wall as though he were a magician. For a few seconds all eyes were on the mural and they were stunned. Rebe took a look and saw the beauty. What struck her was the realism. The painting looked as though Sam had snapped a picture of all the partners with a very expensive camera that took in every line and crevice. Something that could be done with a high definition camera. She had to admit she was happy for Sam and very proud of him. She wanted to say to everyone there, *Sam's my friend. My friend painted that masterpiece.*

Then details started emerging, Mr. Newton sitting at his desk with cigarette smoke coming from his drawer as he used his hand to fan it away. The law stated you couldn't smoke in office buildings, besides that Mr. Newton claimed to have given up smoking. The partners had been caught in moments when they'd not expected, each one humorous, showing some tiny human flaw. Then as Rebe looked from the wall where the mural resided to find Chase frowning, turning back to the mural she studied it more closely and she saw it, the reason for the frown that was on Chase's face. There was nothing that could have prevented her from laughing.

Sam had portrayed Chase with him admiring himself it appeared in a golden ornate mirror that looked so real it begged to be touch. Chase had a container, an economy size container no less, of hair gel, and was pictured putting a handful into his hair. But it was the image in the mirror that looked back at Chase that made Rebe laugh. It was a frog and he was wearing a crown.

Rebe laughed until tears ran down her cheeks and as she continued to do so, every single person assembled there with the exception of course of Chase laughed. Chase glared at Sam and at her.

"I'm suing you," Chase said to Sam." You're going to change that."

"I don't think so," Sam answered.

"You're changing it."

Mr. Newton was laughing so hard Rebe noticed he also had tears running down his face. He wiped them away with the back of his hand but didn't stop laughing as he tried to bring peace. "Oh come on, Chase, it's all in fun and I like it."

Chase turned his glare on the senior partner. "He didn't have a right to paint any darn thing he wanted. This was intended to be a serious painting. Sam, I'm not kidding. You get rid of that."

"Check with my lawyer." Sam laughed and turned toward Rebe. "The painting stays as is."

Chase moved toward a paint brush but Sam was quicker. In disbelief Rebe watched Sam twist Chase's arm behind his back. "You. Do. Not. Mess. With. My. Art." He said each word slowly and deliberately. "The painting stands."

Rebe stopped laughing when she saw things were getting serious between Sam and Chase. Sam's eyes were blazing a greenish brown fire. It wasn't so funny anymore. Sam could be arrested for assault if he didn't cool it. "Sam, let go of Chase and come with me," she ordered.

"Sure, Rebe. Just as soon as everyone has finished admiring the painting and I have a chance to reset the lock."

She walked closer to Sam and whispered in his ear. "Please let Chase go."

"Only because you asked," Sam replied and dropped Chase's arm, not even bothering to move away from him but instead standing toe to toe with him, until Chase moved away. Sam tilted his head in acknowledgement and then smiled at something one of the senior partners was saying about how much he loved the painting. Then he turned back to her. "Anything else, Rebe?"

She so wanted to scold Sam. But for the moment it would be unwise to continue looking at him because the look he was giving her was making her laugh. "Enjoy your unveiling, Sam. you deserve it. I'll talk to you later when this is over."

For over an hour the door to Sam's space remained open and people came, admired the mural, and partook of the refreshments. The senior partners were extremely pleased with the mural. That was obvious from the smiles on their faces and the comments Rebe heard. When Mr. Black shook Sam's hand and asked if Sam would consider doing his family's portrait if he had the time she'd been stunned. When Sam had replied he rarely did that type of painting thus turning the offer down she was dumbfounded. What the heck was Sam thinking? What was in that champagne the two of them were sipping?

When she was finally able to drag Sam away she headed for Chase's empty office knowing he'd left to meet with a client and shouldn't be back for some time. She stood before Sam trying to frown at him.

"Okay, Sam, you shouldn't have done that to Chase."

"Twisting his arm?"

"I meant the painting. You shouldn't have painted him as a frog. But you also shouldn't have twisted his arm and especially not in front of the entire office.

"He was attempting to destroy my work. What would you do if someone did that to one of your manuscripts?"

Rebe thought about it and shrugged. "I probably would have done the same thing."

"Thank you."

"I know you painted all the partners with flaws, but why did you paint Chase as a frog?"

"I painted him as I see him. You see him one way, I see him another."

"But, Sam, you do realize that you're portraying the wrong thing. The frog always turns into a prince and gets the girl. You should have painted the frog and put Chase's face in the mirror."

Shrugging Sam just stared at her. Then he asked, "Is that always the case? You told me that it never happens that way except in fantasy."

"I stand corrected, but what was your message?"

"That I saw his inner being and he's a frog. He will not turn into a prince, or a hero. He's not heroic, Rebe. He's the least heroic man I know."

"And what you did kinda puts you in that same category. Your actions were very unheoric."

"Everyone laughed."

"That still doesn't make it right."

"You laughed."

"And that's going to cost me. Come on, Sam, you know Chase and I are trying to see if we can have a committed relationship. Why did you paint him like that?"

"I already answered that question."

"I wish you'd given me a sneak peek so I wouldn't have laughed right in Chase's face."

"Are you saying it's my fault that you can't see Chase anymore as your hero, that you can't be in a serious relationship with him."

"I didn't say that." Sam was giving Rebe one of those; *I want to kiss you looks*. And she was afraid she might be giving him a, 'please kiss me' look in response. It was time to change the conversation.

"I talked to my parents. I promised them I'd fly out to see them for my father's birthday. That's in three weeks. Will you go with me? I'll pay for your expenses." Sam was giving her such a strange look, one she couldn't decipher. "What's wrong?"

"You're in a committed relation with Chase. Why don't you ask him to go with you?"

Rebe didn't answer. She didn't want Chase to go with her, not to meet her parents and most certainly not to talk about her brother.

"Rebe, are you afraid Chase won't go?"

She hadn't thought of that. She only knew she didn't want him with her.

"If you're in a committed relationship you should want him to do this with you. And he should want to be with you, to go and meet your parents. Come on, all the time you've been together, he should have met them already. Why don't you ask him?"

"But you promised."

"That was before."

"Sam."

"Yes?"

"Are we back to being enemies?" Rebe studied him, her gaze lingering on his lips. Again the image of him standing in his boxers in front of his fridge came to her. She moaned softly. She definitely didn't want to go back to being enemies with Sam. What did she want? *A few more kisses,* she thought and bent her head.

"Rebe, do both of us a favor. You're playing with fire, and if you're not very careful you will get burned. I'm not a yo yo. I'm not going to continue playing kissing games with you. You want the handsome, heroic type, and you want the friend to remain at your beck and call. It's not happening. Besides, a typical alpha male would not allow you to run roughshod over him."

"How would you know that?"

"I do more than paint. I'll talk to you later. I have to check with the partners. By the way do you have that last installment?"

"Yes…but to be honest I don't know if you deserve to be paid. I know what you painted isn't what anyone expected."

"There's only one person complaining, and him I don't care about. Now, may I have my check please?"

Rebe looked on Chase's desk where she'd dropped the file containing Sam's check. She retrieved the envelope and handed it over to him. "Sam, I think Chase is serious about suing you."

"And?"

"And he'll lose. The contract is iron clad."

"Then, Rebe, what's the problem?"

She knew what the problem was. She wanted to keep talking to Sam. She was wishing she'd not agree to try a committed relationship with Chase. And she wanted Sam to kiss her. Again. But she couldn't very well admit that now could she? She went into safety mode and talked about things that might keep him there a few minutes longer.

"I just don't want you to lose work because of this feud you have with Chase. He can't win and that won't even be the point. But he can still sue and make your life miserable by tying you and me up in court. And even though the partners won't like it, and it would look very bad for two lawyers from the same firm to be on opposing sides, I do believe his ego is injured to the point where he might ignore all the reasons why he shouldn't take action. Perhaps if you'd agree to change it just a bit."

The knocking on the office door followed by the handle jiggling made Rebe stare at Sam. She'd not locked the door.

"Sam, what are you trying to do?" she asked as she heard Chase's voice calling her and glanced at Sam who had been in the process of leaving but was now deciding to take a seat. Throwing up her hands in the air she opened the door for Chase.

"There you are," Chase said coming in and looking at Sam and glaring. "I was looking for you. I'm sorry about what happened before. Sam, I want to be reasonable. I'll pay you to change that painting."

"How much?" Sam asked.

"How much do you want?"

"Ten thousand."

"Are you crazy, Sam? You're not worth that much."

"Really? Perhaps you're not aware what a good artist can get for his work."

"How much were you paid for that thing out there?"

Sam laughed. "That's none of your business. Besides, it's really rude to ask what a person makes."

"I got you the damn job," Chase countered. "You should be a bit more grateful. Rebe, help me out here."

Rebe looked from Chase to Sam then back to Chase. But she didn't say a word.

Sam shrugged his shoulder. "Chase, perhaps you should check out a couple of galleries and price great art. By the way there's an art show—"

"Forget it. If you have something to do with it, no way am I going."

Chase paced a few steps around the office throwing his hands up in annoyance. He stopped before Rebe and gestured toward Sam.

After a few moments he glared again at Sam. "Would you leave us alone please?"

For a moment it looked as if Sam had no intentions of leaving or of answering Chase. But the moment he turned toward her and gave her that, 'I want to kiss you look,' Rebe knew whatever came out of his mouth wouldn't be good.

"Rebe, don't forget that thing we were talking about." Sam smiled then finally left the room.

The instant the door closed, Chase was glaring at her. "Rebe what's going on? You know Sam did that deliberately and after I got the job for him. You'd think I'd done something to harm him. I was trying to help him."

"I'm aware you were trying to help Sam by recommending him to the partners. And I'm sure he does appreciate it. It's just...well; Sam is not one of your biggest fans. I have to be honest. He doesn't think you're going to keep your end of the deal. He doesn't hold out much hope that you can be faithful. And he is still pretty ticked about what he thinks was happening at the restaurant."

"I don't care what Sam thinks. You're clear on our arrangement aren't you?"

"I'm clear, but I guess to outsiders it does look pretty creepy."

"Are you saying you don't want us to work together?"

"I'm saying perhaps we should stop using sex appeal to get clients. To be honest just saying it sounds a bit sleazy. I didn't really put that much thought into it before. We were having fun and playing a game that only you and I were aware of. Of course I know you'd never expect me to ever leave with one of our potential clients." Rebe frowned and licked her lips. "At least I hope not."

"Rebe, do you truly think so little of me?'

"It's been a strange day, and I'm a little anxious right now. Let's forget it. I told you, you should have apologized to Sam earlier. Perhaps all of this drama could have been avoided."

"At least tell me this, isn't Sam behaving a bit strangely for being just your friend?"

"Perhaps."

"I've thought about this, Rebe. The only possible explanation for Sam to have gone off the reservation is something we both want and something that only I have. That would be you. Or do I have you? I hope you haven't changed your mind about us. Are we still together?

Are we committed?"

"We are," Rebe said softly

"Then why would you laugh at that painting?"

"I'm sorry, Chase. It took me by surprise. But I wasn't just laughing at you. The entire thing was funny, not what I expected. I thought it was going to be a stiff and stodgy painting. I actually like it.

"You're kidding me!"

"No. I do."

"I wasn't kidding. I'm going to sue Sam. There has to be some clause in his contract."

"Sorry, but there isn't." Rebe shrugged her shoulder. "If you don't mind my saying so, you're making this worst by appearing to be such a bad sport. Take it in good humor, the other partners did."

"He didn't portray the others as a frog."

"But did you see how he had Mr. Black starring at the behind of a woman in a magazine? For sure I thought he'd be in trouble for that. But Mr. Black laughed it off. Even if he's furious, he had the good sense to not let everyone know he was crazed."

Oops. The tension amped way up. Okay so maybe she shouldn't have used the word crazed. Chase had stopped walking and was staring at her. And if she didn't know better the look he had in his eyes was a bit crazed. She almost laughed at the thought. "I'm ready to change the subject. We've done enough talking about Sam."

"Not quite," Chase replied. "What were you doing in here with him with the door locked? This is my office."

"I'm aware of that. I needed to talk to Sam in private." Chase was glaring at her so she slanted her head finding it amusing that he was behaving like a baby. "If you must know, I was asking him to redo your painting."

Chase was staring at her as though he wasn't sure if she were telling the truth or not. Rebe couldn't really blame him. She'd sounded more like she was on Sam's side than his. She sidled up to Chase and caressed his back while placing light kisses around the corner of his mouth. "Baby, I'm on your side," she purred. Finally Chase was giving the tiniest of smiles.

"And Sam said no to your request same as he did to me, right? Darn him anyway," Chase sighed and returned Rebe's kisses. "I'm telling you, he's gone from hating you to having a crush on you. What did you do to that guy? You shouldn't have ever kissed him."

"I don't think there's that much power in my kisses," Rebe teased. That stopped Chase. He returned to glaring and moved her a bit away from him. She needed to be close to his body in order to not think of Sam. Chase was still glaring but a look of confusion was on his hero handsome face. He was trying to figure out if she was having fun at his expense. "Seriously, Chase, my kisses never made you behave in a strange manner."

He walked closer to her. "I've never had any complaints with you in the bedroom." He tilted his head slightly. "Are you ....faking it?"

"Of course not."

"Then what's going on? Every time I turn around you're kissing Sam, and you keep defending him. We're a couple. You should be defending me. Where on earth did he ever come up with the idea to use a frog as my image?"

"I'm afraid that might be my fault."

"You told him to paint me that way?"

"No, but when he took me to the dance, I may have called him a frog prince and…"

"And he's getting back at you through me." Suddenly Chase was all smiles. "I get it. That was a good one, Rebe."

Rebe looked away wondering why the idea of Sam being a frog had gone over so much easier with Chase. Then before she could stop herself words she'd had no intention of uttering came from her mouth.

"I'm going to fly and visit my parents in a few weeks. I need to talk to them. It's really important. Do you think you could go with me?" She watched as a panicked look came over Chase's face and he turned as red as though he'd been out all day in the sun.

"Rebe, we're in a committed relationship, but not that serious. A man only goes to meet a woman parents when they're talking marriage. We're nowhere near being at that juncture. Besides, I'm pretty sure I'm booked solid for the next two months."

He gave her a quick swipe on her lips. She couldn't really call it a kiss. Then he glanced at his watch.

"Listen, I have a client coming in a couple of seconds. I need my office."

"Sure," *you liar,* she was screaming in her head. She'd sat behind his desk and like any good lawyer, or fiction writer, or even a woman, his appointment book had been opened and well to heck with it, she'd looked in it and she'd flipped the pages for several months. And it wasn't because of the trip to her parents which she'd had no intention of inviting him to. It was because in her heart of hearts she still believed Chase was a cheater and wouldn't be able to change even if he really did want to.

Without sparing another look in Chase's direction Rebe left as quickly as a woman walking in too high stilettos could. She had no wish to further embarrass either herself or Chase.

Rushing back to her cubicle Rebe halted. She should have known Sam would be there smirking at her. But she wasn't in the mood to be teased, she had a real problem. She'd given the man she was in a committed relationship with, the opportunity to prove what they were after was more substantial, and he'd failed, miserably she might add. And the truth of it was Sam had been right. It was past time for her to see her parents face to face. She loved them like crazy and because she'd waited so long to return home it was going to be hard. Being there without Jamie would be even harder. She didn't want to return alone to the place where she'd had so much happiness and a feeling of safety. Like a big baby she wanted a buffer, a safety net. She wanted Sam to go with her.

She might as well get it out of the way. She wasn't a coward. Okay, she was a coward, but she wouldn't behave like one with Sam. "What do you want, Sam?"

"I'm sorry." Sam walked directly in front of Rebe and spoke quietly so no one else could hear him. "I'm the one who told you to go to your parents. And I did tell you, I would go with you. I'll still go with you." Her head was down and she didn't look up, so he added, "Even if the hunk is going with you, I'd still like to go."

He saw the slight quiver of her lips and the way her hands curled into fists. She was going to cry. For two weeks she'd cried in his arms and he damn well knew her telltale signs. He tried to run his misdeeds through his mind. Sam wouldn't be able to take it if he was the cause of her tears. He battled with pulling Rebe into his arms and consoling her, or making her laugh. He didn't think pulling her into his arms was the right choice, not out here where so many would see them. She'd be embarrassed and later she'd fight with Chase over Sam's actions. Not that he'd mind that. But he didn't want to cause Rebe public humiliation.

"Hey, I forgot to tell you, I added a fairy princess to the mural."
Sam watched as her fists released and she raised her head. The shine
of tears remained in her eyes but a smile was on her lips.

"You did not add a princess," Rebe said. "And if you did who is
she supposed to be?"

"Why you of course."

Rebe wiped her eyes with the back of her hands. "You haven't
had time to add in a princess. Why did you say that?"

"You were going to cry and I didn't want you to. I also knew you
didn't want to cry in the middle of your office. I had a choice to hold
you, or make you laugh." Sam took in a breath and released it. "Rebe,
I'm sorry if I hurt you."

"Is that the reason you're saying you're going to go with me?"

"If you remember, I said that before the waterworks."

"I didn't cry. Besides, how did you know I was on the verge of
tears?"

"You have this telltale thing about you before you cry."

"Do I?"

"Yes."

"Sam, how in the world do you know so much about me?"

Sam smiled but didn't answer, at least not that question. "Would
you still like for me to go with you?"

"Yes."

"And as for Chase, I promise I'll do my best to get along with
him."

"Thanks, Sam, but you don't have to worry about Chase. He's not
going. He's booked solid for the next couple of months and since
I've made up my mind to go and told them I'm coming I'm doing
just that." Rebe attempted to walk past him, but Sam reached out his
hand and stopped her.

"Instead of flying how would you like it if we drove? We can take
a few days, take our time and make stops along the way. I think it will
be a lot more relaxing. Besides, I know you're not that keen on
flying."

"I fly all the time."

"That doesn't mean you like it. So, are we driving?"

"Sam, come on. Please tell me. How do you know so much about
me?"

Sam pulled in a deep breath wanting badly to not only kiss Rebe but to kiss her until she regained the use of her brain cells that had left her in search of a hero and had found Chase instead. Letting the breath out slowly he studied Rebe, wondering what it was she was truly after. He noticed the movement of chairs around them and knew as long as they'd stood there talking, others, were more than likely making them the focal point of office gossip. It would be wiser to just answer her question.

"Rebe, you're behaving as though my knowing things about you is some kind of magical trick. I know about you, because I care enough to find out. How are you doing with finding out five things about me?" Sam grinned. "Yeah, I know. You haven't had the time have you? Don't worry, Rebe, it's not like you're on trial or anything."

But that was exactly how she felt. And when he asked his next question Rebe was aware Sam wanted her to have that feeling.

"Are you telling Chase that I'm going to drive you home?"

She hadn't thought about it but knew she would. Now she wondered what kind of reaction he'd have and if she gave a darn about it. Lifting her eyes she held Sam's gaze. "Yes, I'm going to tell him."

"And if he says he doesn't like it?"

"What are you really asking me?"

"You're a smart woman, Rebe. I take that back. You were able to finish law school, pass the bar and take care of your clients. And you were able to put together a rock solid deal for me. So you should be a smart woman. I shouldn't have to answer questions you already know the answers to."

"Sam, I didn't appoint you to be the voice of my conscience. You've wiggled yourself into my life and you've been manipulating me for almost five years," Rebe protested.

Sam frowned and a smile appeared on his lips, his beautifully shaped, wonderful, kissable lips. Now where the heck had that thought come from? And why was she wanting to throw her arms around him and kiss him like crazy? She couldn't even use the excuse of being on rebound, because she was still in a relationship. A serious relationship. Rebe groaned. Sam was eying her in a way that made her catch her breath as she wondered what he was going to say.

"I have a question for you, Rebe. You're the expert on romance, and especially on heroes. Tell me in this situation what exactly would a hero do? Would he leave you to your own devices? Or would he think you deserve better? Would he think you're still grieving your perfect hero?"

For a moment Sam thought not to finish his thought, but he'd been skirting around the issue for the past two years. It was time to say it. "Rebe, no one can replace Jamie in your heart. A man would be crazy to try. But I know your brother wouldn't want you settling for less than you deserve because you're afraid of loving too much and getting hurt. That's life."

"Why do you care?" Rebe had wondered why after the way she'd treated Sam he still cared. She was hoping since they were having an honest discussion he would be honest with her.

"The answer should be obvious. You're worth my caring. Why wouldn't I help you? But I'm going to give you this one for free. Your brother asked me to look out for you. You've never wanted to know anything past his funeral. But we were friends, and Jamie knew if anything ever happened to him how hard his leaving would be for you."

"Why would he ask you that? Didn't he know you couldn't stand me?"

"He knew."

"Is that why you kissed me? Why you keep kissing me?" Oh crap if she could take the words back she would. Rebe closed her eyes briefly as she heard Sam laughing softly.

"Kissing you didn't have a damn thing to do with your brother. That, I can promise you. By the way, I like kissing you. You have the softest lips. And you taste so good. It was really hard to stop. But of course I wouldn't have had a ton of experience with women, or kissing. And I definitely haven't been magically changed by any woman into a prince, so…"

"You're weird, Sam. And I don't believe you. No way in the world would my brother ask you to look out for me? Why on earth would he ask a man who hated me?"

"Why indeed?" Sam replied. "Just so we're clear, I never hated you. I found you annoying, self-centered, a featherbrain airhead. I couldn't stand you. But I never hated you. Rebe, how many times do I have to reassure you of that? Why don't you ask yourself why it's important to you how I feel about you? Look… enough talking. I have a project to work on. I'll talk to you later. Just let me know when you want to leave"

Walking away from Rebe at that moment was the hardest thing he'd ever done, but Sam had caught Rebe in a very vulnerable moment. Something had happened with Chase. He knew Rebe so well. More than likely he'd said he didn't want to meet her parents and there was no way she wanted Sam to know that, considering he wasn't a big fan of Chase. The thing of it was, Sam would never take advantage of Rebe in that way. When, and if she ever came to him, it wouldn't be because of something that bonehead Chase had done to hurt her.

CHAPTER ELEVEN

It had been too long since Rebe and Kandi had had a girl's night out. Sure they'd gotten together in their apartments and had been with Sam in attendance countless times. But it had been before Jamie died that the two of them had gone alone for dinner and clubbing. It was about time. As always when they were together they were having a good time. They'd enjoyed a fantastic dinner and had danced until they were breathless. It felt freeing to do nothing more than fend off would be suitors and laughing together. It also felt good that she'd dressed in a sexy short skirt and silk blouse and had done it for no other reason than she liked the outfit. No Chase, wanting her to look sexy, or Sam criticizing her for showing a little skin.

"This feels good," Rebe said. "Just the two of us. It's been way too long."

"Yeah, it's been too long," Kandi agreed.

The sudden sadness Rebe noted in Kandi's voice and in her eyes had her feeling guilty that she'd pulled away from her best friend as well as everyone else she loved. She didn't want to think about the possible damage she could have done to their friendship. She was thankful that those who loved her had understood. Reaching her hand out, Rebe took Kandi's hand in hers. They remained as they were for a long moment just enjoying each other's company. When Kandi focused on her, Rebe was certain she knew what it would be about.

"Sam told me he's driving you to see your parents. Do you mind if I tag alone?"

She'd been wrong. She'd thought her friend was going to ask about Chase, not Sam. Before Rebe could stop herself or even figure out why she was doing what she did, she'd pulled away from Kandi and sat staring at her, unable to speak, but her eyes opened wide.

Rebe couldn't believe her reaction to such a simple request and from Kandi no less. She wouldn't have believed it, but knew it was a good dose of truth, the way it hit her in the chest with such force.

For heaven sake, Rebe didn't want her best friend to make the drive with them. WTH? They'd been born three days apart, had lived next door to each other their entire lives, and had gone through school together, even opting for the same college. And had left home together and now resided in the same city. They were family. But she still didn't want her with them on the trip. She couldn't look at Kandi, couldn't say the words. How would she explain it when she didn't even know the reason?

"Oh my, God," Kandi yelled. "You don't want me to go, do you? Rebe! What in the world is wrong with you? You're going home. I live next door. Why don't you want me along?" A light suddenly went off and Kandi screamed. "You want to be alone with Sam. Why?"

"I do not."

"Rebe, you're such a liar. You're falling for Sam. He's everything you don't want and you're falling for him." Kandi pounced on her and began squealing. "This has taken way longer than it should. I'm so happy."

"Don't be. You can come on the road trip with us. In fact I insist that you come."

"Now, you're afraid. Well, guess what? Sam's afraid also. He's the one who asked me to tag along. I think that boy has it bad for you, and I don't think he trust the two of you together for such a long trip there and back."

"Sam asked you to come?"

"Yes."

"I'm not surprised. When we first discussed the trip, he said it would be great if the three of us could make the trip together."

"Then why did you act so surprised, or as though you wanted to kill me and stuff me in the back of Sam's car?"

"Cut it out. Did I tell you that Sam has added a few words to his opinion of me? He called me a featherbrain and an airhead. He's so mean to me."

"Yet, he's always there when you need him."

"Because of my brother. He told me he'd promised Jamie he'd take care of me."

"Please, Rebe, do you think Jamie didn't know how Sam feels about you, or for that matter how you feel about him? You're just too stubborn to admit it. And Sam's got way too much pride to beg."

Though the laughter in Kandi's eyes was contagious Rebe refused to give in to it. "I don't want Sam to beg me. You both seem to forget I'm in a serious relationship."

"Oh, please. Do you think because you keep saying those words it will make it come true? Chase is so not for you and you're not going to marry him. Yes, you like that he's good looking and he can be a lot of fun. And I get it, he gets the job done and you get the big 'O'. But that's not all there is to a relationship. I mean you could sample Sam, and see if he can get the job done before you dump Chase."

Disbelief made Rebe's mouth drop at what Kandi was proposing. "You can't be serious. I am not sampling Sam."

"You've sampled his kisses. Tell me something, can he kiss?"

"I will not answer that question," Rebe responded indignantly feeling her nether regions heat up. "That is so none of your business."

"You've told me things about Chase."

"Not really intimate things?"

"Get real, telling me how he makes you...cry for Jesus is about as intimate as one can get. Besides, kissing isn't intimate. Well, I'll take that back. It depend if it's your lips, or you're being kissed a bit farther south as to whether it's intimate. Has Sam kissed your southern regions?"

This time Rebe was unable to hold back the laughter. She hit out at Kandi.

"Come on tell, Rebe, tell me, how Sam kisses?"

"If you're so interested in how Sam kisses, why don't you kiss him and find out?"

"Because unlike you my friend I know when a man is smitten with another woman. Even if said woman is unaware of it. Besides, I prefer my kisses to be something he and I both want to do, not something done as an experiment, or because the guy might not be what I've imagined in my mind he should be."

"You're talking about me obviously, and you're beginning to sound like Sam. I haven't changed in the kind of guys I likes since high school. Why are you acting like Sam, like I all of a sudden decided on a type?"

"You were never this bad. You didn't behave like this until you began writing romance novels. It was then you started this nonsense about having to be with a heroic looking guy. I think you're forgetting that it's much better to be with a hero than someone who looks like a preconceived idea of one. I don't get it. Why don't you take a look at your behavior and take a look at Sam's. Pretend you're both fictional characters. Wouldn't he be in love with you? Wouldn't you end up falling for him? I've read your books and I know how the story would end. You'd live happily ever after?"

"Enough of this." Getting up to return to the dance floor Rebe turned and said over her shoulder. "There is no such thing as happily ever after. If there were our group would still be a foursome. Jamie would still be alive."

When the phone rang waking her early on Sunday morning Rebe was sure it would be Chase. For some reason he was always more interested when he was unable to reach her. And for Friday and Saturday she'd been out of touch. Yes, it was childish. But she'd been hurt and annoyed that he didn't want to meet her parents,' that he didn't think they were that serious. Wasn't that the point of them being in a committed relationship? She'd gone back and forth with her logic, hating that she vacillated.

She took a breath on looking at his number at the caller ID. It would have been even more childish of her to not answer, so she did. "Hi, Chase," she said trying to make sure there wasn't the least bit of enthusiasm in her voice.

"Where have you been all weekend. I came over twice, and I've called you repeatedly. And I've left you a dozen texts, none of which you even bothered to answer."

"Kandi and I had a girl's night on Friday. Saturday I had things to do." She waited knowing for the first time in his life Chase was feeling jealous and his confidence was wavering. She'd said what she had in the manner she had in order to make him wonder. That was mean of her. Or was it? If he were truly a hero he would have told her he'd love to visit her parents. And if she were truly a heroine she'd let him off the hook. LOL. She never claimed to be a heroine and had no plans at the moment of letting Chase off the hook.

"Rebe, I'm getting the feeling that you're pissed at me. Is it because of what I said about going to visit your parents? I'm sorry if I hurt your feelings. I've been thinking about it and I don't think what I said to you was my being a good boyfriend. I'm sorry about that. I'd like very much to go with you to visit your parents."

She needed to give Chase one more shot. Sitting up in bed Rebe glanced across her bedroom to the vase of roses Chase had sent to her. A heroic move, right? What if it was fear of the things she'd had with Chase for the past two plus years that had her thinking of Sam?

It could be possible. Why hadn't she thought of Sam in a romantic way before Jamie died, before she was with Chase? *She had thought of him that way, for only a nano second,* she realized but pushed it away.

"I think you're being a bad girlfriend at the moment. I've never refused your calls, never not told you where I was going to be. I thought we made a pact that the weekends were for us, no matter what," Chase said in his calm lawyer voice.

He did have a point. And what the heck? Did she not have a voice? Shouldn't she have told him how she'd felt about his not wanting to go to a place where she didn't want him to go? She was nuts. Crazy.

The sudden realization of her mental status brought the beginning of an internal battle between her head and her heart. Her heart was screaming, 'no, don't do it. End it and run to Sam'. Her head was screaming. 'Chase is safe; you don't want to become lost in another person. You'll never become lost in Chase. He may break your heart, but he'll never be able to break your spirit, or take away your will to live.'

"Rebe, your mind is so far away. I can tell you're not even listening to me. It's only fair that if you have me on trial I receive a chance to redeem myself. We haven't had a fight. I haven't cheated. I had a moment of panic. Will you condemn me for that? I was serious when I told you I wanted a commitment with you. I'm trying and I've come more than half way. Are you willing to take the next step?"

Chase was right. Oh crap. He had a point and she wasn't a quitter. She did owe it to him and to herself to see if there was anything to their relationship besides the fact that they looked good together, had fun, and were great in bed. Not bad really, not when she'd always sworn she wanted nothing more.

Darn it to hell. It was all Sam's fault for suggesting if Chase really cared, even a little bit that he'd want to go with her. Well heck, she'd not wanted him to care enough to do something big like that. She wasn't sure if she wanted him to care at all. The most she wanted was the fun loving Chase without the cheating. That would have been enough for her. But no, Mr. But in her business had ruined all of that.

Sam was forever making her question the things she thought she wanted. And she couldn't get it out of her mind that he wanted her to …well what, be better, more unselfish… more what? And what the heck was it about her brother asking Sam to look after her. She was having a hard enough time living without her brother in her life.

Once again Sam was right. Jamie had been her perfect hero. His death had left a huge hole in her heart, leaving her unable to talk about Jamie with anyone but Sam. She'd not had to put on a brave face with Sam, or even make attempts to get him through his own grief. He'd been close to Jamie and like her parents and other family and even Kandi and her family, they'd all hurt. She'd not been able to be there for any of them. She'd been selfish and had taken from Sam without a single worry. And because of his allowing her to grieve she'd been able to continue living. Two years later he remained the only person she'd ever talked to about Jamie.

In more ways than one, Sam was different. He made Rebe do things she didn't want to do, like question her relationship with Chase. She wanted to be in 100%, but she wasn't. The strange thing of it was, she didn't think her actions or lack thereof had any bearings on the fact that Chase had cheated on her, over and over again. She wasn't stupid. Well, not the way Sam meant anyway. She knew Chase was a dog and she'd been okay with it. Sure, she'd not played around on him. But that was because it wasn't who she was. Or it hadn't been. Now all of a sudden one kiss from Sam had turned into several and she found herself wanting more from him, more from Chase and more from herself. Darn it all. Whenever she got to thinking about Sam she found it hard to stop. She heard a tapping on the phone and realized once again in their conversation her mind had wandered away from Chase and she'd left him hanging.

"Rebe, please answer me. What's wrong?" Chase pleaded, something Rebe was not used to him doing.

"I've been thinking."

"About us?"

"Yes."

"Are you afraid?

"I think I might be, Chase. I'm not sure if we can, or even if we should be attempting this. Look, if you're worried about our working arrangement I promise that doesn't have to change."

"It's not our working relationship at issue here. It's our personal one. I want more. If I'm going to be a better boyfriend then you're the one I want to be one for."

"That is such a strange way to put it."

"I know it might be. But you're a writer; you have to know what I mean."

"Okay, maybe I do. You want to improve yourself and somehow you have me and our relationship tied into it. That doesn't sound very romantic."

"Come on, Rebe," Chase pleaded.

It was time for Rebe to come clean. She had to admit it. Chase had been trying. Her state of flux was not entirely his fault. With a soft moan of apprehension she decided to attempt to explain to Chase what was going on. The thing of it was she didn't entirely understand it all herself.

"Chase, I'm not even sure exactly why I'm upset with you. All of it doesn't have to do with my going home to see my parents. Some of it has to do with the way you behaved at the unveiling of Sam's mural. I'd expected you to be a better sport. I think I've given you qualities I wanted you to have. That's my fault, not yours."

"People can change, Rebe. I can change if the stakes are high enough, if I want to badly enough. I want to change, for you and for us."

Rebe knew she should ask Chase once more if he wanted to go with her to visit her parents. Heck he was practically asking her to. Didn't he say he wanted a second chance? Didn't he say he wanted to change? She thought about it, but couldn't get past the fact that he'd already said he had no interest in meeting her parents. Still for some unknown reason she wanted to give them another chance to prove they were in a semblance of relationship. With a half sigh she decided to go at it from a different angle.

"I decided instead of flying to see my parents, I'm going to make it into a road trip. Sam is going with me." Silence greeted her for an unbearably long time.

"What you're not saying is that now I have to worry about not only hurting you, but I have to worry about Sam's feelings as well? What about mine?" Chase asked. "Neither of you appear to care that it's improper for you to continue playing kissing games. I'm almost positive that you never cheated on me in the past. So I've been wondering if this thing you've got going with Sam isn't pretense on your part. Perhaps you're getting even with me for my past shabby treatment. If that's the case and you've been kissing Sam out of revenge, Rebe, you need to wake up. Sam is in love with you. This isn't a joke to him. He's out to wreck our relationship."

"That's not true," Rebe replied softly, not altogether sure that wasn't exactly what Sam had in mind.

"Yes, Rebe, it's true. I don't know how Sam went so quickly from not being able to stand you to being in love with you, but it happened. I was thinking about it and I figured that perhaps I owe you the couple of kisses you've shared with Sam. It may not even up the score between us, but the divide isn't nearly as great. Still, I think what you're doing is going overboard and it's not fair to me. The point of our making a commitment meant *We*, as in you and me, were going to get closer together. What are you going to do, run off any time you get upset with me about something? That's being passive aggressive."

"You're right." Rebe waited for the information to sink in, that she'd actually admitted she was wrong in being angry with him and not telling him.

"If that's the case, then I don't get it. You've never had any problem reaming me out, telling me you were pissed. Since you've been hanging out with Sam, you've changed. I don't like it."

Laughter was Rebe's answer. "Chase, you and Sam have a lot more in common than you might think. He thinks I've changed since we've been dating and not for the better. So it would appear neither of you are my biggest fan."

"Rebe, I'm not joking."

Sighing, Rebe made herself comfortable. "I know," she said. "I'm not doing this because I'm angry with you. I already told you that I was going to give us an opportunity to make this work."

"So, why is Sam going with you to see your parents?"

"Sam has met my parents several times. Don't get upset, but I had asked Sam to go with me before I ever thought of asking you. It was weeks ago. Actually Sam was the one who told me that considering we were in a relationship, I really should ask you to go with me. I asked, you said no. So I asked Sam again and he agreed."

"Rebe, you have to admit you came at me from out of nowhere with that. And to top it off you were locked in my office with Sam. I was pissed. Can I come over? And we'll discuss us. I'll bring breakfast."

"And coffee?"

Chase laughed. "Sure, I'll bring coffee."

With a bit of a groan Rebe didn't have to wonder how the conversation with Chase would go. She would ask him once more if he wanted to accompany her home and he would say yes. Better yet, he would ask if he could go with her and she would be the one to say yes. Either way she knew by the time he left her apartment he would be going with her. And she knew Sam was going to want to kill her. She had no choice but to call Sam and advise him of the changed circumstances and let the chips fall where they may.

Sam hung up the phone from talking with Rebe and went immediately across the hall to Kandi's apartment and banged on her door. He could barely contain his annoyance until the door was open. One look at Kandi's face and he knew she already had the information he'd come to give her.

"I don't believe her. Did she really nearly beg me to take her to see her parents? Did she not tell me her boyfriend had better things to do and couldn't make it? And now she does this big turnaround because he's suddenly had a change of heart. She told Chase we're taking a road trip and asked him to come along. What nerve. I simply cannot believe she did that. I'm not going. I am just not going."

"Come on Sam, Rebe needs you. It's the first time she'd been home since Jamie's funeral. You know she had to ask Chase if he'd go. Matter of fact she told me you first suggested it."

"I did and he said no. He doesn't deserve another chance to make things right. He only changed his mind when she told him I was going. I do not want to be bothered with him. I can't stand him"

"I know. I also know that you're doing this for Rebe."

Sam was dumbfounded. He'd planned to tell Rebe how he felt about her and see if there was something there between them. He thought he'd sensed it on several occasions and most definitely when they kissed. Then again that could be mutual attraction or lust. He wanted to see if there was more.

Sam glared at Kandi. "I could strangle Rebe. I really and truly could seriously strangle her." Kandi was giving him a funny look before she turned and walked toward the kitchen. Taking two mugs from the cabinet she poured them both coffee then took out plates and placed powdered doughnuts on them. "Have breakfast with me."

"Do you really think coffee and doughnuts will make this go away?"

"Give her a break. She doesn't know what to do. Rebe's in over her head and she's thinking that as a good girlfriend she needs to give Chase a chance to step up to the plate."

Sam sighed and took a sip of the coffee before looking at Kandi. "Chase is never going to step up to the plate. He's never going to be what she needs. Why can't she see that?"

"Rebe sees it, believe me she sees it. She just doesn't want to acknowledge it."

CHAPTER TWELVE

It was the longest three weeks of his life. Sam had remained holed up in his apartment working on a painting. Once they'd narrowed the details down to when they would leave and how long they would be gone he'd adjusted his timeframe on a special project. He'd not spoken to Rebe since she'd given him the details. He may have been a bit gruff with her but that couldn't be helped. That was wrong. It could have been helped, he'd just chosen not to. The same as he'd chosen not to see or talk to her until he absolutely had to.

Now he had to.

Wrapping up the finished Canvas he took it to his car and came back up for Kandi. Together they waited on Rebe and Chase to arrive. The moment Rebe stepped out of Chase's car smiling, Sam thought as he had in the past, Barbie and Ken. Granted Rebe wasn't your typical Barbie, but she was Barbie none the less. "Please," he halfheartedly prayed. "Let them get in the car without speaking to me."

Chase glanced at Kandi and Sam then smiled at Rebe. "Sam, I wanted to tell you that I love long distance driving. So at any point when you feel tired let me know and I'll take over."

Take over. Hadn't he taken over enough things? With a half growl Sam finally answered. "This is my car. I think I can drive it. Besides, we're not driving straight through. This will be done at a leisurely pace."

"I wasn't trying to stop you, and I wasn't implying that you'd need the help. I offered because I'm trying to be nice to you. Rebe asked me if I'd try. I decided I would."

For a moment there was complete silence. It was the longest complete silence Sam had ever witnessed. Even the birds in the trees had stopped chirping to listen to Sam's answer. He would not kill Rebe, not out here in front of so many witnesses. And he wouldn't punch Chase, something his fist was itching to do. But he wouldn't do it because he wasn't a kid, just a jealous frog prince who would forever remain so it seemed.

Sam did the only thing left to him to do. He stared at Rebe hoping she could read his mind and know the things he wanted to say. He sighed at the look in her eyes. Sure she knew what he was thinking. Why in the world did you bring Chase? And why are you forcing him on me? Why didn't you fly if you wanted Chase to go? Rebe, we did not all have to be in this car together. I am going to be sick.

As Sam continued to half stare half glare at her, Rebe steepled her hands together underneath her chin and pleaded with her eyes for him to be nice. Hell, if Chase could do it, so could he.

"Listen, Sam, do you mind if I sit in the front with you so I can stretch my legs out?" Chase did a sweeping hand motion to show his height as if that were necessary.

"And what about squishing Rebe and Kandi?"

"They will survive."

"And so will you. No, stay in the back with your girlfriend."

Rebe sidled alongside Sam and touched his arm. He looked at her and blinked at the look in her eyes.

"Please, Sam, it's okay. I'll sit behind him," Rebe pleaded.

"You're aware he's going to take the seat back as far as it will go right?"

"I'll put my legs on the seat."

"You're going to get leg cramps," Sam muttered.

She smiled. "I'll be okay."

Three hours later Rebe was regretting those words. Sam had been right. She had legs cramps. She'd tried not to moan. It had just slipped out. Sam heard her and glanced in the rearview mirror. His gaze connected with her. Annoyed wasn't the word for the way Sam glanced at Chase in the passenger seat beside him.

Sam had known Rebe was going to get leg cramps. He shouldn't have listened to her about Chase sitting in the front and taking his seat back as far as it would go. Hell, Chase shouldn't have come on this trip. Sam should have insisted if Rebe really needed Chase along that the two of them take a plane and skip the long drive. But she'd wanted to drive, and she'd wanted Sam and Chase both to go. Sam had known it was going to be sheer disaster. When Sam pulled off the toll road to a restaurant he was livid. Before any of them knew what was happening he was out of the driver's side and yelling for Chase to move out the way. He opened the dash, retrieved the pain spray he'd brought along for Rebe and swore.

"Everyone get out, we're going to take a break," Sam

commanded.

"Come here, Rebe," he ordered ignoring the others. He rolled both legs of her pants up to her knees and sprayed feeling a slight satisfaction when she gave a little scream from the frigid liquid. "Don't move. This will help. I think we need to find a place to rest."

"Sam, we've only been driving for a few hours. At this rate we won't get to Atlanta until next week. Can't we at least drive a few more hours?" Chase stared at Sam and waited.

"If you would like to trade places with Rebe then we can try it. Otherwise we're stopping so she can rest."

"When they returned to the vehicle Sam looked at Chase with disgust. "You can drive now. Rebe, take the front seat." When she made a move to push the seat back up he stopped her. "I'll sit behind you."

Rebe smiled and out of the blue gave him a hug then a kiss on the cheek. "I wouldn't dream of being that selfish. Thanks for the spray, Sam. My legs are feeling better already."

Damn it, why couldn't Rebe have left well enough alone? Sam wondered. Why couldn't she have gotten in the car without touching him? The hug made him unhinged, the soft gentle kiss shattered him and an instant erection happened. There was no way in hell he would be able to sit calmly behind her. Moving over to the other side of the car he nodded at Kandi. He took in several breaths trying to calm his wayward thoughts. When that didn't help he frowned, then he bit his lips. He turned his full gaze to Kandi until he was certain she'd get his meaning. "Would you sit behind Rebe?" he asked.

For once Kandi didn't ask questions, she just moved. For several minutes there was an awkward silence as they all got back into the car and Chase began driving. Well, it would have been silent if Chase wasn't humming. Sam and Kandi exchanged looks and shook their heads, both looking at their watches then giving a quiet chuckle.

Before Sam knew what Chase was doing he'd lifted the armrest and popped in a CD Sam had made for the trip, for Rebe, when he'd thought it would be the two of them making the drive. Damn. He had to find a way to get Chase not to play the damn music without making a big deal of it.

"Chase, if you don't mind I have a headache. Please turn the music off." Sam asked."

"I'll keep it low, don't worry." Chase answered.

Before Sam could say another word a stupid love song was playing. Why hadn't he gotten rid of the damn thing?

Sam sighed hoping that no one would know he'd made the CD especially for Rebe, and read his feelings into it. But hell that wasn't to be. Kandi was staring at him, he could feel it. He turned slightly and their gazes locked, he wanted to plead with her not to say a word. How he wished the song would end, but when it did there would be another sappy love song that told just how he felt about Rebe. She drove him crazy, most of the time he absolutely couldn't stand her, but somehow in spite of all that, he found himself in love with her. He groaned. The one time he'd taken Kandi's advice to tell Rebe of his feelings for her. He'd thought the idea cute to make the CD and play it for her on their road trip. Now it was torture. *Please, God, don't let Rebe figure it out.*

"What a sappy song." Chase laughed. "I mean seriously, it's filled with contradictions."

"It's beautiful," Rebe challenged. "It's meant to be filled with contradictions. Love is never straightforward and problem free." After several songs had played Rebe was singing along.

"Rebe, you can't really like all of these sappy songs."

"I do. Matter of fact I wasn't aware that all of the singers were singing of the things I want in my life until I heard their words."

Again Chase laughed. "You have got to be kidding."

"I wish I was."

"Well, at least one of them got something right. You are crazy. And you're driving me out of my mind." Chase gave a quick peek at Rebe and laughed.

"Me? What about you?" Rebe responded. "And what about the part of giving your whole self to the other person? Surely you agree with that?"

"There is no way in hell you have ever given me all of yourself, except maybe in the bedroom," Chase teased.

Rebe was aware Chase was teasing her but still she wanted to ask him a question. "And you, Chase, have you given that to me?"

Chase turned his attention from the road and stared at Rebe. Immediately all three passengers screamed, "Chase, watch where you're going."

"Rebe, are you serious? Are you wanting more?"

"I don't think we should have this conversation right now."

"It's a simple question. We're in a committed relationship. Are you thinking marriage?"

"I'm thinking of the singer and the song. I believe whoever wrote the song was writing it for the woman in his life. Even so, I find that he's speaking to my heart. Those aren't things that a woman or a man asks a person for. It's just something that happens. You can't make it happen. It's either there, or it isn't."

Rebe sang a few more lines of the song that was playing then she said, "Sometimes I wonder if I've been wrong in the way I've thought about love and relationships. What if hurting is a natural part of love?"

Don't listen Sam chided himself. *Don't listen; you don't want to hear her answer.* Sam's heart was thumping wildly, and then Rebe continued.

"But I suppose you can be in a committed relationship and not have that deep and abiding love. It's a bit scary to give your all to another person. But there are times when I would love to be someone's end and their beginning. And in those moments of weakness, I'd love for someone to be mine I suppose."

"I'll tell you what, as soon as we get to a hotel room I'll give you a massage and I'll be your end, if you'll be my beginning." Chase laughed and glanced toward Rebe quickly turning his eyes back to the road before anyone could yell out.

For the next hour Sam barely breathed. He closed his eyes wishing he were anywhere but in the car wanting Rebe, longing for her and having to listen to her ask Chase again and again to return the CD back to the sappiest song of all. There were other songs on there. Why the heck couldn't she request those?

"Sam, you have great taste in music," Rebe said at last. "The woman you fall in love with will be very lucky."

"Why? Who in their right mind would want to marry a starving artist?" Chase countered.

"A woman who sees his vision." Rebe grinned. "A woman who can look in a mirror and see what's really there."

Chase glanced at Rebe then into the rearview mirror. "Thanks for that, Hon. See, Sam, I could care less about that painting you did of me. Rebe sees the real me."

"I can only hope that she does."

"What does that mean?"

"Just that I know Rebe is smart. And I know she sees the real you.

Since you no longer have a problem with the painting I guess I'll forget about redoing it."

For about ten seconds that shut Chase up. Sam smiled to himself. He had no intention of redoing the painting

Chase glanced up into the rearview mirror and looked at Sam. "You were going to change it? Why?"

Sam hunched his shoulder. "You didn't like it."

After a brief pause Chase shrugged his shoulder and said, "Thanks, Sam. But, I'm good with it now. Besides, Rebe told me that I'm the handsome prince in your little fairytale and that's what the other women at the office think. They seem to think my part of the mural is what makes it. You might say you've made me a star. So, thank you."

The laugh from Kandi's corner of the car made Sam give her a sharp look.

"I'm sorry but I have got to look at that painting that's caused so many changes in the three of you." Kandi glanced at Sam. "I mean first there's anger then down right praise. When we return home that's one of the first things I'm going to do."

Chase laughed. "Good, Kandi, and maybe you'd like to go with us to an art show. You too, Sam. Rebe and I are going to see a really famous artist. I hear the guy makes a hundred thousand dollar a pop for something as small as an eight by ten. Maybe you can get a few tips. Now this is one artist that could afford to get married if he wants. But why bother. He has enough money to do what he wants. He should just continue playing the field."

And just like that without any help from Sam, Chase had firmly inserted his foot into his mouth. For once he realized it when the car became eerily quiet.

Chase coughed a couple of times. "Of course if he's in a serious relationship then that's a different matter."

"Nice save," Kandi purred.

Sam laughed and bumped fists with Kandi and sat back to contemplate his life. For a couple of hours the ride was fun. If Chase wasn't dating Rebe and they were in some alternate universe he could possibly see a time where he wouldn't want to punch Chase out. With a sigh Sam admitted to himself what was bothering him. Chase was dating Rebe. And Rebe had been laughing at his corny jokes for the past hour. It didn't seem that she had any plans on dumping

Chase. As far as he could tell, Rebe couldn't even see she had options.

"Chase, next sign you see where there's food please get off," I'm getting hungry. Anyone else hungry?" Rebe asked.

"I brought a ton of food," Sam said without thinking and immediately wished he'd just allowed Chase to stop for food. When Rebe turned eagerly back to ask him what he'd brought he had no choice but to name the array of food he'd prepared for her.

"Thanks, Sam. I'll have the chicken salad sandwich. I still need to make a pit stop though." She turned to Chase. "Would you like anything?"

Sam was in love with her. It wasn't just a case of lust or that he liked her kisses. A shiver raced across her body and Rebe felt deliciously happy, heck she was euphoric with happiness. What a time to find out when they were on a trip with her boyfriend. Everything Sam had done had been for her, She'd enjoyed the music. She'd listened carefully. All of songs were favorites of hers. Even the food he'd prepared including snacks had been things she liked.

She thought of the pain spray for her legs. No one else had used it including Sam. She remembered the road trip they'd taken to Jamie's funeral. Her parents had insisted Jamie be buried in Atlanta. Kandi had flown home to accompany the casket. Rebe had not wanted to fly, she'd become freaked at the thought, so Sam has driven her to Atlanta. Now that she thought about it, she remembered her legs had cramped then too. But it had taken her awhile to realize it, she'd been so distraught. It had been Sam who'd noticed her swollen legs and immediately pulled off the highway at the next exit and had gotten ice for her legs and ordered her to stretch out on the backseat. Ah. It was as though a light bulb had gone on in her head. Her leg cramps was the reason Sam had promised her they would have fun and they'd stop and make the trip, a leisurely one. And the CD, it was a mix of artists. Darn it, she should have known. He'd made it for her.

Singing from the driver's seat brought her attention back to the man she was committed to. How ironic that she was committed to a man who would never put her needs first, would never think to buy pain spray in case she got a cramp in her legs, or make her chicken salad just the way she liked it. Sam was all the things she'd said she didn't want in a relationship, real love, real caring. Now that she was getting a taste of it, it wasn't so bad. Still, she was in a bit of a pickle. It wasn't as though she didn't care for Chase in her own way. She'd always liked him. She didn't want to hurt him. And especially not when he'd agreed albeit a bit reluctantly to visit her parents with her.

Oh darn, her parents. They were bound to think things were more serious with her and Chase than they were. And she owed that to Sam as well. He'd egged her on saying Chase would never agree to meet her parents, until she'd wanted to know the answer and asked. *Please God, don't let Daddy ask Chase his intentions toward me. I'll just die.*

"Chase, don't forget I need to make a pit stop." Rebe looked toward the backseat. "I'm sure Kandi does also. Right, Kandi?" Rebe arched her brow and gave Kandi a stern no nonsense look until she got the hint and agreed she needed to stop.

Moments after they'd pulled into a rest stop Rebe grabbed Kandi's arm and pulled her into the ladies room. The door was barely closed before she blurted out her information. "Sam is in love with me."

"What else is new?" Kandi asked unconcerned.

"I mean, he's really in love with me."

"You do know you knew this already. So what are you going to do about it?"

"What am I supposed to do? I have a boyfriend."

"Please."

"Kandi."

"How do you feel about Chase? I mean really feel about him. Do you love him?"

"Yes, I love him."

"Rebe, are you in love with Chase?"

"I'm in a committed relationship with him."

"Stop stalling. We've known each other since birth. You may try to lie to me, but we both know I'm aware of what you're doing."

"Come on, Kandi, you know I like Chase. I've told you that a thousand times. I have fun with him. He's really not as bad as you and Sam thinks. And I promised him I'd give our relationship a real shot."

"So what's the problem with Sam? If you don't have feelings for him don't worry about it."

Rebe didn't answer, in fact she looked away.

"Rebe, oh my God. You love Sam."

"Of course I love him. He's my friend and has been for almost five years."

"You know what I mean. Stop using legalese on me. Are you in love with Sam?""

"I can't answer that. Things are too confusing at the moment. I can't be analyzing how I feel about another man when I'm in a relationship, but I wish...."

"You wish you'd come alone with Sam."

"Yeah. I do. We need to talk also. Some of this is my fault."

"Would you listen to yourself? Sam is in love with you and you think it's your fault. You can't control his emotions. Who do you think you are? Besides, you love who you love, and apparently Sam loves you. And you...well you don't have any idea who you're in love with. Or maybe you do, and just don't want to admit it. Rebe, the idea that you don't trust me, your best friend to share the truth with really hurts. This is the second time you've pushed me aside. The first time with Jamie. And now with Sam. What gives? Are we best friends or not?"

Rebe was aware Kandi was playing her, but still there was some truth in her statement. They were best friends. They didn't have secrets. Rebe groaned.

"What am I supposed to do? This is so beyond awkward. Just tell me, Kandi, what am I supposed to do? Chase came on this trip to support me, and to meet my parents. I keep telling you that I promised him I'd give us a real try. He's trying, he really is."

Kandi didn't answer just listened to Rebe with her head tilted slightly allowing a sigh to escape from time to time. When Rebe finally ran out of steam she gave her a look before asking the obvious.

"Come on, Rebe, tell me please. Even if you don't tell Sam, tell me. Are you in love with Sam?""

"I'm not sure I even know what being in love means. But I do love him. And like you said I've always known Sam had feelings for me. I've known in spite of the nasty little names he's lobbed at me through the years. I'm not stupid. His opinion means the world to me. He's the one person who can get me through the hard times. He makes me challenge myself and do things I would never do without him needling me. I can depend on him. He makes me sound like a darn romance novel."

"Are you ever going to tell me what happened between the two of you when your brother died? Why was Sam the only one you wanted to be around?"

Rebe reached out and gave her friend a hug. She'd never meant to hurt her feelings by not seeing her after Jamie's funeral. Just as she'd not meant to hurt her parents. She sighed and pulled away to answer Kandi.

"It was instinct. For those two weeks I was weak and I allowed it because I knew Sam would be my strength. He was my haven in the stormiest time in my life. I knew Sam loved me and I knew I loved him. I know you're wondering if anything happened between us. Yes, but not what you think. I laid in his arms, in his bed, and gave my heart permission to grieve and to begin to heal. There wasn't so much as a sexual look that passed between us. He was my rock, my protector and my love."

"Then why did the two of you go after each other after that time was over?"

"That was my doing. Sam was so deeply in my heart and I loved him so much that I had to end it. I had to find a way to make him stop loving me. I had to stop loving him. It would hurt too much for something to happen to him. Besides, as much as I was aware that he loved me, I also knew because of my brother's..." Rebe's breath hitched. She still didn't like saying the word. Then she took a deep breath, let it out and continued.

"Because of Jamie's death there was this sense of obligation on Sam's part to take care of me. I wasn't going to fall into something with him because he'd saved me."

"So the mutual hate you guys participated in for the last couple of years, was it all an act?"

Rebe laughed. "Definitely not on Sam's part. Though he says he never hated me, he just couldn't stand me. I think if I'd never become involved with Chase, Sam never would have examined his feelings for me."

"And just what brought on this revelation? Why now do you know he's in love with you?"

"It was the music. But before that when he had the spray for my leg cramps…well, when Jamie died and Sam drove me home, my legs hurt, and were swollen. He remembered."

"How do you know he didn't have the spray for himself?"

"He didn't. And all the food he brought. They're all my favorites."

Kandi thought about it. "That's such a random thing."

"You might think that, but the thing of it is Sam thinks about me, my comfort, my likes and dislikes. But the thing that let me know for sure was when Chase put the music on and I heard the song. I knew Sam had brought the CD to tell me how he felt about me. I wish …."

"That he'd not brought it or that Chase had not played it?"

"I wish we'd been alone when he did."

"What are you going to do?"

"I'm not going to do anything to hurt Chase's feelings. Even though he didn't want to come, he did, and I don't want my parents worrying about me. So, I'll have to think of some way to keep the peace."

"Good luck with that. But I think the idea that we're going to stop at a hotel and get a room is driving Sam crazy thinking you're going to be with Chase in the biblical sense, and probably in the room next door to Sam's."

"Yeah, it's even awkward for me. How am I going to all of a sudden tell a man I've been sleeping with for years that I'm not in the mood? The truth is with Chase, I don't have to be in the mood. He touches me and well…"

Kandi covered her ears. "Enough already. *TMI"* She. thought for a moment and snapped her fingers. "We can say we'll *get two rooms to save money.* You and I can take one and the guys the other one."

"Please, Chase will offer to pay for all three rooms."

"Oh yeah I forgot about him being super rich."

"Don't start. Besides, there is no way in the world I'd ever attempt to put Chase and Sam in a room together. For sure only one of them would emerge alive."

"Well, it looks as if you might have to make a decision."

"I don't know why we need a room. We only have a few more hours until we get home."

Laughing Kandi said, "Because Sam knows you're tired and need to take a break. He could care less about the rest of us. Even when he's pissed with you, he still looks out for you. I wish I had a man who cared about me the way Sam does for you."

"How did this happen?"

Kandi laughed. "That's a conversation for another day. Right now we'd better get back outside before Sam and Chase stop playing nice and start trying to kill each other instead. I have to tell you even though I understand why you had to ask Chase if he wanted to come, it was still a dumb idea to have them both in a car together for so many hours. I have no idea what is going to happen when we make it home. Sam could always stay with us."

"No, that's not going to work. After everything he's done for me, that would hurt his feelings and I can't do that. Besides, he's familiar with my parents." With another sigh Rebe headed out the door.

When she reached the car she went to stand next to Sam. "It's okay if we keep driving. I'm okay."

Sam smiled. "I know what you're trying to do. Thanks. I'm an adult. You're here with Chase and that's that. We're going to get a room and let you rest…all of us could use a bit of rest. Driving has been kind of tense."

Within an hour they'd found a hotel and checked in. True to her word Kandi had tried to make a case for the girls sleeping together and the guys sharing a room. Chase had looked at her, reached for Rebe's hand and laughed.

As days go, the next morning wasn't nearly as bad as it could have been. Everyone's mood seemed to have improved and they actually managed to have fun, to joke and laugh. Not one barb or snide remark was made. When they stopped for lunch and Chase treated, Sam and Kandi accepted. Chase was sitting in the front with Sam and pulled the seat up without being asked in order to give Rebe more leg room. Sam saw and almost smiled. So yes, Rebe considered it a very good start to the day.

Finally pulling up in front of her childhood home, Rebe took in a breath trying hard not to allow the memories of the last time she'd been home to overwhelm her. She teared up but was determined not to let them fall. She should be ashamed of herself for being such a coward and not coming home to visit her parents. And she was, she acknowledged as she exited from the car. Her gaze collided with Sam. He had a worried look on his face.

"Are you okay?" Sam asked

She smiled at him. "I want to be. I have to be."

"I'm here for you," he assured her. Rebe glanced at Chase who was giving her a WTH look. Sighing heavily, and biting her lips, knowing without a doubt she should shift her gaze away from Sam, but was unable to do so. As much as she didn't want to cry she was crying all the same.

Before she could move or even take her next breath, Sam was there cradling her in his arms holding her to him, caressing her, whispering words of comfort. And when she felt strong enough she lifted her head and he kissed her gently on the forehead then chucked her underneath her chin. Kandi and Chase were staring at the two of them with a dumbstruck look on their faces. While they stared at them a sort of metamorphosis appeared to be taking place in Chase. He walked toward them and inserted himself between her and Sam. It appeared the truce between the men was ending. Rebe could understand Chase's point.

"I've got this, Sam. If Rebe is in need of being comforted, I'm her boyfriend, I'll do it."

Sam's eyes blazed. "You have no idea what's going on, or how Rebe is feeling. But you're right about one thing. She's with you and I'm sure you can comfort her."

Going to the back of the car Sam removed his bag along with a heavy wrapped object. Ignoring all of them he walked to the door of Rebe's parents' home and rung the bell. When the door opened Rebe's mother looked at him in surprise and burst into tears hugging him to her. It was several long moments before she pulled away and Sam took her hands.

"I brought Rebe," he said and watched as mother and daughter stared at each other.

What the heck just happened? Rebe wondered. Though Sam wasn't a stranger to her parents she'd certainly not thought he'd receive the kind of welcome her mother had just given him. Turning toward Kandi she tilted her head

"Kandi, what was that? Why was my mother so happy to see Sam? She didn't even notice me standing in front of the house. Kandi gave her a hug but no answer. Then she hunched her shoulder.

"Good luck with everything. I have to go in and see my parents." Grabbing her luggage, Kandi made a beeline for the house next door. Rebe watched as she made her way to the door of her home and opened it with her key.

"Are we going up or what?" Chase asked.

Rebe didn't know why she wasn't running up the stairs to her mother or why her mother wasn't running down those same stairs to her. She gave Chase a tiny hint of a smile. "What's the rush? You said you we weren't serious enough to meet my parents?"

Chase stopped. "After last night I know this isn't about me, or even our relationship. Rebe, what's wrong? Are you feeling pressure from your parents to marry? Has Sam offered you that?"

When Rebe didn't answer, Chase sighed, pulled her in close and whispered in her ear. "You have to admit I've been trying."

"Yes, I'll have to admit to that. *But should you have to try?* Should I? she wondered. Should love be as hard as the two of them were making it? Taking a deep breath, Rebe placed her hand in Chase's and walked up the stairs of her childhood home. Before she could utter a sound her mother was crushing her in her arms, and her father hearing the noise had joined in. Her plan had been not to cry anymore, but just like a few seconds ago, here she was bawling like a baby. Luckily the tears were tears of joy. When she could catch her breath she pulled away from her parents to make the introductions. "Mom, Dad, let me introduce you to Chase McGuire."

Rebe held her breath as her parents smiled at Chase and shook his hand. Then both of them glanced toward Sam. Rebe saw the question in their eyes. What the *heck* was going on? Why had they thought…then she wondered again. Why were her parents so overjoyed to see Sam?

Before she could put more thought to the question they were ushered into the house. Within moments after removing their coats, mugs of hot chocolate had been given to them. Rebe hadn't had a moment to adjust. She was too busy watching Sam talking to her mother. They were in a small alcove off the living room. He was giving her mother the wrapped package he'd brought in.

Rebe stared while her mother opened it, gasped in amazement then threw her arms around Sam again, and appeared unable to talk.

"Mom, what is it?" Rebe had to know what was going on so she rushed toward her mother, turning the painting so she could see. She ended up doing the same thing her mother had done. She'd always known Sam was a good artist. The realism in his paintings was one of the reasons she no longer wanted to go into his apartment. There were too many memories.

She found herself staring in awe at the painting. Jamie's face was smiling back at her. Her gaze moved to her own image while instant memories flooded her body. It was one of the last pictures she'd taken with her brother before the accident. The painting was so lifelike she could swear she sensed her brother near. She could even smell the scent of the cologne she'd bought for his last birthday. The blend of citrus and spices tickled her nostrils.

With an almost silent groan she found her body swaying, her hand raised to touch the canvas. She wanted badly to reach out and touch her brother's face, wondering if he'd feel as alive as he looked. Finally the urge to find out overcame how irrational the act would appear. It didn't matter. She couldn't stop what was about to happen. It was as though she were in a dream as she watched her fingers gingerly trace her brother's face. Her gaze went to Sam. She had so many questions to ask him. She'd have to be a blind fool not to know the relationship between him and her parents was solid. Was this one of the things he'd wanted her to learn about him? Did it count that it had just happened?

Glancing back at the canvas she noted the bracelet her brother had given to her was around her wrist. She'd not had it on when they'd taken that picture. Then she looked at the earrings, the ones Sam had given her, the same one's she'd worn when he'd taken her to the dance. She blinked and one tear after the other slid down her face. "Thank you, Sam."

Sam shrugged, feigning an indifference he didn't feel.

Rebe couldn't stop looking at Sam. Even when Chase walked up to her and slid his arm around her waist, she continued staring at Sam. "It's so beautiful. When did you paint this?"

"Who's the guy?" Chase asked breaking the spell.

Three pair of eyes turned to her with identical quizzical expressions. She knew what they were thinking. Why had she never told her boyfriend anything about her brother? And no, she hadn't hidden him away.

A thrumming pain shot to her temples and she paused as she thought about it. Yes, she had hidden her brother from Chase. She'd removed all traces of Jamie from her apartment, taking their pictures that had resided on the mantle and putting them away, refusing to look through family albums, or to visit her parents. For almost three years she'd not spoken his name to anyone but Sam. Everyone was staring at her, waiting for her to answer Chase. She couldn't help her nervous habit of licking her lips.

"That's Jamie, my brother."

"Oh, where is he?" Chase asked.

Darn it she should have told him. Now was not the time, but she needed to answer before Chase asked anymore questions.

"My brother was in an accident a couple of years ago…almost three years. He didn't make it." Rebe's eyes swung back to Sam. "He and Sam were good friends."

Snapping his fingers Chase's gaze turned quickly toward Sam. "Now, I get it. So that's why you tolerate Sam's interference."

Really, could they have chosen a more inopportune time to have the conversation they were on the verge of having? Rebe took Chase's hand intending to lead him away while answering him. Chase wouldn't budge. She was forced to answer.

"Sam's wasn't only Jamie's friend. He was my friend as well. He's been there for me while my brother was alive and after. He's always been my advocate. There was just a period of time that I forgot about that and treated him as though he were my enemy."

She glanced toward Sam. "I'm sorry, Sam. That's a beautiful picture. I'm sure my parents will love it."

"He started painting it for you," her mother answered. Sam touched her mother's arm and her mother stopped the explanation. This was getting to be a bit too much. She had to get away from Sam, she couldn't and she wouldn't be rude to Chase. He was her boyfriend, not Sam.

"Chase, let me show you the rest of the house. Is it okay if Chase takes the upstairs guest room?" she asked over her shoulder, somehow knowing that Sam would be taking over the basement, the place that used to be her brother's domain. She wished for a moment that she'd not been goaded by Sam, and had never asked Chase to come.

With a sigh she headed toward the stairs. This was another thing Sam had maneuvered her into. Well, in spite of what Sam had thought, Chase came. Did that mean he cared? Or did it simply mean he was trying to make sure Sam didn't score more hero points?

It was funny how in a few shorts months both her and Chase had been affected by Sam. Both were looking at him as being a hero, and all because of her second occupation of writing about heroes and heroines.

Rebe took in a breath and exhaled. Being home again brought up so many happy memories. It had never been about her not wanting to come home. It was about the loss being renewed and tripled. Her brother wasn't home and would never be coming back. She missed him like crazy. Even now she didn't think she could stand being in their parents' home knowing he was gone.

"What really happened to your brother, Rebe?" Chase asked.

"He had a car accident."

"You two were close?"

Rebe stopped in her little tour of her home and turned to face Chase. "Very close," she finally answered. "He was my perfect hero. He loved me fiercely and would have protected me with his life."

Chase smiled. "And I remind you of him. See Babe, you chose me because of him. We keep getting back together because of him. I'll bet if he could, he'd put his seal of approval on our relationship."

Tears flooded Rebe's eyes at just how wrong Chase was. If her brother were alive she would have never looked twice at Chase. Would have never taken his cheating, and her brother would have *beat the crap out of him for cheating on her, and ....suddenly Rebe could see it so clearly*. Jamie would have been disappointed in her for wanting so little. He would want her to find a man who loved her as much as he had. That wasn't Chase.

"Let me show you where you'll be sleeping." Rebe turned and made her way toward the stairs, saw her parents and Sam staring at her and wondered what was going on. Sam walked right up to her, tilted her chin and stared into her eyes, then he wiped away a tear with the pad of his finger. "Are you okay?" he asked.

No, she wasn't okay. She wanted to bawl like a baby the same as she had almost three years ago. She wanted to fall into Sam's arms and allow him to comfort her, but she wouldn't. She needed to talk to her parents. She regretted her actions towards them. Sam was right. Skypeing didn't take the place of a face to face visit. She should have come home sooner. Every second she was in her childhood home made her terribly aware of that. She'd been a selfish brat for behaving as though she was the only one who'd suffered a loss when Jamie died. She had to apologize to her parents.

"Sam, would you take Chase upstairs please? Give him the bedroom next to mine."

Glancing at Chase she hurried with an explanation to the question that was on his lips. "Sam has spent a bit of time here with Jamie. I need to talk to my parents for a few minutes."

She gave Chase a light kiss before turning towards Sam. "And be nice to him," she managed to whisper.

Moving toward her parents Rebe hugged first her father then her mother. "Mom, Dad…I…I'm sorry."

"We know why you haven't been home, honey." Her father said.

"Did Sam tell you?"

"Sam?" Her mother laughed. "You're our baby. We didn't need Sam to tell us why you didn't come home, or why you didn't want us to visit you. But you do have Sam to thank for us giving you time to grieve and sort it all out. He's been assuring us you were okay."

"But I call you guys almost every day. We even skype."

"And you think that's the same?"

"No…but…I didn't know you were so close to Sam."

"Honey, I'd say the last three years you haven't been too aware of anything that's been right in front of your eyes."

"You're talking Sam right?"

"So, you've finally figured it out."

"I have a boyfriend." Rebe studied her parents. Her mother was biting on her lips as though trying to prevent a laugh while her father rolled his eyes and gave a snort of disgust.

"I like Chase. He's a lot of fun. He's just what I need in my life. Fun."

"He's your hero."

"Good heavens no. I know that came from Sam, but he has it wrong. Chase is the kind of man I write about, tall, handsome, rich and fun. And he does make my…" she laughed trying to find the right word without shocking her parents. After all they didn't need to know every little nuance of her life. "Chase makes me swoon."

"Right," her mother laughed. "What about Sam?"

"He behaves as though he's my jailer. He's disgusted with me, and for the past couple of years he's practically hated me."

"Yet he's still been looking out for you, hasn't he? Look how long we tried to get you to branch out at the firm. Did you do it until Sam coerced you? No. And your writing, you were going to stay underground and not participate as though your writing was some sordid secrets. He's forced you to admit you love it."

"He's annoying. I can't stand it. Sam always thinks he knows what's best for me. He remind me too much of—"

"Say it."

"No."

"Rebe."

"How will I ever know for sure? I don't like that Jamie may have picked out a man for me. I don't even like that you two approve of Sam, or that he's had a secret relationship with you and you've never mentioned it. How many times has he been here in the past three years? Don't try and deny that he's been coming here often. I could tell right off the bat. He's too comfortable with you."

"He came home with your brother. You know that, you were here."

"But I'm talking since. How often has he been here? Does he call you also?"

"He's been here several times, and yes he calls us, and we call him. So what?" her mother asked.

"It's like he's been spying on me for all of you. Doing a favor for his friend. Taking care of Jamie's little sister. Sam told me that himself. He said Jamie asked him to take care of me."

"If Jamie asked Sam to take care of you it wasn't so he'd spy on you. He knew Sam loved you. He didn't think you'd ever see that, or that you'd even want Sam, because he'd told you not to date him."

"He thought I was too flaky to date Sam. I know that," Rebe laughed.

"Sam was his best friend. You were Jamie's world from the moment you were born. I've never seen a bond like the one you had with your brother. You were very fortunate."

Rebe went silent for a moment thinking back over her brother's protectiveness. "But, Mom, Jamie was so adamant that I not date Sam."

"He didn't want the drama that comes with relationships to mess with his friendship with Sam."

"Then why would he ask Sam to take care of me?"

For a moment the room was silent. They all knew the answer to that one. Jamie was aware he wasn't going to make it. Her father gave her mother a stern look, then came and took Rebe in his strong arms and patted her on the back.

"Your brother wanted you to be happy. That's all that we want baby, is for you to be happy. I don't give a damn if you don't want either of these guys. Don't allow your brother, or your mother to pressure you into making a decision you don't want to make."

When her mother shot her father a dirty look Rebe laughed and put up her hands. "Let's call a truce. The thing of it is that I do have feelings for Sam. I'm pretty sure I'm in love with him and that he's the one. But I've made a commitment to Chase, and I want to honor that."

She looked to her parents for some parental advice. It felt good to be talking to them in person. It was different than skypeing. She'd have to admit that. "Mom, what do you think?" she asked.

"If you're in love with Sam, why are you with Chase?"

"Sam would want more from me than what I've given so far to Chase. He'd demand more. There would be drama and tears and breakups. He has the power to break my heart and make me worry about him. If anything ever happened to Sam, I don't think I'd be able to survive it."

"And Chase?"

"Like I said, he's fun. But he doesn't have the power to break me. And I doubt that I hold that power over him. When he's cheated on me it didn't even hurt my pride, not really. I've behaved as though I was enraged because Kandi and Sam thought I should be, but I never was enraged. If I had been, I would have never been able to take him back time after time."

Her mother walked around the room pointing toward her then returned to walking. Until finally it was as though she'd figured things out. "So it's fear?" Her mother asked at last.

"Yes," Rebe answered. "And I know what you're thinking. I'm not afraid to admit it. Fear is holding me back. I know what's at stake and you two can't talk me out of it. So whatever you're going to say, you may as well save your breath. I like fun and keeping my heart intact.

"Rebekah Johnson, you're being silly," her mother laughed. "There are more than two men in the world. You don't have to settle for either one if you don't want. I agree with your father on that. It doesn't matter if Sam loves you. If you don't want to love him, if he doesn't turn you on and make you want to be with him, then you're right to reject him. And if Chase is what you need, then go for it. Stay with him until you no longer need him. If that leads to marriage we'll be happy for you."

Psychology? Seriously was her mother trying reverse psychology on her? "Thanks, Mom. If Chase asks me to marry him, I'll say yes." When Rebe saw her mother's gaze flick over her shoulder she turned knowing it would be Sam, Chase, or both. If only she'd not taken the bait and spoken. She didn't want either man to hear what she'd said.

"Your boyfriend's taking a shower," Sam informed Rebe. "He said he was feeling grungy. How are your legs?"

"Better."

"So, Rebe, you're thinking of marrying Chase?"

"My mom said it would okay with her if I did."

Suddenly Sam's eyes lit up and he smiled at her, the most wonderfully endearing smile Rebe had witnessed in a very long time. He was aware of what she'd done, just as her brother would have been. But with one big difference. Sam was looking at her in that way that told her he wanted to kiss her and darn if she didn't want him to, but not in front of her parents. They would begin wedding plans if she did that.

"Are you staying downstairs in Jamie's apartment?" she asked.

"If you don't mind. If you'd rather I didn't..."

"No, Sam. I'm glad you're staying there. That's where you always stayed, so why should you change that? I just wanted to go down for a few minutes and...I don't know. I just wanted to go down."

"Do you want to go alone?"

Rebe shook her head and held out her hand to Sam. As much as she probably needed to do this alone there were too many reminders of her brother in the home. She needed Sam.

Walking into the area was like a blast into the past, the huge cream colored sofa, so plush that she always fell asleep watching movies on the 70 inch screen, the popcorn machine, the fridge stocked with soda, beer, and wine, the cabinet with all sorts of teas and coffees and a cappuccino maker along with a coffee pot.

The room was airy and cheery. She could see her parents hadn't cordoned it off, but were using it. Good for them. She went to the sofa and sank into the butter cream leather. When Sam sat beside her, she pulled him to her and kissed him like there was no tomorrow.

Suddenly Rebe heard voices, her mom was talking loudly. Her mother was one smart woman. She was warning them Chase wanted to come down. Only she didn't want him to do so, not until she'd had time to feel her brother and release him.

"Sam…"

That was all she had to say, that one word, and Sam was racing for the stairs. "Sam," she called out again. When he turned back she gestured for him to wipe his lips. He laughed and continued up the stairs.

Closing the door to the basement behind him, Sam glanced in Chase's direction. "I thought you were taking a shower."

"And I thought you were going to stop kissing my girlfriend."

Sam shrugged. "Rebe made you that promise, I didn't."

"Get out of my way. I need to talk to Rebe."

"Not now, Chase. Rebe needs to be down there alone for a while."

"You were with her."

"Chase, I shouldn't be telling you this because I do think it's Rebe's place to fill you in. But since she's downstairs I guess the job falls to me. Rebe had a very hard time dealing with her brother's death. She's been unable to come home, or to even talk about him with anyone. Think about it. She never told you about her brother. Don't you think that should tell you something? And just so you know it, we weren't making out. She just needed someone to hold her for a moment."

"If she needs someone to hold her, then that will be me. Thank you very much, Sam, but I've had all the help from you that I need." Chase moved to walk down the stairs and Sam moved to block his way.

Rolling his eyes Sam stared at Chase for a moment. Seriously, for a lawyer Chase was dense. Couldn't he see Sam belonged here, whereas Chase was an interloper?

"Let's sit down for a moment, Chase." Sam smiled and turned toward Rebe's parents. "Do you mind if Chase and I have a private talk?" He waited until they'd moved toward the kitchen.

"Listen, Chase, I'm going to do my best to remain calm and tell you this again. Perhaps you thought I was bulling you. I'm not. Rebe is having a hard time with being home. She hasn't been here since the funeral. She was extremely close to her brother."

He moved his ring finger over the little finger to show Chase how close the brother and sister had been. She has to do this without you. Just give her a few minutes. I'm sure it won't be long, ten, twenty minutes, I'm guessing."

"But you're okay to be with her?"

"You really are dense aren't you, Chase? I thought if we talked about this, man to man you'd get it. But since you're stuck on why I was with her and you're not allowed, I suppose I'll answer that question for you. Yeah, I'm okay."

Chase glared. "Screw that. I'm going down and if you try to stop me…"

Sam sprang up so quickly one would have thought he was a super hero with special abilities, like super-fast reflexes. "If you attempt to go down there and bother Rebe, I will stop you. So stop being a baby and wait until she comes back up."

"Get out of the way, Sam."

"I'll tell you what. You either go ahead and take a swing at me or sit your ass back down. What's your pleasure?" When Chase sat back down Sam narrowed his eyes and glared at him. He'd had no intentions of hitting Chase, not in Rebe's parents' home anyway, so Rebe's hero backing down was appreciated. Sam paced for a moment for affect and to allow some of his anger to flow away, then he too sat

"Are you in love with Rebe, Sam?"

"Are you?" Sam asked.

"That's none of your business. Rebe and I are a couple. You should respect that. We're in a committed relationship. How many times do we have to repeat that to you?"

"Until I believe you. By the way you never answered the question. Are you in love with Rebe?"

"Screw you, Sam," Chase hissed.

"You can't say the words can you? Listen, Chase, if it's true it's very easy to say. I love Rebe. And yes, I'm in love with her. Can you even say you love her as a friend?" When Chase refused to answer Sam laughed. "Go take your shower. I'm going back down with Rebe. And for God's sake be an adult and don't make a scene in her parents' home. Just so you know, I have no plans on telling Rebe about this childish discussion."

Sam turned to walk away, thought better of it then turned back toward Chase." The door will be locked. When Rebe is ready to come up, we'll come up. With those parting words Sam opened the basement door and locked it behind him. Shaking his head he moved toward Rebe wondering how much longer it would take for her to dump Chase.

"Is everything okay with Chase?"

"Sure. But I thought he needed an explanation about what was going on with you. I told him as soon as you can handle it you'd be up. He hadn't taken his shower, so I'm thinking he's going to do just that."

Rebe was giving him a look as though she wanted to ask a question but she didn't. She sighed and continued looking through a photo album she was holding. *Progress,* he thought and joined her.

CHAPTER THIRTEEN

A couple of days with her parents had turned out to be the very thing Rebe needed. After the first day when she'd disappeared into Jamie's apartment and had reemerged she'd known instinctually something had happened between Sam and Chase but decided not to deal with it. By nightfall Chase had done what he did best, charming women. Her mother had become enamored of him. While her father was reserving judgment, he was friendly. With time whatever had happened between Chase and Sam appeared to have smoothed over.

Sitting at the breakfast table she caught Chase staring at her and smiled in his direction. "What's wrong?" she asked.

"I was wondering if you'd tell me about your brother. I know he's no longer here, but he was important to you and I'd like to get to know him."

Shock wasn't the word, Rebe was flabbergasted. Daring a glance toward Sam she could see the surprise in his eyes. It was as though everyone was on pins and needles waiting for her to collapse with the mere mention of her brother. Had she really gone that bonkers? Had she really done that to her family? Well, not anymore.

"I'd love to tell you about Jamie," Rebe said and smiled.

And for the remainder of breakfast she continued to do just that with everyone telling stories. They were laughing the entire time and it felt good, cathartic. Rebe smiled again at Chase when finally they dispersed. Turning to him she gave him a kiss and squeezed his hands. "Thanks, that was just what I needed."

For the first time since he'd known the man Chase had done something right as far as Sam was concerned. He'd shown genuine interest in Jamie and had helped to get Rebe to open up. *Just what I needed*, he'd heard her say to Chase, and he'd swallowed the lump in his throat. She'd then kissed Chase and had looked at him as though he were her hero come to life. Sam had not realized until that moment how much he'd hoped Chase would show his true colors. Who would have expected for a man concerned with his own comforts would have a moment of sympathy for Rebe, or would be able to get her to talk freely and openly about Jamie.

Inwardly Sam cringed wondering if he were jealous of having that special bond between him and Rebe breached. For all this time he'd been Rebe's only ear. She wouldn't speak of Jamie to Kandi or her parents, only him.

And now Chase, the cheating boyfriend who bargained her off to clients, who pushed his seat in the car back so far that Rebe's legs got cramped had suddenly gotten a clue. He was being sensitive and Rebe was eating it up. He wanted to turn away from them, not look at Rebe beaming at Chase, but he couldn't. He continued watching them hoping that if Rebe really did feel something for Chase; it would deaden his own feelings for her. He sighed and finally turned away. That would never happen. He'd loved her for much too long. And Rebe had warned him he was the frog in this three way drama hadn't she? There was one thing left to do. He needed to apologize to Chase, he'd been out of line. His main focus especially since Jamie died had been to protect Rebe. But even he had to admit he'd gone overboard. And somehow he'd have to do what Chase suggested and stop kissing Rebe. With a groan he walked away.

Taking Chase to all the places of interest had been fun. It had been much too long since she'd done the sightseeing angle. It was fun doing it with Chase. And it was fun going out to a nightclub with Chase, Sam and Kandi. It almost felt like the days when the original foursome enjoyed each other's company. While it was apparent Chase would never replace Jamie, Rebe was beginning to think maybe it wouldn't be so bad if the four of them tried a bit harder.

One more day and they would be returning home. She'd been right to give Chase a chance. He'd stepped it up. He was really trying and she was pleased. When they woke that morning everyone was up and there were tons of flowers in the dining room.

"What's going on?" she asked.

"We thought you'd like to go with us to put flowers on Jamie's grave," her mother responded.

Say what? Panic took over before Rebe could control it. "No," she shouted. "I'm not going."

"Kandi and her family are going."

"No, I can't. I don't want to go." Rebe stopped. She was sounding like a whiny child. "Mom, I'm not into that."

"Excuse me. None of us are into that."

"Don't get upset, Mom. I didn't mean it like that. I don't want to go to a cemetery to lay flowers on my brother's grave while all of you stand around to watch my reactions. I've been enough of a basket case. That's over, but I'm still not ready to do what you ask." She glanced at Sam. "Sam, help me. Please. I know you understand."

Before Sam had a chance to speak, Chase was besides her caressing her shoulders gently and smiling at her. "How would it be if you decide to do this later on, when it's just the two of us, no crowd? You could well...sort of introduce me to your brother. It would be just the two of us, easy breezy, and then after we'll go do something fun."

"Chase, thank you. That's a great idea. And it's a compromise. Mom, you all go ahead with your plans and if I change my mind, Chase and I will go later."

"Would you like for me to leave you some flowers?"

"I don't think that will be necessary," Chase answered. "We can always stop and get some if Rebe decides she wants to go."

Where the heck had this man been for almost three years? This caring, easy, fun, man, who made her laugh. Who was now smoothing over a very rough patch for her, and had her mother smiling, totally different than what her mother was doing five minutes before. They had been headed toward a major fight and Chase had put an end to it just like that.

But something was wrong. Sam was...Sam was what, sad, disappointed in her for not going with her family? More than likely he was big on her facing her fears and overcoming them. This one wasn't his call, Rebe decided. This one was hers.

"I think I'd like to go out for breakfast," Rebe said suddenly grabbing Chase's hand and leading him out the door. "Sam, would you like to come with us?" she asked. She ignored his look, the one asking if she'd completely lost her mind. She gave him a quick hug. "Come on, Sam," she said. "I think we need this. I need this," she said.

"Then you go," Sam answered.

For less than a second Rebe held Sam's gaze. There was so much she wanted to say to him. He'd helped her live and if anyone could have gotten her to go to the cemetery, to Jamie's grave, she would have bet anything it would have been Sam. And she would have fallen apart in his arms. No thanks. She didn't want to fall apart. She wanted to heal. She wanted Chase.

Sam stool at the door watching Rebe interact with Chase. For the first time since he'd met the man he knew for this moment in Rebe's life Chase was just what she needed, like she'd said, he was easy breezy and fun. He stared after them, this time not upset that Chase had given to her what she needed. The main thing was that he had. Chase had taken what could have become a volatile situation and turned it around.

While he had no idea if Chase and Rebe would actually go to the cemetery or not, he was definitely not going to push her. If she went he thought it would be good for her. If she didn't, well, that only meant Rebe had come as far as she could for now. He wouldn't press her on it.

With an exhale the thought came to Sam that perhaps Chase did care for Rebe in his own way. Perhaps he could learn a thing or two from Chase, to be easy, breezy and fun. He laughed. Right. Someone had to be the responsible adult. Someone had to do the worrying in a relationship or nothing would get done. Then again this was Rebe and Chase's relationship and they could handle it in whatever manner worked best for them.

When Sam turned from the door he found Rebe's parents staring at him, a worried look on their faces.

"Are you okay, Sam? You could have gone with them if you'd wanted," Mrs. Johnson said with a concerned expression creasing her face.

"No, I'm fine. Right now I think Chase is exactly what Rebe needs. She doesn't need to be forced into doing things she's not ready for. With Chase, if she decides to go to the cemetery none of us will need to worry about her. As much as I hate to admit it, Chase does have a certain way with Rebe. He makes her laugh. It doesn't seem to matter what's wrong, he smiles at her, and she caves. Then she smiles back at him and things are fine between them. I never knew how he did it, how he could get her to keep taking him back after he continually cheated. And to be honest, I still don't get it. But whatever he has, it works. For that reason I'm glad Chase is here. I want Rebe to feel safe."

"That's what you've done for her since Jamie's death. How does it make you feel that Chase may be taking over that role in her life?"

"There're trying to make a go of it. At least that's what they both keep stating and very emphatically I might add. If that's the case, then that's as it should be."

"Do you think they're in love?"

"I think whatever they have works for them." And on that Sam was not lying.

"Thanks for getting her to come home, Sam."

Sam smiled but didn't answer. Today would be a very long day. Tomorrow they would return home.

After beating Chase in a round of miniature golf Rebe looked at him. "Okay, let's go buy some flower and I'll introduce you to Jamie, though I don't think of my brother as being there. I suppose I must do this, or Sam will think I'm a coward."

"Is Sam's opinion of you really that important?" Chase asked her, a puzzled look twisting his features.

"It is."

"Is it because he was your brother's best friend?"

"Some of it is. "

"And the rest?"

"I don't know, it just does."

"Rebe, are you in love with Sam?"

How did she answer? Honestly, she decided. "I'm not sure."

"What about us?"

"I'm still trying to figure that out. We've never talked about our feelings. Are we in love, Chase? Are we even heading in that direction?"

"I care about you, Rebe and I know you care about me. I've seen many couples who claim to be in love and have a lot less going for them than the two of us?"

"But I think couples who are in love try fidelity."

"You or me?"

"Both of us. The kissing, it's not all Sam. I like kissing him."

"I never thought it was all him. So, if you like kissing Sam and you're unsure of your feelings toward him, where exactly does that leave us?"

"I'm not ready to give up on us. I think you're right, I think neither of us ever demanded anything of the other. I think we just might be entering a brand new phase."

"Are you going to continue kissing Sam?"

"I think it's time for me to stop playing games with you, Sam and myself. If we're going to have a chance at doing this I have to be all in. You're right I've not given it my all." She shrugged. "And before you ask, no, not all of it was your fault."

"You know, Rebe, I do think if we make it, we have Sam to thank. I haven't liked the way he's gone about trying to make you fall in love with him and being the man you turned to. But I wasn't that for you. It was my own fault for not realizing how much I did care about you. The fact is, I think we complement each other in so many different ways. Maybe the things we have are what lead to long and successful marriages. I don't know if that romantic kind of love you write about is even for real. So far I've seen no evidence of it. Everyone in my family has been divorced at least once, some as many as four times. I've never hungered after being in love. I've always wanted a woman who was my equal, who thought as I did, who wasn't that hung up on romantic love. And until you went to that damn dance with Sam, you and I were a perfect match."

"To be honest, I thought the same thing." Rebe turned from Chase and began walking back toward the parking lot. This was the first time they'd ever had a serious conversation. It felt good. It felt right. Perhaps this would be the first step in their cementing a lasting relationship. Briefly she thought of Sam. If she was going to have a shot at a relationship with Chase, she'd have to stop depending on Sam. And she'd definitely have to stop kissing him.

"Rebe, we've never talked about any of this. I think it was long overdue. Why do you think we haven't talked about this before?"

"I'm not sure."

"Why do you think we're doing it now?"

"I'm not sure. But I can't help wondering if we both haven't been selling ourselves short. I think I do want more than we've had. I'm not trying to pressure you into anything because being in love is not something you can just order up. But I'd like more. I'd like to be there for you, and for you to be there for me. I want us to be able to count on each other if we're really going to try this."

"In other words, you want me to be more like Sam."

"I'm sorry, but yes, Chase. I want you to be more like Sam."

"I can see now that I made it easy for Sam to take the position of being the man who looked out for you. I was so damn selfish in my treatment of you. I never did it to hurt you though, Rebe. I didn't think you cared, not really. And perhaps I was beginning to feel closer to you than I wanted. So, I fought it by running to other women. I'm not running anymore. I thought about it after Sam and I talked and realized that there were so many things about you that I didn't know. I want to know more about you, Rebe. I want you to be able to depend on me." He gave her a half smile then bent to kiss her.

Kandi and her family were over and they were having a cook out. By now it didn't surprise Rebe that Sam was well acquainted with all of Kandi's family. When she found that Sam's parents had visited her parents though she was flabbergasted. What the heck was going on? She would worry about all of that later. For now they were sitting on the porch enjoying a very pleasant evening. When Kandi turned toward her with a smirk on her face, she could only hope the evening would continue to be pleasant.

"What did you two do all day?" Kandi asked.

"We had fun. I showed Chase the highlights of our little piece of the world. We played miniature golf." Rebe paused. "And we swung by the cemetery." As she'd known they would, all eyes turned to her.

"We stayed a couple of minutes. I made introductions, then we went to a movie."

"Really. Which one?" Kandi challenged.

Rebe smiled. "I can't remember. But the day was a lot of fun. All in all it was a very good day."

Actually after the cemetery they'd went to a local motel and made love. She smiled at Chase. "It was a very good day," she repeated and moved away from Kandi to sit next to Chase.

Chase looked around before wrapping his arms around Rebe. "You're right. It was a very good day. I'm so glad I came with you to meet your parents and to learn about your brother. It seems I have you to thank for all of this, Sam, so thank you."

Now was the time for Sam to issue Chase the apology he deserved. He stuck his hand out to Chase. "I'm sorry for what went down between us. I was looking out for Rebe. Perhaps the trip has been good for all of us. From this moment on I will do my best to attempt to butt out of your life and your relationship with Rebe. I'm glad you were here and more importantly, that you were able to give her what she needed." They shook hands and Sam looked around. Rebe was beaming at him while Kandi was looking as though he'd lost his mind.

"It seems we're leaving so soon. I'm not ready." Chase looked at the group and sighed. "But we all have to return to work, except you, Sam."

Sam glanced up and smiled. "Yes, except me. Though this is fun, I don't think we should stay up too late. We have a long drive ahead of us and we need to be rested." He stared for a moment at Chase then glanced quickly at Rebe.

"Speaking of long drives, Rebe, I was thinking how you got leg cramps on the way here. Like Sam, I'm concerned about you getting fatigued. I was wondering if you'd like to fly home. We'd get there in a couple of hours, and you wouldn't have to go through the long drive."

Stunned that was what Rebe was. She stared at Chase for a long moment wondering how on earth with one offer he'd managed to be totally heroic and totally uncaring, rude, and unheroic at the same time. She'd never leave Sam. The thought pinged in her head. That wasn't the way she'd meant it, was it? Of course it wasn't. Luckily Chase didn't possess ESP. Still she'd never fly home with Chase after Sam had planned this trip especially for her.

"What the hell?" Sam began, "Rebe doesn't," Kandi's hand on his leg stopped him. He'd wanted to remind Chase that Rebe hated flying and only did it when she absolutely had to. He glanced toward Kandi. She whispered, "No, don't say anything. Let Rebe handle this." She was right of course. Sam sighed and looked away from Rebe wondering what she'd say to Chase. He could tell from the way she was hesitating that she was trying to be diplomatic.

"Chase, that is so sweet," Rebe cooed. "Thank you. But no, I want to drive back with Kandi and Sam. You do remember they came because of me."

"And I'm sure if you wanted to fly home because of the leg cramps, they wouldn't mind. Would you guys?"

"No," Kandi and Sam both said.

"Really, Chase, I wouldn't think of doing that," Rebe repeated. "Besides, we had fun on our way down here, and we're going to have fun on the way back too. You are getting so sweet and thoughtful though. I do appreciate it." Rebe glanced first at Kandi then Sam. "Wasn't that thoughtful?" she asked.

Was Rebe really and truly asking him for his opinion? Sam needed to puke right this second, Chase, sweet and thoughtful? Hell no, no way. For a couple of days Chase had fooled him by being caring and concerned for Rebe's comfort. Now he knew it was all an act to make sure Rebe didn't depend on Sam. *Touché* he thought, thinking he really couldn't blame Chase. He'd given him more than enough reason to do what he'd done. He would have done the same, only sooner. Ignoring Chase and Rebe, Sam walked across the wrap-around porch and began a conversation with one of Kandi's brothers. It was safer that way. And it remained safe when they finally went to bed, and even when they woke, had breakfast and prepared to leave.

After all of the goodbyes had been said, all the happy tears shed and promises that they would return soon, everyone climbed into Sam's car, Chase in the driver's seat without any complaint from Sam, and Sam riding shotgun. Driving back was fun. He'd have to admit that. He'd made sure by removing the CD's and placing them securely in his bag which was stored in the back.

And when the trip was over Sam had actually asked Chase and Rebe up. They'd declined, but at least he'd offered. If Chase was going to be in his life since for sure Rebe would be Sam was glad he could at least pretend to be a grown up and stop challenging the man to a duel. Maybe he'd have to think about no longer kissing Rebe.

CHAPTER FOURTEEN

Eating Chinese food with Kandi was a treat. Instead of eating in Kandi's kitchen with a huge mirror to dissuade you from enjoying the meal they were curled up on the sofa at Rebe's apartment. For the past hour the two of them had gone back and forth about Chase and Sam. Kandi refused to let go of the idea that Rebe should dump Chase in favor of Sam.

"Why are you behaving as though falling for Sam is the end of the world, like there's a law against it? What gives?"

"Jamie."

"What the heck are you talking about?"

"Jamie didn't want me with Sam."

"They were best friends."

"Exactly, we had a long conversation about it. He told me in no uncertain terms that friends' sleeping together was a very bad idea. He didn't want to know who I was sleeping with, but he made it plain he didn't want it to be Sam. He thought I was too flighty to be serious and he liked Sam. He didn't want our becoming involved to mess up their friendship."

Kandi shook her head and stared at Rebe. "Are you for real?"

"Of course. I've told you this before."

"I'm not trying to be mean, but your brother is no longer here. If you're with Sam, even if you break up in the future that would have no effect on your brother."

"But…he—"

"He was a hypocrite."

"Excuse me?"

"Don't go getting ticked. Let me explain. Jamie and I slept together for about six years. It started before we left home. When Jamie decided to move to Chicago, why do you think I badgered you so much to move here? And why do you think when Jamie and Sam decided to move into a larger apartment and you refused to take an apartment in the same building in order to get away from your brother's prying eyes, that I decided it was time we each had our own apartments? Why do you think I took the apartment across the hall from Jamie and Sam?"

"You and my brother? But Jamie told me everything."

"Apparently not."

"Why didn't you ever tell me?"

"It wasn't any of your business."

"Like we haven't talked about things that weren't the other's business."

"Okay, you're forcing me to say this. Your brother didn't want you to know. We weren't in love with each other and knew it. We were hot for the other, that's all. It was purely physical. And he threatened to end things with me if I so much as hinted at our physical relationship to you. I enjoyed being with him. So, I kept my mouth shut. Simple as that."

"I seriously can't believe this. You and Jamie. Ewee."

Laughing, Kandi hit out at Rebe. "Jamie was my Chase. I loved him madly. I'd had a crush on him for years and had thrown myself at him more times than I care to remember. One day he was in the right mood. He'd broken up with Amy and was angry and lonely. And just a wee bit drunk I might add."

"You got my brother drunk."

"I had to. If I hadn't he wouldn't have touched me." Again Kandi laughed. "After it was over I told him it didn't have to end, that I didn't want it to end."

"And you never fell in love with him?"

"I thought I was in love with him when it started, but realized later it was a teenage crush. I still loved him, but he was my friend. I could talk to him about anything. He always gave me great advice. Our being a foursome made it easy. You never questioned the times Jamie and I did things alone. To you we were just friends hanging out."

"So, why was he so against me being with Sam?"

"Jamie flipped a lot on that. I think because the two of us weren't in love, he didn't want you to become just a sex buddy for Sam."

"Seriously? Didn't that tick you off? I mean he had these lofty goals for me as though he wanted to keep me unsoiled and at the same time he was …well, doing things with you. I would have been ticked."

"Some days it did annoy me. Some days it didn't. I knew Jamie loved me and worried about our relationship. I also knew he wasn't in love with me. But he was so gentle, so loving, so everything I wanted in a man. I really wanted him to be in love with me in the beginning. But as time passed, it was the excitement of hiding it from everyone. We were both adults, neither of us took anything from the other that we didn't want to give. Besides, you know Jamie. He was constantly asking me if I was okay with what we were doing, telling me that at any time I could stop. He even tried to fix me up with a few guys who he thought would be good for me. I couldn't have asked for a better, more loving relationship."

"How about being in love?"

"What about being in love?"

"What about it?" Rebe shrieked. "Kandi, don't you want to be in love?"

"You're willing to give up on the idea even though you've found the man you're truly in love with. So far I haven't. When I do though, Jamie taught me exactly how I should be treated by a man."

"Sneaking around. Lying to everyone, dating other people." Rebe's voice was raised in annoyance.

"Let me think, sneaking around, lying and dating other people, does that not ring a bell for you? That is Chase, Rebe. But for your information Jamie and I were not in a relationship. My God, we were not. He sat me down with an entire book of rules for how we were to conduct ourselves. And every single rule had to do with how something would make me feel. When he did have an occasional date he'd tell me about it before hand and asked me after if I were okay with it. He bugged me so much about it, that sometimes I almost wanted to end things. But I never did. I enjoyed being with him. In that way, Jamie was my Chase."

"So why are you so down on Chase? You and Jamie had the same kind of relationship."

Kandi was slowly shaking her head. A sad look came into her eyes then the sheen of tears.

"Jamie never said he wanted to try and have a committed relationship with me. He was always committed to me. And he had no problem telling me he loved me. He did, and I always knew it. Chase was unable to tell Sam that he loved you, even as a friend."

"It wasn't Sam's business."

"Rebe, don't be angry at me or Sam. We both love you. Can you say the same about Chase? He should at least love you as a friend. You're cutting yourself short if you don't at least have that."

"You were never jealous when Jamie went out with other women? I mean for real, not once?"

"There were a few times that I was hurt in the beginning. And I cried over it in Jamie's arms. He felt so badly about it that he didn't touch me for over a year. We both started dating. It was only in my times of extreme need that things ever got physical between us."

"Yuck."

Kandi laughed. "Rebe, grow up."

"So now I know why my big brother was so worried about me. I supposed you were worried about me for the same reasons."

"It was Sam I worried about. I knew he was in love with you and I knew you were…well, perhaps a bit of a flake, but a loveable flake. I knew you could hurt him and I didn't want you to."

"And now?"

"You're still a flake. You're admitting that you're in love with Sam, but still you're with Chase. I told you to go ahead and sample Sam. I know if he can get the job done, then you win, and you can drop kick Chase to the curb."

"I will not sample Sam, and I will not drop kick Chase to the curb. I told you I really like Chase. And yes, I like other things about him too." They both started laughing and only stopped when a knock sounded on the door.

"Come on in, Sam," Kandi yelled out and looked at Rebe. "You two can't keep avoiding each other forever. Bedsides, I've been missing Jamie too. I miss how things were. I miss the four of us." Kandi ran her hands down the side of her body and gave Rebe a wink. "I really miss Jamie. I loved him too. I don't think he'd like it that the three of us can't be friends."

"It sounds like you may have been in love with Jamie after all."

"Of course I was. A part of me always was. And always will be. That was the reason I accompanied Jamie's body home. I knew that would be the last time it would be just the two of us. I knew once we reached Atlanta, your family would take over and I'd have to pretend that we've never had a special relationship."

"Kandi, I'm so sorry, what you had with Jamie had to be hidden. I'm sorry the two of you never fell in love."

"I wouldn't have minded if we'd had the kind of relationship where we wanted to be married and raise a family together. But that wasn't what we had. You have that, my friend. All you have to do is reach out and take it." The last Kandi whispered because Sam was walking into the room.

"Rebe, why in the world are you sitting here with your door open? That's dangerous. Aren't you aware of that? What is wrong with you?"

"I didn't know it was open. Apparently Kandi left it open for you. I didn't know you were coming over."

Sam glared at Kandi. "Next time lock the door." He turned back to Rebe. "Do you mind that I came over?"

Rebe's gaze landed on Sam. "Did you know Kandi and Jamie were involved?"

"Of course. I don't know how you missed it."

"Enough about my personal life," Kandi complained before changing the subject. "Sam, we were talking about how close we all were. We were wondering if perhaps we could get back to that. I'd really that," Kandi said, but Sam remained quiet.

Glancing toward Kandi, Rebe turned slightly and her gaze collided with Sam. "Things are a bit complicated. I don't want to be a downer, but let's face it, neither of you like Chase. So how in the world are we going to be a new foursome?"

"I wasn't exactly talking about Chase joining us. I meant the three of us should continue our tradition." Kandi lowered her gaze.

"Oh," Rebe said in surprise.

"I won't object to your bringing him." Sam shrugged his shoulder and sighed.

"Sam, you can't stand Chase."

"I'm trying to be nice."

"You're always threatening to beat him up."

"He's the hero. He shouldn't be worried about me, isn't that right? Chase should be able to easily flatten me."

"And this is what you think I want to do all night if he's there with us?"

"I was kidding, Rebe."

"Yeah right."

"Children, children, this is supposed to be us, three friends, three adults making an attempt to preserve our friendship come hell or high water," Kandi scolded.

"I was being nice. Rebe misunderstood my intents." Sam grinned knowing he was telling only a half truth. "I have an idea. Look, how about we pick a date for…perhaps dinner. I'm thinking we should ease into this new relationship. Perhaps the first time just a couple of hours. I think we'll be able to handle that."

After deciding on a night, Rebe exhaled, not knowing if she'd fought with her friends to include Chase in their group for no good reason. For the past month things had not been right with her and Chase. Not that they fought, they never fought. But they hadn't been having fun either. She'd been too busy reevaluating her life. It was much harder to be contented with what she had with Chase when she'd finally admitted at least to herself that she loved Sam.

Clearing away the mess they'd made gave Rebe something to do with her hands. Part of her wished her friends had not left. She was being a coward in not just ending things with Chase, but every time she'd tried he'd remind her that he was trying and that if Sam wasn't in the picture things would be better. So yes, she had doubts that things would go well with Chase becoming part of their group.

The one thing that always worked for her and Chase had also failed. Since returning from the visit with her parents she'd found herself unable to make love with him. She'd given excuse after excuse. But a month for them to be together and not make love was unnatural. And knowing Chase's sexual appetite she wondered if somewhere in the back of her mind she wasn't giving him a chance to cheat so she'd have reason enough to break it off.

Rebe truly hoped she wasn't that much of a coward. No, she wasn't a heroine, but who the heck wanted to be a coward.

Two down and one to go. If Chase was to become a part of their group Rebe had to broach it to him in a way he'd accept. She made his favorite meal and bought a nice bottle of wine to put him in the right mood. When she could no longer delay the inevitable she asked him about joining the group.

"Seriously, Rebe? You want me to have dinner with your friends, who both hate me by the way. And let's not forget, Sam is in love with you. And you…well; we're not exactly sure where you stand."

Rebe didn't bother denying it. It wouldn't have done any good. "They're in my life and they've both agreed they'd like to behave like adults. I don't want to lose either of them from my life. They're important to me."

"Why don't you just admit that you're in love with Sam? Things haven't been the same for us since we went to visit your parents. It's hard to believe that you're now comparing me to him and I'm losing." Shaking his head Chase paced a few steps then turned and paced in the other direction. "I seriously can't believe it."

"I never intended to compare you, just as I never intended to do it the opposite way. I do apologize for that. I think as a romance writer sometimes things get mixed up in my head and I live this sort of fantasy life. I've been looking at both you and Sam as my heroes."

"Both of us? I would have thought I'd at least have Sam beat on that score."

"You are on the outside anyway what a hero represents. But Sam is what a hero represents on the inside. Lately you've been behaving a lot more like Sam and Sam has changed. I don't see him as I used to. He's very attractive."

"He looks the same as he always did to me."

She laughed. "I'm a writer what can I say. Plots are always spinning around in my head even when I don't want them to. And now I'll admit even his outside is pretty good.

"I don't want a part in your fictionalized story. I think you're more hung up on Sam than you think. I can't think of a good reason for me to want to hang around him. If it's for more comparison forget it."

"It's not that. I promise. I want us to succeed and I want to keep my friends. We have to learn to co-exist."

"Why don't you admit it, Rebe? You have this sort of contest going on in your head, Sam and I are your would be champions. You want us to duel for you."

"That is so not true."

"You've changed."

"So have you."

"Yes, but I've changed with regard to being a better boyfriend. You're turning into…well, the old me." Chase laughed. "I liked the old you. Please come back."

"I promised to give us a real try. I intend to do just that."

"You do realize that's not a very good reason right. I don't want you to be with me because you promised to try."

"I know, but it's all I've got right now."

"And the reason we haven't made love in a month?"

"It's not like I had some elaborate plan."

"No, it's more like when I touch you, or kiss you, you're thinking of Sam."

Rebe's eyes widened in disbelief. "I'm not sure if that's true."

"I know my past behavior has something to do with your feelings for Sam. I've given you reason not to trust me. I know that. But I still think we're good together. Lately it seems that I'm the only one who's invested in this relationship. I'd hate for us to give up without trying.

"Chase."

"You say our not making love has nothing to do with Sam and that you've not shunned me deliberately. I beg to differ. Don't forget I know your body intimately and your body has not been responding to me. Something is holding you back and I think its Sam." He kissed her then soft and sweet, not the kind of kiss he usually gave her.

"You've always turned me on, Chase. That hasn't changed."

"If you say so." He let out a breath. "If it's important to you to remain friends with Sam, then I'll give it a try. Yes, I'll go to dinner with them."

With that matter taken care of they settled in to watch a movie, Rebe in his arms, him lightly caressing her thigh and every so often a kiss between them until finally, it was time for bed. Chase's hand moved to her breast and pushed aside her bra. He began caressing her and she remained still. When he suckled her, she barely moaned.

Chase raised his head and said "I think I'll head home."

"You okay?"

"Yeah. I'll see you tomorrow." He kissed her lightly. "I enjoy being with you. I think we're great. I want you to be happy though. I'll see you at the office tomorrow. "

He gave her another light kiss and left. Rebe stood at the door wondering if she was missing something here, some clue. She'd better hurry and make up her mind before it was made up for her. She didn't want to dump Chase because she wasn't sure she wanted what a relationship with Sam would mean.

Darn it all. She was a coward. She should write a story about her dilemma and get a clue from her fictional heroine to see what she'd do. Sighing and heading for the shower she didn't have to write the scene to know what her fictional character would do. She'd break things off with Chase and take a chance on being in love. Rebe smiled. She'd never been in love, never had anyone in love with her.

The thought was scary but exciting at the same time.

CHAPTER FIFTEEN

Things appeared to be getting back on track. Chase had been out of town for several days for an important meeting with several of the senior partners. When he returned it was with the offer of a big case that he wanted Rebe to partner on with him.

Putting on the finishing touches to her makeup Rebe couldn't help but remember the last time she'd gone on a business dinner with Chase to woo a client. She was glad Sam wasn't standing around scrutinizing her dress and more delighted that he wouldn't be at the restaurant with his sketch pad.

Chase was watching her so intently that she turned toward him to ask, "Is there anything wrong?"

"I was just remembering how things went with our last business dinner. I'm glad Sam won't be joining us."

Rebe laughed. "That was pretty crazy wasn't it? Thank God we still landed the client. We're a good team, Chase. I like working with you. I realize you could ask any of the other lawyers at the firm to work with you. I want to thank you for choosing me."

"Just so we're clear on something, I chose you because you're a fantastic lawyer and your research is impeccable. I never have to worry about carrying you when we work together. You always hold up your end."

Chase's comments made Rebe smile. It was nice to hear she wasn't being handed cases because they were sleeping together. "Thanks, Chase."

"For what? I like working with you too. There are other things I like doing with you, Rebe. I love kissing your belly. I love moving slowly down your body and having you part your thighs for me. I miss the taste of you. I miss the way you hold me, touch me, and the way you make me come. Rebe, I miss you and I miss our making love. Neither of us are that busy that we can't find time to be together. I feel you're pulling away from me. I think we should be getting closer. I think your parents even approve of me. Take Kandi for instance, she doesn't hate me as much as she did. So, I'm wondering what the problem is. As far as I can tell Sam is the only hold out on our being together. Even he seems to have accepted that we're a couple. He still doesn't like it, but he has accepted it. I need you to tell me what's going on. What's wrong with us, Rebe? Hot and heavy is what our lovemaking has been for three years, at least in another month it will be three years. I've kept my promise. I've been committed to you, even though you appear to have cut me off. What's wrong? We haven't made love since we left Atlanta."

"We're doing okay. I don't think we have a problem."

"No?" He ran the pad of his finger over her body then moved behind her pressing his hardness into her rear end. "So tell me why I'm not ripping your dress off right this second and making love to you?"

"Because you don't want to be late for the client."

Chase tilted his head back and began slowly licking the side of her neck. "I want you, Rebe, in the worst way. I can't take much more of being celibate."

"Then why don't you rip my clothes off. We can make love right now and make an excuse to the client."

Rebe turned around to face him and cupped him. She saw his jaw clench, saw the lust in his eyes. But the moment he closed his eyes she was aware he was deciding which was the most important, his lust being slaked or the customer.

"We have to go. This will be the biggest case we've brought to the firm, if we can land it."

"I know. Chase, I promise when we get home tonight we'll make love. I've missed you too." And she had. She wished they would have done what came naturally to them. A few months ago they would have at least had a quickie. What had changed she wondered? Were they both looking for more?

Sam was standing in Kandi's hot pink and lime green kitchen staring at Kandi in shock because of the scheme she'd just asked Sam to take part in. "You want me to do what?"

"I want you to call Rebe and tell her you need her."

"She's on a date with Chase, another one of those dinners where Chase tries to use Rebe's body to close the deal. You told me about it a couple of days ago. So why are you all of a sudden wanting me to call her?"

"Your family's in town. Do you realize in all the years we've been friends they've never met Rebe. They've met me, Jamie, my family and even Rebe's family. But they haven't met the woman you're in love with."

"How the hell would I have even gone about introducing her?"

"Don't you want her to meet your family?"

"There's only one way I want her to meet them, and I don't think that's going to happen."

"It's not going to happen unless you make it happen."

"You told me this meeting was important for Rebe, that she was really excited Chase asked her to be on the case with him. Is that true?"

'Yes, it's true."

"Then tell me why you want me to interfere."

"If you don't you're going to lose her. She's trying to convince herself that Chase is the man for her. We both know he isn't. Come on, Sam, you have to make a move before it's too late. Call Rebe and tell her you're desperate, that you need her to go with you to dinner with your family. Tell her they're determined to set you up and she'll be saving you. Even if she says 'no' call her on it."

"But if I tell her I want her to meet my family, she might not come. She might think..."

"That you're in love with her and want her to meet them."

"This could blow up in my face. I'm trying to think of what other name she would call me beside a frog."

"What does it matter if she shows up? If she does you know what it will mean."

"Yeah, that she's keeping her word about being my last minute date if I ever needed her. And that Chase will be sitting somewhere pissed at the both of us. He'd be pissed at you also if he were aware of your meddling."

"Sam, come on, don't be a coward. Rebe needs an out. This is your chance to give it to her. You can play it off like it's no big deal if you want to, but do it. Your family needs to meet the woman you're going to marry."

"Or the woman whom I've told them to keep bail money, for the time when I'm going to kill her. Besides, I'm not sure I want to give Rebe an out. Why would I want her that way? Why can't she just be honest with me and with Chase?"

"Because she's nuts. And because she still thinks real life should happen in the same manner as the books she writes. She needs you to rescue her."

"She likes alpha males."

Kandi laughed. "Believe me Sam, you are the alpha male. You just practice restraint. It's time for you to make a bold move, if not Chase just might marry Rebe and you'll have to wait a few years for both of them to admit they've made a horrible mistake. Think of it like this, you'd be saving a member of your sex from marrying a woman who doesn't love him. You'd be doing Chase a tremendous favor."

They laughed together and Sam thought harder about it. "I'm supposed to pick my family up. I made reservations for eight. What time did Rebe say they're meeting their client?"

"Seven thirty."

"Kandi, that doesn't give me or her much time. I told my family I was bringing you."

"Which only means you won't have to spring for more money. I'm assuming it's your treat."

"Of course. My father will attempt to pay and both of my brothers, but my mother will smile and hand me the check. She's the only one who seems to understand I'm really not starving. By the way, you could still come."

"And if I did it would take away the significance. It would reduce Rebe to being just another one of your female friends. That's not what you're going after."

"You've got this all mapped out in your head. I didn't agree to do it." Sam began pacing as he thought the matter over. "This is going to be beyond risky."

"Then I'd say go for it. Rebe's not going to disappoint you, Sam. You may have to do a bit of begging to get her to leave Chase and their client, but I'm counting on her doing it."

"I have no plans on begging Rebe."

"Then don't beg, but for God sake, call her."

Sam paced about Kandi's apartment. "If I decide to go along with you hair brain scheme, I have to time this right. I need to pick a restaurant that's not too far from where she will be. I want her to be sitting down with the client, maybe even having a drink. I want to interrupt her at the moment she will be most invested in the client and in Chase. I want her to choose."

"Sam."

"Yeah, I know. She might choose me because of the agreement.

But that will be a start." Instantly the horror of what he was about to do hit him. "I'm manipulating her. I'm as bad as Chase. Neither of us are heroes."

"There is a difference in you and Chase, Sam. Do you love Rebe?"

"Yes, I love her. You already know that."

"And are you in love with her?"

"Hell yes, I am. But still, this isn't right. I sort of promised Chase I'd stop interfering in their relationship. Besides, in their own insane way I do believe they care about each other. I don't think I can go through with it."

"Look at it this way, you'll only be making the call. Rebe has a choice."

"Maybe if I don't pour it on so heavy. And maybe if I leave off the nonsense about my family trying to find a wife for me. I could just tell her I'd like for her to meet my family." He smiled. "I think I can handle that. Where is she having dinner with Chase?"

"Juseppia."

What's the closest restaurant to, Juseppia, that's nice?"

Immediately Kandi went on the internet and showed Sam more than a dozen restaurants that were within a few miles radius. "Take your choice," she announced.

"Okay, let me call and see if I can get reservations some place on such short notice."

Sam had been pacing for twenty minutes, ever since he'd made new reservations. His family wouldn't remember which restaurant he'd said he was taking them to so he wasn't worried about that. He was worried about Rebe's coming and at exactly what moment he would tell her what he'd done. Because there was no way he'd end the night without telling her. He knew he should have left to pick up his family. But he wanted to call Rebe first. He rubbed his hands feeling nervous.

"Make the call," Kandi yelled.

Turning in Kandi's direction Sam sighed and took another breath before taking out his phone. "I'll text her and ask her to call me."

"Coward."

"Yes, this time I am."

The three tables surrounding theirs had diners who were talking loudly enough to be overheard. Rebe hated people who carried their phones with them and talked during dinner with others. She thought it was beyond rude. But still she kept her phone close to her and kept it on vibrate. She had parents who might need her. There was no way she didn't want them to be able to reach her.

When her phone vibrated against her body she smiled. It seemed if you thought about something it always happened. She just hoped it wasn't anything too serious. She saw SOS from Sam and tilted her head wondering what could possibly be wrong.

"Excuse me," she said to Chase and their client. "I have to return this call." There was little need to explain it was merely a text, that would take much too long, and she didn't want to get into anything with Chase about calling Sam. No, it was better this way.

As soon as she was in a private area she placed her call. "Sam, are you okay? What's going on?"

"Rebe, I have a huge favor to ask. I know it's a lot, but I would really appreciate it. Forgive me for the timing, but..."

"What is it?"

"My parents and my brothers are in town. I think I mentioned it to you."

"No, you didn't."

"Sorry about that. Anyway, I intended to."

"What's the problem, Sam? Why an urgent SOS?"

"They're leaving tomorrow. I've been telling them about you for years and promising that I'd introduce you. I know this is last minute. Anyway, here goes. I'm taking them out to dinner tonight. I have always wanted them to meet you, and they'd love to meet the woman who called me a frog. Would you be available to have dinner with us?"

"Sam, I'm having dinner with Chase and a client. We've already put in our orders. If I'd known sooner—"

"Thanks, anyway, Rebe. I shouldn't have waited until the last moment to ask you. Good night, enjoy your dinner."

Clicking the phone off, Sam turned toward Kandi, "She said no." The moment the words were out of his mouth his phone rang again. Seeing it was Rebe he mouthed the word to Kandi

"Yes," he answered doing his best to sound nonchalant.

"Sam, where would you like for me to meet you?"

"You're coming?"

"Of course I am. I owe you."

"Forget it, Rebe. This was a really bad idea. Thanks anyway." Sam clicked the phone off and turned toward Kandi and glared at her.

"I shouldn't have listened to you. This is so wrong and definitely not the way I want to get her."

When his phone rang for the third time Sam groaned and released a breath. Closing his eyes he answered. "I don't want you to come because of a debt, or because you promised you would."

"I get the feeling this is something that's important to you. Is it, Sam?"

"Yes, it's important to me that you meet my family."

"I would like to meet your family."

"What about Chase and your client?"

"Chase, will be ticked off, royally so. And the client will be disappointed. But they will both survive. Your family is important to you."

Rebe took in a deep breath and released it knowing full well what she was about to do. "And, Sam, you're important to me. Where are you taking them for dinner?"

"Carter's Steak House."

"I'm at Juseppia, so that's not too far away. What time?"

"Eight."

"Eight! Are you crazy, Sam? You really did cut this close. Like I said, I'm not too far from there, but I don't have my car. I'll have to catch a taxi. There is no way I'll arrive in time and I have no plans on taking the hit for being a flake who doesn't arrive places on time. You, Kandi and Jamie all thought I was a flake and I'm sure one of you relayed those thoughts to your family. You make sure you tell them you didn't ask me to come until the last second."

"How about I tell them, you'll be meeting us about 8:20."

"That will work."

"Good, then problem solved."

"Sam, don't think I didn't notice that you didn't say you hadn't told your family I'm a flake." He laughed and suddenly Rebe was floating on air. She hadn't admitted it even to herself, but she'd felt a bit hurt and maybe a tad bit jealous that everyone had met Sam's family but her. Meeting them felt right.

"Thanks, Rebe." Sam pocketed his phone then turned toward Kandi, his heart bursting with joy. It was past time that his family met the woman he loved. Swinging Kandi up in his arms he laughed.

"Thanks."

Rebe cringed when she returned to her table. Some of her joy was tamped down. Chase would be livid, and he had every right to be. She didn't blame him, but this was something she had to do. She couldn't believe that her parents, and even Kandi's family had met Sam's family and she never had. How could that be possible?

Taking in a breath she smiled at the client, then glanced at Chase noting his annoyance—not concern. That triggered something within her. He didn't know if she'd left the table because of a medical emergency. He should at least wait until she told him what was going on to be annoyed with her.

There was no way around it. She had to tell him. Taking in several breaths hoping they would fill her with courage she nervously bit her lips before turning her gaze on Chase.

"Chase, I need to speak to you in private for a moment." Turning slightly to her left she held out her hand. "Mr. Stone, I'm so sorry about this. I promise I'll make it up to you after you're a client with us. But right now I have to leave. Please forgive me." She pulled on Chase's hand and he reluctantly followed her

"Rebe, this had better be good."

"It is," she said and continued walking toward the door of the restaurant. She was stalling. She didn't want to tell him. She waited until they outside before turning to face him.

"What is it? Who's ill?"

"It's Sam."

"Sam! Damn it, Rebe, he'd better be dying."

Rebe's mouth fell open and she stared at Chase. "I hope you didn't mean that."

"Rebe, we're with a client. You know how important this is to us, to our careers, to the firm. I didn't even make love to you because of this meeting. And you and I both know how much I wanted to. Now you're here, and you're leaving because of Sam."

Chase was angry, no doubt about it. Suddenly Rebe wasn't feeling so badly about it. "Look, I can give you a key to my apartment and you can let yourself in when you're done here." Chase didn't answer, he merely glared.

Rebe opened her purse and fished inside for a spare key which she handed over to Chase. "I'm sorry, Chase, I have to go."

"What's wrong with Sam?"

"He wants me to meet his family." Rebe didn't dare look at Chase. She walked to the curb and stuck her hand in the air waving for a taxi. For the first time in her life she was able to grab a taxi in the blink of an eye. Once inside she heaved a sigh of relief. "Drive," she said to the driver, wanting to get away from Chase's scowling face as quickly as she could. Once the driver pulled away she calmed down enough to tell him where to take her.

Relaxing a bit she did a bit of soul searching and realizing it, admitted the truth. She wanted to meet Sam's parents. She wanted to finally do something nice for Sam. And she was telling him the truth. It wasn't because of the promise she'd made to him when he'd taken her to the romance dinner. It was because since they'd returned from her parents she'd barely seen him. He'd been avoiding her and she missed him.

Rushing into the restaurant Rebe spotted Sam immediately. He was standing, scouring the restaurant, watching for her. The smile on his face made her stop in her tracks and her heart pounded. Suddenly her entire body was overcome with emotion, joy, happiness. She began walking toward Sam, smiling as his family turned toward her. But it was not them she was interested in. It was the look in Sam's eyes, the pure wonder, and love.

Ah, she thought, would it be too corny, too much of the romance writer in her to say it was adoration on Sam's face? But who cared about that? It was total and complete adoration. No one had ever looked at her in that manner. She was very nearly drowning in the feelings coming from Sam. She could barely wait to reach him. Sam came forward and held his arms open. To her surprise she went into them easily, as though it were the most natural thing in the world. With her head pressed against his chest she could hear his rapid heartbeat.

"Rebe, thank you," Sam whispered.

"Thank you for asking me."

She brought her head up slowly and their gazes met and held. A moment before Sam's lips touched hers, she whispered to him. "I promised Chase, I would stop kissing you."

After the kiss was over Sam laughed and said, "Did you now?" Then he took her by the hand and introduced her to his family.

Her family a voice whispered to Rebe. This was how it was meant to be. Sam was who she was meant to be with.

They sat for hours laughing and talking as though they were all old friends. It appeared his family already knew a lot about her from Sam, Jamie and even Kandi she learned. She glanced toward Sam. "Why didn't you ever introduce me to your family before?"

Sam shrugged. "Timing," he finally said.

Before Rebe knew it, it was after one and Sam's Parents were saying they had to leave. For some reason she didn't want the night to end. She thought about Chase. She'd told him to wait in her apartment for her, that they would make love when she returned. But she'd turned off her phone and had no desire for the evening to end. When Sam's brother asked if they'd like to continue talking in their hotel room, considering Sam had to take his parents back to the hotel and would be Rebe's ride back to her apartment. Sam looked to her to see what she wanted to do.

"Sure," she answered. And just like that her decision had been made. She'd never had so much fun in her life. It was seven in the morning by the time Sam was driving her home. When they pulled up in front of her building, he smirked.

"I see Chase is waiting for you."

"Yeah, I guess I might as well go in. Thanks, Sam, this was one of the best nights of my life. I wouldn't have missed this for anything." She gave him a quick hug before he attempted to kiss her.

When Rebe walked into her apartment the last thing she expected to see was Chase standing in the kitchen making breakfast. He glanced at her and turned his attention back to his cooking.

"Chase, I'm—"

"Save it, Rebe. Would you like a cup of coffee? I just made it."

"Thank you."

She stared at Chase before walking into the kitchen and taking a seat at the kitchen counter.

"Did you sleep with Sam?" Chase asked as he sat the coffee down in front of her.

"Of course not." Rebe answered, insulted. "Why would you think that?"

"Take a look at the clock, Rebe. You made me a promise last night. Yet, you didn't bother to come home, or to call. Not only didn't you bother to contact me, I'm not a fool, you turned your phone off in order for me to not be able to reach you. Tell me, is Sam still alive?"

"Why don't you say what you're trying to say?"

"Rebe, if you want out of this relationship, why don't you just say so? What do you think is going to happen? It's not as though either of us will die. We will move on. But this time, I want you to remember that I kept my promise to you. I've been trying." Chase turned from her and returned to cooking.

"Are you making enough for me?"

"Of course. I was going to make a plate for you and put it in the microwave, but now..."

"You know when we're done eating we could take a shower together and get back into bed."

"Back into bed?"

"You can get back into bed. Chase, I wasn't in bed with Sam or anyone. I went to meet Sam's family. I was having a good time with them. I'd already screwed up with you and knew you were annoyed. I gave myself permission to enjoy myself. I knew you'd be angry no matter what time I returned. So, I stayed."

"You left a business meeting in order to meet Sam's family. Do I have that straight?"

"Yes."

"And that's your only excuse?"

"Yes."

"Did this have anything to do with the favor you promised Sam several months ago when he took you to the dance?"

"He thought it was the reason I said yes. But I really did want to meet his family. They're leaving tomorrow. Chase, I'm not sorry I went."

"I can see that." Chase dished the food up into plates and handed one to her, then he began to eat. "About that shower, Rebe, I think I'll take it at home."

"How about tomorrow? Will you still have dinner with Kandi and Sam?"

"Of course, Rebe. I'm not that petty. I'll meet the three of you at the restaurant."

Rebe wasn't getting a good feeling about any of this. She knew she'd been wrong in the way she'd treated Chase with utter disrespect. He didn't deserve that. Neither did their client. They ate in silence and when they were done Chase took the plates to the sink kissed her on the forehead and left.

Rebe had been too afraid to call Chase the next day. She'd have to wait and see if he would really meet them for dinner. If he didn't she wondered what kind of excuse she would make. More than likely he was still ticked. If he didn't show, it wouldn't be a total surprise. In fact she'd forgive him for it. He did owe her one because of the way she'd treated him the night before last.

They were sitting around the table waiting for Chase when he called to say he couldn't make it. No one said too much about it just ordered drinks.

When they were on their second round of drinks, Sam's body stiffened. He'd gone from smiling at Rebe to glaring. But it wasn't at her. Rebe followed Sam's look and saw he was also not glaring at Kandi. Her instincts screamed for her to turn around. A slight chill danced up and down her spine. She didn't want to turn to see who Sam was glaring at. She was pretty sure what she'd see. There could be only one thing that would have made Sam so angry.

Finally Rebe turned. It was just as she'd thought. Chase with his tongue down some woman's throat was the culprit for Sam's rage. But that was crazy. He was supposed to be having dinner with the three of them, at this very restaurant where he'd called to say he couldn't make it.

The light finally came on for Rebe. Chase was being the good guy, the hero. It might have looked like payback, it might have even been payback. But Rebe was sure Chase's motive was to get her to make a decision.

Before she could explain Sam was up and marching toward Chase, and Kandi was following. Didn't they know what was going on? Chase was making things easier for her.

"Sam, stop," Rebe reached for him and attempted to hold his arms, but it was like holding a piece of steel. "No," he said. "You stay out of this." Then he turned to Chase and Rebe froze.

"Seriously, Chase, I told you what would happen if you hurt Rebe again."

Again Rebe attempted to plead with Sam. "Sam, please don't. Stop okay. It's okay."

"It is not okay," Sam roared.

"It's not your business. I'll take care of this." Rebe saw the anger in Sam's eyes and almost stopped. "Sam, I'm not in need of rescuing. I don't need a hero, real or otherwise. I never did."

Then she did something that surprised all of them. She put both of her hands on Sam's back and shoved him. "Please just go back to the table." Turning to face Chase she said, "Chase, we'll talk tomorrow. Just do me a favor and go someplace else for dinner. She stood between Chase and Sam as Chase got up and escorted the woman he was with from the restaurant. Then she calmly went back to the table and perused her menu. She couldn't help smiling at what Chase had done. Maybe he'd done it for her, himself, or for both of them.

Kandi and Sam were looking at her as though she'd lost her mind. They were both glaring at her.

"Look you two, Chase knew this was where we were going to meet. He's not stupid. He was giving me a way out."

"You're crazy. If that was what he was after, he could have just broken it off with you."

"And I could have broken up with him. But I didn't and neither did he. Instead I chose to stay out until seven in the morning with you, Sam. And I chose to turn my phone off after I'd told Chase I'd meet him back at my apartment. He did this for me. Don't either of you see that? He was being heroic."

"Oh God, not that again. Please don't tell me you're even thinking of going back to him." Sam held his fisted hands in the air. "I could joyfully strangle you, Rebe. If you fall for this…I promise you, I will—"

"Chase and I are going to talk, Sam. What happened tonight is my concern, not yours. Look, this dinner was supposed to be about the three of us renewing our friendship. Stop glaring at me and let's order. "

"This dinner was not about the three of us. It was supposed to have been for us to try and stomach your boyfriend. Now that's totally gone to hell," Sam shot back.

"You may as well get over what happened tonight and order, because I'm going to eat dinner."

Neither Kandi nor Sam bothered to order dinner just another drink. They both stared at her the entire time. And she could just imagine they were both thinking she was going to like the hero aspect of what Chase had done. To be honest she did. She couldn't help smiling. And the more Sam and Kandi glared the more she smiled.

CHAPTER SIXTEEN

Monday morning was the beginning of a new phase in Rebe's life. She knew what it was she was finally going to do. Knocking on Chase's office door, she waited patiently until he told her she could come in. His eyes wouldn't meet hers, but she was about to put his mind at ease.

"Chase."

"I'm sorry, Rebe."

"I didn't come in here to ream you out. I came to thank you for the last three years. You've helped me to get to a place where I can open my heart and take a risk. You've prepared me to love and be loved in return."

"You're not talking about me are you?"

She laughed. "No, I'm not. I'm ready to tell Sam that I'm in love with him and have been for a very long time."

"I was holding out hope that you were too afraid to fall in love with me because of my past behavior. I didn't want to believe you were seriously in love with Sam. How can you be sure?"

"Because he's everything I need. He loves me, Chase. I am his main concern. My happiness is what matters to him."

"You're just angry."

"For once, I'm not upset with you. We have had fun together and I've enjoyed most of it. But we were never in love. We couldn't even pretend to be. The most we could do was take a stab at having a committed relationship, and we failed miserably at that."

"You mean I failed."

"We both failed. All the kissing I was doing with Sam was wrong, no matter what you had done. Since my brother's death I haven't wanted to feel anything. I could do that with you, Chase. Neither of us wanted all the emotions that go along with being in love. That's not us. We do care about each other, but our thing has been fun. Now, I want more. I'm finally growing up."

"I'm guessing that what you're really saying is I haven't grown up. You're wrong about that, Rebe."

"I wasn't trying to say that. In fact, I do believe you've changed. It's just…we've taken too long to get to the same place."

"Do you believe Sam is mature enough to be the man you want?"

"Sam has been so patient. He's waited for me to see him. I see him, Chase. I'm going to duke it out with him and I'm going to accept all the crazy things that go along with being in love. I know Sam is going to make me crazy, but I want to give it a chance."

"Like you gave us?"

"I'm sorry, Chase. I do think if we had tried to have a monogamous relationship before I realized I had feelings for Sam it would have gone a lot smoother. I want you to know that you played an important role in my life and I'm grateful. You're fun and I enjoyed our time together. I don't want it to be awkward between us."

"But what can Sam give you? He doesn't have any money. He can't help you advance here at the firm. He has nothing."

"That's not quite true. He has me."

"Are you really okay with me?"

"I'm okay."

"Were you telling me the truth when you said you hadn't slept with Sam?"

"I would have never done that without breaking up with you first." A smile was trying to break out on Rebe's face and she allowed it. "You forget, I'm a romance writer. I have to follow the rules. The heroine can't sleep with two guys. She's required to break up with one before she begins a relationship with the other. But now that I've done that, I plan to do everything in a bed with Sam that two people can do."

"I guess if you're the heroine that would make Sam the hero, and me, the villain."

"You were never the villain."

"I gather you haven't told Sam yet that you're in love with him."

"It wouldn't have been right."

"I take it he's the reason we didn't have sex for over a month."

"Probably, but it wasn't anything I planned. I really wanted things to work between the two of us, Chase. I was too afraid of what being in love with Sam would mean."

"And now?"

"And now, I plan on giving him my heart. It's a bit scary because I know what that means. I'm going to give him the power to break my heart and even to break me."

Rebe moved closer to Chase and smiled when he jerked away as though he'd thought she was going to strike him. She chuckled and threw her arms around him, hugging him.

"I did want to be committed to you, Rebe."

"I know. But I also know one day you're going to fall in love. It's going to happen out of the blue. As for the two of us, we both tried and love shouldn't be about trying. I've been looking for a hero. All along I had my hero and didn't know it. One day you're going to find your perfect woman, your heroine, Chase, and I'm going to be happy for you. I promise when it happens you're not going to have to try to be committed to her. You just will."

Rebe pulled away and Chase brought her back and kissed her hard, then he pulled away.

"I had to try. You're serious aren't you?"

"I know you had to try, you didn't believe me."

"And I owed it to Sam to kiss you. After all, he kept kissing you while I was doing my best to be committed to you."

"You're not going to blame Sam are you, Chase?"

"I'd like to. It would make me feel better about hurting you, and you turning to him as your rebound guy."

Rebe laughed and shook her head. "Seriously, you didn't hurt me. That's part of the problem. Your cheating should have hurt me, but it never did, not really. By the way, Sam is not my rebound guy. He's my guy." She grinned. "I love him. I really do. By the way I know what you did last night. That's part of the reason I wanted to talk to you. I wanted to thank you."

"What did I do?"

"You forced me to make a decision. You were being heroic."

"Yeah, but you were supposed to choose me."

"I'm not sure at all if that was your plan. But you were right. For the last month I've been sitting on the fence. You've helped me to see that. Thank you."

She wasn't sure if Chase really understood, but he was pleased that she wasn't making a scene. Turning to walk away he stopped her.

"Mr. Edgar wants us to go to see a client in New York, this afternoon. We're taking the company jet. That won't be too bad. Remember that swanky art show he gave us tickets to? Well, he forgot to mention it's also in New York. He wants us to select a piece of art for the office. I think since you've aligned yourself with a penniless artist perhaps it would be good to see how the really good artists live. We leave at four."

"Are you serious?" Rebe was distressed. She had planned to tell Sam she was in love with him, and to finish it off with a long slow evening of love making.

"We've got a crazy busy day today. We have a meeting with Mr. Stone in about forty-five minutes. I arranged to have him give us another shot. I told him you had an emergency the other night when you left the restaurant. We can still win him over. This time you shouldn't object. It's in the office. We need to get started. We have back to back meetings. There's also a partners' meeting that I haven't been invited to. It looks like something big is going down, but I don't have any details."

"Why not? You're a partner."

"I guess being a junior partner doesn't give me access to whatever the heck is going on." Chase shrugged. "Are we going to be able to continue working together? I hope so, because we really are the best team around."

"You still want me to work with you?"

"Of course. Rebe. I meant it when I said I didn't choose you to work with me because we were in a relationship, but because you're a damn good lawyer."

Chase's words made Rebe beam. "Thank you. Yes, I'd love nothing more than to continue working together. I think we may have to change things around a bit though. Sam goes absolutely crazy with even the thought of me bringing in clients by being sexy. I had never looked at it that way before, but I'm seeing a lot of things differently these days. I'm seeing things through Sam's eyes."

"Oh, God, No…" Chase laughed. "We've lost a good one."

Rebe laughed also. "Stop it. It matters what Sam thinks of me. I told you that. It matters a lot. So yes, I want to continue working with you. And no, to me dressing sexy and giving our male clients the idea that I might be available."

"And our female clients?"

"I don't think you should give them the idea that you're available either. We're both good lawyers."

"Sam doesn't think I am."

"That doesn't matter. You are a good lawyer. We're both too good to use sexuality to bring in clients."

A hard knock on the door made Rebe and Chase turn toward the sound in the same instant. Chase called out, "Come in," and Rebe waited.

Mary Ann, the office receptionist, stuck her head in. "Rebe, Kandi has been trying to reach you. She said your cell wasn't on and that it's an emergency. There's been some kind of accident. I put the call through to Chase's office. You can take it on three."

Barely glancing at Chase for his approval to take the call in his office, Rebe was snatching up the phone. "Kandi, what's wrong?"

"Rebe, Sam's been in an accident, a three car pile-up. He's at Edward's Hospital in Naperville. I don't have any more details. I'm on my way there."

Cold sweat ran over Rebe's body and she closed her eyes. She was trembling. Chase came over to her. "Rebe, what's wrong?" he asked. "Are your parents okay?"

"It's Sam. He's been in a car accident... a three car pile-up. He's at Edward's Hospital in Naperville." She held Chase's gaze. "I have to go."

"Rebe, we have an important meeting with, Mr. Stone. We can't blow it, not twice. If we don't take the meeting, he's not going to sign on with us."

"I'm so sorry. I know it's not fair to stick you with this, but you know I have to go. I know you can handle it. I'm going to the hospital." She took off running toward the parking lot. Before she could reach her car, Chase was there.

"You're in no condition to drive. I'll take you," Chase said taking her arm and directing her to his car.

"What about the meeting?"

"I asked my secretary to try and arrange it for later in the week. She'll call me and let me know. But I'm not going to let you go to Naperville alone. We're a team. This is an unavoidable emergency."

"Thanks, Chase." Rebe remained silent for a few seconds before turning to Chase. "What if Sam doesn't make it?"

"Don't think like that. You don't even know how bad it is."

"But I'm worried."

"He's going to be fine, Rebe."

"That's what they told me about Jamie, only he wasn't fine, Chase. He died."

"Come on, Rebe, not every accident results in death," Chase snapped.

For a moment Rebe was stunned unable to utter a word, her eyes watered and the first tear fell.

"Don't cry, Rebe. I wasn't trying to be harsh. I'm just trying to get you to stop worrying."

"I know."

"You really do love him don't you?"

"But I've never told him. I've told Kandi, my parents and you. But I haven't told Sam. I'm so worried that…"

"You know this is a bit odd that you're talking to me about this right?"

"I know, but I also know you're my friend. I know you don't want anything bad to happen to Sam."

"You're right I don't," Chase sighed. "I hope he's okay. He has to be. I want you to have your hero. I know he'll be a much better boyfriend that I ever was."

"Chase, you are a hero. I realize what you did for me. I was being a coward. I was having a hard time saying the words that needed to be said. But I have to tell you this. I do love you Chase."

"Wow, you are scared aren't you?"

"Yeah, I am. But I also realize that I've waited too long to tell Sam how I feel. I don't want to do that with you."

"Rebe, it's not necessary. I'm okay. I promise."

'It's not okay. I may never get the chance…I have to tell you all of this." She glanced out the window and thought of Sam and all the things she hoped she'd still get a chance to tell him. Then she turned toward Chase and spoke softly.

"I love you as a dear friend of mine. And I really meant it when I told you I'd enjoyed the time we've spent together. I also appreciate your wanting to try to have something more. The thing of it is we had almost three years of a devil may care relationship. We didn't demand nor did we need anything from the other. That made it almost impossible to transition into an adult relationship."

"But why? Haven't you ever wondered why we couldn't make the switch?"

"You're an only child and that alone makes you innately selfish and self-centered. I on the other hand had three people fawning over me, the youngest in the family, and a girl to boot. That made me selfish and self-centered. It would seem we should have been perfect for each other."

"Are we really that bad?"

"Yes." Rebe smiled then and touched Chase's arm. "I've thought about it and I want you to know none of his had anything to do with you, or that you were, or were not a good boyfriend. You were as a good a boyfriend as I was a girlfriend. I was in love with Sam long before you came along. I just didn't want to admit it because I didn't want it to be true. Sam is so different from either of us. He challenges me to be more, to want more, to think about others first." Rebe laughed. "All the things I hate. I like the way I am, or rather I thought I did. I just want you to know a couple of things. I think you're good boyfriend material. You stepped up when you decided to change. Keep doing that and you're going to find the right woman for you. Had I known how deeply I was in love with Sam...I don't know... I probably would have never admitted it. So, I'm sorry for the last few months. And I'm sorry for kissing Sam and hurting your feelings."

"Stop, Rebe."

"I'm almost done. The other night at the restaurant, neither Sam nor Kandi understood what you were doing. They thought I was being stupid, again. Kandi wanted to kill you, but I knew you were giving me the opportunity to end things and it tells me you are heroic. You are, Chase." She gave his hand a squeeze.

"I think we should say a prayer for Sam," Chase whispered.

The moment Chase dropped Rebe at the emergency room entrance she ran into the building and straight to the desk asking about Sam. They didn't have any information about him and said no one with that name had been brought it. She was worried to death that Kandi had gotten the information wrong. Within minutes Chase joined her followed by Kandi. They rushed into each other's arms.

"I don't have any news on Sam. They don't even have his name listed," Rebe wailed. "They said no ambulance had called in about anyone with that name. What the heck is going on? Kandi, are you sure he was brought here?"

Kandi began pacing. "I'm sure. Let's just stay here and wait."

Patient after patient was wheeled in. As Rebe watched her thoughts were of her brother and she began to cry. Within seconds she was surrounded by Kandi and Chase. Chase held her in his arms lighting caressing her back and neck. "Don't worry, Rebe, Sam's going to be okay." She wanted to believe Chase. She even wanted to believe Kandi, but her friend had a strange look in her eyes that she'd never seen before. Rebe was positive it was because she was trying to get her not to think about Jamie. It wasn't working.

For an hour they paced. Rebe was facing the door when the hairs on the back of her neck stood up and she turned around. "Sam," she yelled and raced toward him.

"Rebe," Sam stopped at the sight of her racing toward him wondering why she was there, if there was something wrong with her. Then she hit him with a thud landing on his chest and began crying. "Rebe, are you okay? What's wrong?"

"It wasn't me, it was you. You were the one in a three car pile-up."

"Me?" Sam glanced toward where Kandi was standing with Chase and the picture became clearer. He'd not told Kandi he was injured, nothing close. In fact he'd told her it was a minor fender bender. But he'd followed the ambulance to the hospital because his friend had complained of neck pain and they'd taken him in to check him out.

"Rebe, stop crying. I was never in any danger and I told that to Kandi. I didn't ask her to call you. I only wanted her to know where I was because the two of us were meeting for lunch."

They both turned and glared at Kandi. When Rebe began trembling Sam threw her close loving the feel of her in his arms, but not like this. "Rebe," he whispered. "This isn't anything at all like what happened to Jamie. I promise." Still she cried.

"Kandi," he called and glared in her direction. Instead of answering him or helping him reassure Rebe, he watched as she turned to Chase.

"Chase, how about if you show me that mural in your office. I'll follow you. I think Sam and Rebe can handle this."

"I need to make sure," Chase answered.

"Chase," Kandi laughed. "You really are dense aren't you? Go ahead, make sure Rebe's okay."

Chase tilted his head and glared at Kandi before sighing as he looked on at Rebe in Sam's arms. She was in good hands he realized. Still he asked. "Rebe, are you going to need me to take you home?"

Rebe stopped her tears and smiled at Chase, so did Sam and Kandi.

"Okay," Chase admitted. "I get it. I'm no longer needed. I've been replaced. Come on, Kandi, I'll show you the famous mural," he said and headed for the door. "We're going to have to have a talk though about your part in trying to replace me with Sam in Rebe's life." With a wave to Rebe and Sam, Chase and Kandi headed for the door.

Sam used the pad of his finger to tilt Rebe's chin up and looked deeply into her eyes where a few tears remained. "Are you okay now?"

"Sam, I don't know what I would have done without you...I need you in my life. You're you're..." She threw herself in his arms and began crying again. "They didn't have your name listed anywhere. I was beginning to panic." She felt his fingers caressing her back then he moved her from him.

"Rebe, why can't you live without me?" he asked glancing toward the door where Chase and Kandi had just existed.

"I love you, Sam. I'm in love with you and I want you to be in love with me. I want you in my life."

"I thought you were afraid."

"I was. I still might be. I don't know, but I'm more afraid of not having you in my life than I am of what could happen."

"Why now, Rebe, because Chase cheated on you again?"

"Are you crazy?"

"No, but I don't want to just start a rebound relationship with you."

"Chase didn't cheat, Sam."

"Yeah, right."

"He didn't. I talked to Chase—"

"Chase doesn't deserve to have you say one word to him. He's going to beg you and give you the puppy dog eye and you're going to think about the heroes in your book and take him back. I can be your hero, just take a better look."

"I have taken a better look. You are my hero. You were always that. I want us to be together."

"I think you need to officially break things off with Chase. You'll have to before we can be together."

"You're not listening to me, Sam. I already broke things off with Chase. Didn't you notice that Chase brought me here? He wasn't cheating on me last night. He was…he knew I was in love with you and he knew I was trying to honor our agreement. He really was being a hero. He wanted to make things easy for me to leave him."

"You just made my point. That's the only reason you decided you're in love with me, because Chase made it easy for you, and Kandi exaggerated. Oh hell, she lied to you, thinking you'd rush here and fall into my arms. She was right. Because that is exactly what happened."

"Does it really make a difference how or why I got here? I'm here. I love you, Sam. Are you saying you don't want me?"

Before Sam had a chance to answer her, his lips were on hers, his kiss hard, demanding. "Let's go," he commanded and pulled Rebe toward the door and into his car.

"What about your friend? Doesn't he need you to take him home?"

"His wife is here. Did you really break up with Chase?"

"Yes."

"And you did it because you want to be with me?"

"Yes,"

"Rebe, please tell me you did this before Kandi lied to you that I'd been hurt. I'd hate to think that your thinking about Jamie, and worrying about me is what made you do it."

"Sam, I did it because I finally came to my senses. Now why don't you kiss me again?"

After several passionate kisses Sam put the car in drive. Every time they got to a light he kissed Rebe. It seemed it was taking forever for them to reach her apartment. The moment they got to Rebe's apartment she ran up the stairs and opened the door. And at that moment her cell rang.

"Chase."

"Since Sam is okay I wanted to tell you the good news. Mr. Stone is flying back to L.A. He has appointments with two other law firms. He said if we can give him a lift to the airport we can have our meeting with him in the car."

"Are you serious?' Do you still think we have a chance to get the account?"

"I do. He didn't sound too upset. I think he may even be a bit intrigued that we've stood him up twice. Do you think you can make the meeting? Mr. Newton wants us both to handle this. Of course if you can't, I'll make an excuse."

"I'll do it."

"Have you told Sam that you dumped me?"

"That wasn't the way it happened."

"It was exactly the way it happened. Give me an hour and I'll pick you up. That should be long enough for you to talk to Sam. I'll admit I don't want to give you time to do more."

"You know if that's what we wanted it would be more than enough time."

"If that's true maybe you should reconsider your choice. The two of us would never be finished in an hour."

Rebe started laughing. "Come and get me in an hour."

"Was that Chase?"

"Yes, we have an important meeting. Mr. Stone, the client we were supposed to meet when I ditched the meeting to meet your family. He rescheduled for today. Right before the meeting I got the call from Kandi and ran out. Now Chase says he's intrigued and wants to give us another chance. We're going to take Mr. Stone to the airport. Chase is picking me up in an hour."

"Rebe, call Chase back, tell him I'll bring you to the office. What I have in mind might just take longer than an hour. Tell him you have a new hero now."

"Sorry, Sam. Chase has been covering for me a lot lately. I like my job with the firm. I'll continue this with you later"

Rebe looked into Sam's eyes and his gaze locked on her like a laser. Sam was kissing her before she could take her next breath. She wanted him to stop. She had to tell him the many things she'd held inside. She wanted him to know he'd long been her hero.

But Sam was making it difficult for her to tell him anything. Before she knew what was happening his hand was undoing the button of her slacks and he was pushing them down with one hand while his other stayed firmly around her waist.

"Sam, no, I don't have time for this." He stopped and a pained look crossed his face. "Not you, Sam. I can't blow this meeting with Mr. Stone a third time. I have to get out of here, and knowing Chase he'll be here well before an hour."

"I'll be quick," Sam whispered in her ear.

"I don't want quick." That brought a smile to his face.

"I'll be good."

"Sam."

"Don't you want to? I've wanted you so long, Rebe. I know it hasn't been the same for you, but I think we'll be good together. In fact I know we'll be good together. I love you, Rebe."

His mouth moved over hers and this time the kiss was different. It told her what his words didn't. It told her how very much he loved her. But he was moving so slowly and she really didn't have time.

"Seriously, Sam, I don't have the time. ..." Rebe gasped as Sam's fingers found their way inside her body. A nice haze filled her and she wanted more. "Five minutes," she ordered.

"You are taking all of the fun out of this seduction," Sam complained.

"I don't have time for seduction." She pushed away from him. "Maybe next time."

"Maybe next time? I don't know if I should be insulted or pleased. Here I am thinking of myself as the hero. I don't think that's how this little scene is supposed to go. You're supposed to be panting with desire right now." He saw the smile on her face grow wider. "You'd better not laugh at me, or I swear—"

"You've been reading my books. That's one down for me finding out things about you. How long?"

"I thought we had to make this quick." Sam planted his body and bent his knees putting his arms around Rebe only to be stopped

"You're kidding right? I am way too tall for you to lift. You're going to hurt yourself."

"Remind me again why I want you. That is definitely not something the heroine says to the hero."

"But I'm not a heroine. I'm a flawed, half-crazy, self-centered woman who has been too afraid to accept a real grown up love. Perhaps that's why romance writers write about heroines and heroes. I don't know if anyone could live up to the expectations in real life. I don't know anyone who could pass the test. I know I never would. Then again there is something to be said about real life. It's so darn unpredictable. Sometimes there are no happy endings. Sometimes there are no lessons learned. Sometimes we just keep making the same mistakes over and over again."

"If that's the case why do so many women read romances?"

"To escape. They want to believe in the happily ever after."

"And you?"

"My thinking is too analytical for that. I see all the bumps in the road ahead, and sometimes I hope for the best."

"And me."

"I think you're a romantic and see the happily ever after. I also think you're a hero, a true hero." Rebe tilted her head to the side. "But I'm not sure that you're the kind of hero who can lift me." She ignored him rolling his eyes. "It's not necessary to prove anything to me, Sam."

"I know Chase lifts you, and I know you don't complain or tell him to stop. You squeal with delight." Sam lifted her in his arms and looked down into her face. "Where's my squeal, Rebe?"

"Don't drop me."

"You're very bad for my ego."

"Two minutes, Sam."

Shaking his head, Sam carried Rebe into her bedroom and unceremoniously dumped her on the bed, pulled off her pants then her panties, and then he stood staring at her.

"Stop staring and let's get on with this. I have a meeting."

"You're ruining the mood because you're afraid. I'm not afraid of us. I'm sure enough of this for both of us."

Opening the drawer, Rebe pulled out a condom and held it out.

"I don't want to use condoms you have on hand for Chase."

"Do you have one?"

Snatching the condom from her fingers Sam pulled away his clothes feeling a bit vulnerable, hoping Rebe didn't say anything else, no wise cracks. She was staring at him. "I swear if you're doing a comparison you'd better stop."

"No comparison. If I were, you'd be doing okay. By the way when we're done you're going to have to remake my bed. I won't have time and I refuse to finish this and leave the house with my bed unmade."

Stopping with his hands positioned on either side of Rebe's body, Sam looked down at her. "Do you think you could at least pretend that I'm not forcing you?" He opened the condom and rolled it over his erection. "I'm not forcing you am I?" She shrugged.

"Rebe?"

She pulled the covers back. "Would you come on?"

"Are you afraid I won't satisfy you?"

"Sam."

He'd never imagined in all the times he'd dreamt of making love to Rebe, that he would be doing it with one eye on the clock and her rushing him. He wanted to taste every inch of her body, make her cry out with passion. He saw a tiny smile curving her lips. She was teasing him.

Jumping into the bed Sam pulled Rebe into his arms and kissed her long and hard and very satisfyingly until she stopped fidgeting and rushing him, and began moaning. When his hand found her, she was wet.

"Please," Rebe whispered.

Sam wanted to believe she wanted him to hurry because she couldn't wait to have him inside her. But that would be plain foolishness. Rebe wanted it over and done with so she could get to her meeting.

"Sam," Rebe smiled. "Next time we'll take it slow. I promise."

He smiled back at her. That was enough to make him do what she wanted, what he wanted. Rising up he entered her and for a moment he didn't move as he savored the feel of her. Her heat was scorching him, her legs wrapped around his torso and he began to thrust into her body, going deep and hard.

Two, three, four…what the? He was…his orgasm was fast approaching and there wasn't a damn thing Sam could do about it. This couldn't be happening. He'd lasted longer than this when he'd been a teen and it was his first time. Damn it all to hell. But it was too late, he couldn't stop. His body convulsed and pleasure filled him as he grunted with the orgasm, knowing Rebe had been nowhere near ready. WTH. He fell on her in a slump and attempted to roll her over but she moved quickly getting out of the bed and making a dash for the bathroom.

"Next time it will be better," Rebe yelled over her shoulder as she made her way for the bathroom. "I have to take a shower."

In stunned disbelief Sam stared at her. Did that just happened? Did he really only last four strokes? He groaned and lay back on the bed covering his head in shame, remembering what Kandi had told him about Chase.

Oh hell. Then he remembered Rebe said she was in love with him. That had to count for something. She'd never been in love with Chase. He grinned, he'd made love to Rebe and four strokes or not he'd never felt such intense passion. How unheroic of him to be feeling like a caveman wanting to drag her back to his lair and do it right. Or at the least how about doing it again in the shower, perhaps he'd last a little longer. Before the idea could fully take root he was at the door to the bathroom and was trying unsuccessfully to turn the knob. He couldn't believe it. She'd locked him out.

"Rebe, why did you lock the door? I thought we could try it again in the shower."

"I told you I didn't have time."

"But…"

"Please, how did I know you'd try to come in here and finish the job? I know you better than you think. And that makes two things so far I know about you."

He heard a funny sound. "Are you in there laughing at me?"

"Yes, but not for the reason you think. I think you're very sweet."

"Sweet," he groaned. Sweet was not what he wanted to be with her. Especially not after Kandi telling him why Rebe had stayed with Chase for so long. It was his sexual prowess.

Moving away from the door Sam went for tissues trying to decide if he should take a shower at her apartment or return to his own. He glanced behind his shoulder at the bed thinking perhaps he'd just crawl back in and stay until Rebe returned home. The door to the bathroom opened Rebe came out and before he could say a word she'd opened her drawer and put on red panties. He moved toward her, but she held out her hand and grabbed for a matching bra. Then she ran for the closet snatched a blouse and pants from hangers and redressed.

"Chase isn't here yet."

Rebe glanced at her watch. "Trust me he'll be here in a couple of seconds." As though she'd spoken a prophesy, the horn of a car sounded and Rebe ran for the door. "Make the bed and make sure you lock the door when you leave."

Looking after Rebe, Sam tilted his head slightly as he caught his reflection in the mirror. Rebe had decided for him. It wasn't a wait for me until I come home moment. He should be feeling worse. Why wasn't he? Making a move for the mirror he gave himself a thorough once over. Turning his head in different directions he was looking for the warts.

"Sam, what are you doing?" Rebe asked laughing hysterically.

"Why are you back? I thought you were in a rush."

"I am but I decided to come back for a second. Now why are you looking at yourself so intently in the mirror?"

"Okay, I'm looking for the warts." More laughter greeted him.

"Seriously, I shouldn't have ever said that. You're not a frog." Rebe crossed her fingers over her heart.

"Why did you come back?" he asked.

She pressed her body against his and kissed him. Then she pulled away. "I wanted to tell you that I like it that you wanted me so much you couldn't hold back."

"That was because of your nagging me to hurry."

"No, it wasn't. You wanted me and you wanted me bad. Admit it."

"Yes, I wanted you, but…not even my first time. It's you, Rebe."

"I know that. You're in love with me." She kissed him again. "And I'm in love with you, Sam." Then she gave him a slap on his naked behind and ran out the door.

CHAPTER SEVENTEEN

The impromptu meeting while taking the client to the airport had gone well. They didn't have a definitive answer but at least they'd finally told the client what he could expect from their firm. When they'd returned to the office for the other appointments they had lined up, things were going as though they had divine help.

Rebe was beaming, wanting to hurry the day along so she could be with Sam. She had proclaimed him the hero in her personal little drama. She laughed. She had it wrong. The readers had it wrong. As her mother had always told her, pretty is as pretty does. Yes, Chase was tall, handsome, rich and fun. And she wouldn't lie, they were damned good together. And no, she'd not had the big 'O' with Sam. She hadn't even been close. But it didn't matter. He was a hero in every sense of the word and she loved him. She loved that he wanted her so much that he'd been unable to hold back. And she loved that they both had warts and weren't perfect. It didn't matter, she was just happy he hadn't given up on her, that he'd loved her enough to allow her to get over her mistakes. Chase was her mistake, but he'd served a need she'd had. She glanced up and saw Chase coming toward her. He held his hands up in a defensive mode and gave her a look.

"You're not going to like this but there has been a change in the plans for us. We're staying overnight. We have another meeting in the morning. Mr. Newton has a meeting with a client and he wants us to be there."

"But why?" Rebe stopped, she'd sounded like she was whining. "Chase, come on," She pleaded trying her best not to sound like a little girl pouting.

"You do get that Mr. Newton is head of the firm don't you? I'm merely a junior partner. If you ever want to make even that, you've got to learn how to play ball. You don't have a choice but to go to the meeting and neither do I."

After giving Rebe the remaining details Chase dropped the final bombshell. "I already booked our room."

"I suggest you book one more." Rebe walked away her heels clicking. No way would Sam believe her. Heck she wouldn't believe it either. Still she had to call him and let him know she was flying to

New York and wouldn't be home until the next afternoon.

When she was almost done with the call she took a breath. She was determined to tell Sam all of it. "Chase is going on the trip with me, but nothing is going to happen. I promise."

"I was already aware that Chase would be with you on the trip. After all, this is really his case, he's just allowing you to help him. Besides, you don't have to promise me nothing will happen between you and Chase. I trust you."

"Seriously?"

"Yes, seriously."

"By the way, Chase and I are going to an art exhibit while we're in New York. Seth Alexander Martin is having a private showing for some of his most exclusive clients. It's a really posh event, something I'd never go to, but the boss bought tickets for us. The artist is one of his favorites. He asked that Chase and I go and pick out a new painting for the office."

Rebe thought for a moment how that could possibly hurt Sam's feelings and rushed on to soothe ruffled feathers. "He loves your work though, Sam."

Sam laughed.

"What's so funny?"

"Nothing much, but I'm thinking Chase is probably thrilled to be going to the exhibit of a famous artist. I know he's been saying for months that both of us should see how a really successful artist is treated, and that I should probably be able to pick up a few pointers. I really don't mind that Chase thinks you should see a successful artist."

"You can't blame him for making a crack. I mean you did paint him as a frog. But just so we're clear, Chase didn't buy the tickets to the exhibit. Our boss did. Don't worry, I'm pretty pleased with the artist I have. I don't care if you never become famous, or make tons of money. After all it's not your money I love, but you."

For a long moment Sam was silent then he asked, "What time are you going to the gallery?"

"I think it's about eight. Chase and I are having dinner first. They are supposed to have snacks at the exhibit, but you know how these things are. If you don't eat you'll end up starving. But I think the exhibit starts around eight."

"Have a good time."

All in all the day had been pleasant with the exception of thinking something really bad had happened to Sam. But even that had turned out well. They were now a couple. And Rebe had to admit, from the private plane, to the meeting, everything had been first class and all on the company dime.

As usual she was having fun with Chase. Dinner was delicious. And now even though neither of them had been thrilled to attend the art show they were both enjoying it. Rebe stood in awe looking at the paintings, something about them so familiar. She wasn't an art connoisseur by any means but if she didn't know better, she'd swear she'd seen the artist work before.

Then she moved to the next painting. It was her face staring back at her. She looked radiant and happy and she was holding, she laughed, she was holding a frog with a crown on its head. She knew the artist. Looking down at the signature she noticed the first letter of each name was in a larger font. Seth Alexander Martin. Sam. She turned to tell Chase and her eyes met Sam's. She smiled at him. "I figured this one out on my own."

"That you did. But it took you long enough."

"I'm slow, what can I say? It's beautiful." Rebe turned back toward the painting. "It's really beautiful."

"I know. My model is beautiful." His arms slid around Rebe's waist and he nibbled her neck. "Tell me the truth. Doesn't it feel better to have finally and officially broken it off with the other guy?"

She laughed. "Yeah."

"Did you tell Chase the reason?"

"That I'm in love with you?" Rebe asked.

"You told him that?"

"Yes."

"Are you really?"

"Does it come as a surprise to you?"

"It comes as a surprise that you're finally admitting it."

"I know. You've been pretty patient."

"Not always. There have been so many times I wanted to wring your neck, so many times I wanted—"

"To stop loving me."

"Yeah, but I couldn't. It's not that easy to stop loving someone. We both know that."

"I don't want this to be about my brother."

"It never was." Sam drew Rebe into the safety of his arms. "It was always about you."

Neither of them had paid much attention to Chase until he tapped Sam on the arm.

"Sam, I didn't expect to see you here. In fact I didn't expect to see you in New York. Apparently you're jealous and came to check on your..." he shuddered. "I can't say it. It just doesn't seem possible that Rebe would choose you over me. Come on, Sam, tell the truth, you didn't trust us together did you? I can't blame you. After all, Rebe and I were together for nearly three years."

Sam shook his head. "Don't remind me. I was there for the entire three years."

Chase slapped Sam on the shoulder. "Have you had a chance to look at some of the artwork? How does it feel to see the work of a real artist? I don't see a single painting in here less than seventy-five thousand dollars."

Rebe and Sam began laughing simultaneously. "Chase, stop talking and look at the painting in front of us," Rebe advised.

After a couple of seconds of staring Chase turned in Sam's direction. "That's Rebe. Did you paint that? Are you Seth Alexander Martin, the famous artist?"

"Yes," Sam held his hand out to Chase. "I am."

"Then why were you using the name Sam Adams? I don't get it."

"People treat you differently when your name is tied to something. With my friends and the people I care about I use my initials."

"But you were lying."

"Perhaps." Glancing at Rebe he saw that she was staring at him and he knew what she was thinking, why hadn't he told her? He grinned at her. "I'll tell you all, later."

""I guess I was wrong about you, Sam. Well, Rebe, it doesn't look as if you're going to starve."

"I was never going to starve. I have a law degree, remember?" She saw Sam smiling at her as he moved between them.

"Excuse us, Chase, I have another painting I want to show Rebe."

When Sam took her hand and began to lead her out the door Rebe wondered. When they got in the taxi and he gave an address, she wondered even more. When they rode up in an elevator of a swanky apartment building she could barely contain herself. "Yours?"

she asked, as the light turned on and she began looking at the paintings on the wall.

Sam's apartment was beautiful, tastefully decorated in rich jeweled tones, the décor was modern chic, artsy, yet classy at the same time. It was the kind of place an artist like Sam should have, which made her wonder about the messy apartment he'd shared with Jamie. The place practically screamed out happiness.

Looking around Sam's apartment Rebe could see why he wanted to redo her apartment to bring in more energy. She now wanted the life in her living space that Sam had in his. And she was going to put all of her pictures back on the mantles and the walls. All of the people she loved including Jamie would be out where she could see them constantly.

"Take a look at the canvas in my bedroom," Sam suggested as he pointed the way.

Rebe knew what the painting would be before she entered the door. A very tasteful nude of her.

"Are you upset?" Sam asked.

"Depends. I was pretty out of it the two weeks I spent in your apartment. Is this painting from memory or imagination? I mean did you take a peek while I was sleeping?"

"Are you serious? I would never—"

"Sam, I know that. I was merely teasing. Why didn't you ever tell me who you were?"

"Do you seriously have to ask me? You treated me like the scum under your shoes. You were out for a man with money."

"But I've met your family. Your father tried to give you money. I saw him."

"To be honest with you, my father and my brothers think it will only be a matter of time until I starve. They're disappointed that I didn't follow them into medicine, or become a lawyer like my mom. She's the only one in the family who truly believes in what I've chosen to do with my life. She's the only one who insists I buy her the most outlandish and expensive gifts. My father scolds her for doing it. I love her for it. It proves just how much she believes in me.

Rebe walked from corner to corner eyeing the nude of her. "So tell me honestly... did you ...I mean while you were painting me nude... did you ever pleasure—"

"No, of course not."

"I don't believe you."

"Even if I had, do you think I'd admit to doing something so childish? It's been a long time since I used beautiful girls in magazines to find my pleasure."

"Are there more surprises?"

"You're going to have to find out. You've only found out two things about me and I pretty much helped you with those. I thought since you were staying in New York, why not stay with me."

"Chase got me a hotel room." Sam grinned at her and Rebe's heart pounded wildly. "Did you make my bed and lock up my apartment?" she asked.

"Yes."

"I still have to go to the meeting tomorrow."

"I'll get you there in plenty of time. Me, not Chase."

"What are we going to do?"

"I can tell you this much. What we do won't be accomplished in a couple of minutes. Give me your phone," Sam ordered holding out his hand for her cell. "And I can assure you, I will not be borrowing Chase's condoms."

"Was that as in plural?"

"Oh that I can promise you. It will not be quick."

"I almost feel like walking back out so you can carry me to the bed." Rebe glanced down then back up at Sam, and smiled. "Now that I know a little bitty man can carry me."

And wouldn't you know it, the little bitty man had her in his arms before she could say another word. He was kissing her in a way she'd never been kissed and her legs were turning to rubber. "Sam," Rebe whispered, "I'm yours."

"You always were," he whispered back to her. "And I'm yours. Stay with me."

"Sam, are you sure about us? I mean really sure?"

"Am I sure I love you? Yes. Listen, Rebe, you're not the only one afraid. I've been in love with you almost from the moment I met you and I've called myself crazy. You're totally nuts and I know it. So, I have to be out of my mind to want you."

"Well, you've told me there are a hundred things wrong with me. You called me a featherbrained airhead, you've always talked about my many imperfections," Rebe complained.

"Yeah, I have, haven't I? I've decided I love all of your

imperfections. You're perfect for me."

"Am I your end and your beginning?"

"Don't get carried away," Sam laughed. "I'm not a poet, but you are more important to me than you'll ever know. I can tell you this much. All of me does love all of you. If I could not love you, believe me I would have done that. But you love who you love. I tried a thousand times to wipe you from my mind, but you'd still invade my dreams. I guess I did as much running as you, but I'm not running anymore. You're the woman I've been waiting for."

"And what about the rest?"

"If you give your all to me, I promise I'll give my all to you. I'll not hold back one thing. But I'm not going to accept half of you, Rebe, not half of your love, or half of your trust. I want you to love me so much, that yes, you'll be hurt if you lose me. You'll feel pain if we fight, if we spend one night apart without talking. I want all of you."

"I do love you, Sam and I think a part of me always has. But you were my brother's friend and I just couldn't see it happening. I didn't think he'd approve. By the time we lost Jamie, I was sure I loved you. I was even surer that I could never lose another person I loved."

Sam ran his hand lightly over Rebe's body. "We can't know how long we have, but what a waste not to take advantage of the time we do have. What a waste it would be, to be so afraid of living that we just die a little each day in order not to hurt. Do you know why your brother asked me to look after you? Not because we were friends, but because he knew I loved you. I told him I loved you."

"Sam, I have to tell you something. It's very important. You are aware that if you cheat on me, my reaction will be different than it was with Chase."

"You should know I'd never cheat on you. And you should never ever again in life compare me with Chase. Now what shall we do?"

"You know we could have made love in my hotel room."

"That was much too close to Chase. I'm sure he got the two of you an adjoining room."

Rebe laughed. "I wouldn't doubt it. I thought we were going to stop talking."

"And so we were." Sam moved toward his nightstand and reached for several boxes and held them up for her inspection

"That's pretty ambitious."

"I'd say we're going to take the first dozen or so encounters just to take the edge off. After that we'll slow down just a bit, just enough to learn what the other likes."

"I think I'd like to know that going in," Rebe laughed.

"This isn't your game anymore, Rebe, but I can promise you're going to enjoy it."

This new alpha Sam was turning Rebe on. He moved slowly a touch of a predatory smile. His hand moved toward her blouse and he slowly began undoing the buttons. With each button undone he'd kiss her. Her body was heating up. What he was doing felt so erotic. She knew she shouldn't be doing it, comparing men was a definite 'no no' but she did it anyway.

No man had ever undressed her in such a slow and deliberate manner. And no man had ever looked at her the way Sam was doing, as though she was the most wonderful woman in the world. As though he couldn't get enough of her. As though he loved her and she was firmly entrenched in his heart.

He was kissing her, slow, deliberate, soft kisses, no tongue; just him licking at her lips, nibbling, even lightly biting her. Then he moved to pull her earlobe into his mouth and suckled it. Lord have mercy, she nearly lost it. She knew she was wet because she could feel it. She couldn't remember if that had ever happened. In fact it surprised her so much that she'd wondered about it.

Sam was not in a rush that much was obvious. Rebe suddenly felt shy. When he'd finally removed the blouse from her shoulders he was staring at her, then he smiled and his gaze moved to her chest. He was kissing the bra. *Damn man*, she wanted to tell him to get on with it, but she'd rushed him once already and didn't think he'd take too kindly to being rushed again. Besides the silk moving against her skin was erotic. Then she felt his hand moving to undo the clasp of her bra, which thankfully was fastened in the front. He removed it and tossed it into a chair and stood back looking at her. "Beautiful," he murmured. "This is so much better for painting you."

"Are you thinking of painting me right now?" Rebe asked in astonishment. Modeling for Sam was so not what was on her mind and if that was what he wanted she was more than a little peeved. "Sam, are you thinking of painting me?"

"Actually I am. But not at the moment. I'm thinking how much more beautiful you are underneath your clothes, much more than I ever imagined. It's such fun to unwrap you. It's like you're my special present."

That made her smile and forgiveness was instant. "Stop staring at me, Sam, you're freaking me out."

"You're beautiful. Hasn't a man just wanted to look at you?"

"No," she answered.

"In that case, thank God, I am the fortunate one you have chosen to spend your life with."

Did he just say that? Rebe's heart was pounding like crazy. She felt as giddy as a school girl. She wanted to jump up and down and pump her fist and yell, 'yes.' But she had to play it cool, right? She had to keep the upper hand, be the one in control, be the heroine? A heroine would never but never allow the hero, and she had firmly established that yes, Sam was a hero. Anyway she'd never allow him to know how she was feeling. Right?

Wrong. "Sam, you make me feel…cherished."

"You are cherished. It's so hard to believe you find this so unusual. I can't believe any of the men—"

"Hold it. I haven't slept with that many men."

"In the years I've known you, you've had a ton of boyfriends."

"That does not mean I've slept with all of them."

"How many would you say?"

"That is so not your business." He was eyeing her, his head tilted and his eyes slanted as though he was having very erotic thoughts. She made a move for the bed, anything to cover her body. Only she was backing away not knowing how comfortable she was with him seeing her rear

"Don't move, Rebe, just let me drink you in. "You know what, I have a better idea."

Sam went for her discarded panties. "Lift your leg," he said as he tugged the red silk over her calves then moved the material upward where it belonged. A growl, low and menacing came out as he retrieved her bra then fastened it.

"What the heck are you doing?"

"I'm dressing you."

"Why?"

"I should have thought of this sooner. I'd love for you to undress for me."

"You mean strip?" A lazy smile crossed his face. He hunched a shoulder.

"You say tomato I say tamato. Either way I'd love to see you naked."

"I was already naked."

"So you were."

"I've never had a man demand that I get dressed once I was already in the buff."

"Since our relationship is so new I'm going to give that one to you for free. But I will not ever stand for your comparing me to other men." He looked her over. "At the least I don't want you voicing it. I mean I can't know what you're thinking."

Rebe started to laugh and Sam frowned. "But on occasion I can read your mind and you might not know when those times are." She started laughing again.

"Rebe, in case you're wondering, I'm not a virgin." He waited until she'd gotten the message. "Thank you. I won't compare you to other women and you won't compare me to other men. I've figured you out. Chase was a safety net for you in order for you not to love me. But now that you've gotten rid of him, you've lost that net. We're not going to have walls between us. Here are your pants," he said pulling her from the bed and waiting until she'd put them back on. Then he handed her, her top and decided to rebutton it himself.

"Sam, you are awfully bossy."

"A bit too much of the alpha male for you?"

"Okay, cut it out. My books are fiction. Now come on, tell me your plan. Why the heck are you trying to redress me? Is it in order to make you last longer?" She said the words with a smile and just a hint of a smirk.

"To be honest, yes. You do have me a bit paranoid about my performance, and I do want to make the actual loving last a bit longer. But I was a bit premature about how much I wanted to unwrap you. I've done that, now I want you to undress, and yes I'd love to observe."

"You're a freak."

"I'm an artist. I want to put every movement of your fingers into my memory. I want to see how the clothes fall when you take them off. I even want to look at the way they crease. Call me crazy."

"You're crazy."

"Perhaps. How about we go at this a bit differently, a little slower perhaps. How about if you just undo the button of your slacks and perhaps the zipper."

"Just the button?"

"Okay, go ahead, the button."

She did that.

"Now the zipper."

Rebe complied but added an unasked for wiggle of her hips. The slacks pooled about her feet. She glanced at Sam and saw he was breathing hard. She looked down and saw other things were hard as well.

"Now the panties, or I could take them off," Sam suggested.

"Are you going to strip for me, Sam?"

"I'll be happy to."

"I'll bet you will. I'm not going to stand here exposed while you're fully dress, take off your shirt." Within seconds Sam's shirt was off followed quickly by his pants. Rebe began to breathe faster as the two of them moved again toward the bed.

"I'm getting tired of standing, Sam. I think I'll lie on the bed for now." Rebe moved backwards.

"Good idea." Sam was near panting as Rebe's fingers lingered in the band of her panties. "Keep the panties on," Sam said in a hoarse whisper. "I want to use my teeth to remove them from your body. And then guess what I want to do."

Seriously was this Sam with the sexy, dirty talk? she wondered. Was he thinking he had to keep up with Chase? Had she given him a complex?

Together they sank onto the bed. "Ooh Sam," she moaned.

"I'm sorry, Rebe, I really am. I'm crazy, but I have to do this, just indulge me, please." He pulled her once again from the bed. "Just stand right there for me. You're going to kill me, but I have to do this before I forget." Sam dashed from the room and left Rebe standing there. And when he returned he had a sketch pad and began sketching her.

If it wasn't so crazy she'd laugh again. But she was started to feel a bit weird and not so wanted anymore. "Well, of all the nerve," she huffed thinking how just that morning Sam had badgered her to make love when she'd told him she didn't have the time. Now he was doing everything in his power to delay it. The thought entered her mind once more and she knew it was true. Sam really was trying to compete with Chase. She was wishing now she'd never teased him about being a frog prince.

"Sam, seriously I'm not kidding. I'm all for fun and games, but you're making me feel unwanted, undesirable. This morning you wanted to make love to me. Now all you want to do is sketch me. Forget it." She went to the bed in a huff, pulled back the covers and crawled under them, then she glared at him and watched as he allowed the pad and chalk to fall from his fingers.

"Now I know how to get you in bed," Rebe whispered.

"You were getting that already, so you didn't win anything here. I suppose we're going to fight the entire time we make love. Is that your way of hiding from your feelings? I'm not going anywhere, Rebe. That's one thing you won't have to worry about." He watched her. Her brown eyes misted and she pulled the covers to her chin.

"Sam, are you afraid? Have I emasculated you with my teasing?"

Sam frowned. "You think you've emasculated me? No, Rebe. I probably shouldn't be admitting this to you. In fact I don't think a true alpha male would." Sam stopped and smiled at Rebe then he continued. "Perhaps I am a bit afraid to just make love to you considering earlier today my performance was not as either of us desired. And perhaps I am afraid that I might not be able to measure up to Chase. Kandi told me that Chase really knew how to please you. That does put a lot of pressure on a man."

"Kandi talks too much."

"Was she wrong about Chase?"

"Sam, do you really want to hear this?"

"Of course not. But I think maybe we need to discuss it."

Rebe was exasperated. "Are all men hard of hearing? Listen to me, Sam, yes, Chase and I enjoyed a healthy physical relationship. I still want that. But I want it included with love and being in love. I want all of this with you, Sam. Forgive me for making you feel…well…rushed earlier. I get it that you're putting off the moment. This is so important, Sam."

"I know."

"It's different."

"I know that too."

"I want us to…

"Be a match. We are. Don't worry, Rebe, I was teasing you, at least a little bit. I could see you were a bit anxious and I was trying things to make you laugh, to make you a bit angry, to make you horny. We're going to be together for a very long time and if we don't get it right the first couple of times, so what? I'm sure we will eventually. I know I'll never stop trying to please you. And for your information, you are very desirable."

With a flick of his wrist Sam was out of his boxers and heading for the bed. He smiled as Rebe gave him a most appreciative look.

"It would appear you like what you see. Later, you can draw me if you want."

"I can't draw," Rebe admitted.

"Then you can sculpt me. You only need your hands," Sam grinned. "And who knows, maybe a few other body parts." Before Rebe could say anything or utter another smart comment, he was with her under the covers and holding her in his arms.

This time they would take it slow. He'd not rush things though he'd wanted to be inside her from the moment he'd seen her at his art exhibit. Hell, all the things he'd done were to make sure he'd last, now he had her thinking he didn't want her. That was just plain crazy. He'd have to prove that to her and quickly.

"I want to kiss you all over, Rebe. I want to taste you just to see if you taste as good as I've always imagined." Then he began nibbling on her ear using the tip of his tongue to trail a path of want up her body. His hand cupped her breast tweaking her nibbles.

Sam was doing everything in his power to make the buildup last. He was only human and had no idea what would happen when they finally tried it again. But he did know he'd make damn sure Rebe was well satisfied before he entered her. He would never be able to live it down if he went only a couple of strokes before breaking lose again.

After Rebe's third orgasm Sam finally entered her. She held him close. "I love you, Sam. Don't worry. We are a fit. And you, my love, are not a frog. You're a prince."

Okay, so she'd been worried. But in real life one would hope their life partner knew them well enough to know that, and would be able to stop them from worrying. Sure, Sam's antics had ticked her off, confused her and downright frustrated her. But when she began screaming out in pleasure, she'd forgotten all of that, and all she could do was scream Sam's name over and over.

And now she was rounding the base toward orgasm number four, a first for her in such a short period of time. But this time Sam would be rounding that base with her. After all, this was her fairytale. And

Sam was her prince. And what would a fairytale or a romance be without a happy ending?

Hers was just that.

A very happy ending.

ABOUT THE AUTHOR

 Dyanne Davis is a Multi-Published, Award Winning author of 20 novels. She has written dozens of articles for on-line magazines. Dyanne lives in a Chicago suburb with her husband of 43 years, William Sr.

She has been a presenter of numerous workshops. She hosts a local cable television show in her hometown, *"The Art of Writing,"* to give writing tips to aspiring writers. Interviewing many of her favorite authors has been the highlight of doing the show. You can catch some of the clips on Youtube.

Dyanne also writes a vampire series under the name of F. D. Davis

You can reach her at:
> davisdyanne@aol.com
> www.dyannedavis.com
> adamomegavampire@aol.com
> www.adamomega.com

Here is a sneak peek at book two in the Undying Love Trilogy

THE GIFT

Blaine MaDia sat on the jet, his eyes closed behind the dark glasses he wore so often now. It had taken him less than a week to survey the damage in his San Francisco apartment and start the rebuilding process. In the meantime he needed a place to live. So he was heading east to his spacious suburban home forty minutes west of Chicago

Funny when he'd flown to San Francisco he'd had thoughts of staying. Problem was, even with a psychic, life didn't always turn out as planned. For assurance he'd even drawn Tarot cards for himself. Too bad he hadn't asked if he would be burned out of his west coast apartment.

Lifting the glasses a tiny bit from his face to swipe at the sweat that had beaded between his brows, he allowed a deep breath of air to escape. He didn't want to take them off because for the past week he'd taken quite a bit of ribbing, some of it good-natured, some of it mean spirited. Mostly people questioned if he were a true psychic, why didn't he know his apartment was going to catch on fire?

In all honesty he'd answered, 'I'm not God.' Now he was tired of the questions, tired of all the answers. He just wanted to go home undisturbed. If he didn't wear the glasses, strangers would be pestering him with requests for readings. He accepted that as a price for his fame.

On most occasions he handled those requests with a modicum of dignity and humor offering his card to the person asking. He couldn't chance it now; he was in too weak of a state psychically. The fumes from the smoke had wreaked havoc in his body. He needed time to heal. Right now he could ill afford strangers pulling at his energy field. It was all that he could do to keep the barrier of energy surrounding his body, keeping out the thoughts of his fellow passengers.

Sleep was pulling at him when he sat up with a start. He rubbed at his temple feeling the beginning of what promised to be one doozy of a headache. Since the fire, dreams of his mother dogged him raggedly. There were so many questions he wanted to ask. If he could he'd eliminate the dreams, but for whatever reason they continued. *Not now* he thought not wanting to deal with the experience of the fire while sitting on a packed plane.

Trying to push the thoughts from him a searing pain warned what was happening wasn't about him or the fire but about someone entirely different. He closed his eyes in order to better focus his powers, to see who was having such an effect on him. Not since the first time he met Michelle Powers, his soul mother, had he felt such a dramatic reaction. Blaine wanted to know who it was who was having such a strong effect on him. And what was happening to his hard won self-control.

As he focused his energy the feeling became stronger, until at last, he was on his feet, standing, moving forward without wanting to, yet drawn to someone's pain. His hand moved unobtrusively through the air. Since finding his mother he was discovering new powers he'd never known he possessed.

He smiled to himself, the thought that he had only to put out his hand and connect with someone's energy surprising. After a lifetime of dealing with the unexplained, he was comfortable with his gift of clairaudience. He didn't have a name for this newest emerging gift.

The best way he could explain it was mining for energy. He used his hands much the same as he used his mind when speaking to those who had departed this life and were waiting. He focused.

Suddenly he stopped walking, his eyes landing on a woman of petite stature. Even from a sitting position he could tell she was short. He stood over the woman perusing her body in a quick perfunctory manner. She was slender also. His gaze fell on the woman's curly, dark brown hair and a lump formed in his throat.

Blaine stepped back as an irresistible urge to reach out and touch her clutched at his throat. It took all his psychic energy to resist the pull. A tightening began in his groin. Good Lord, not now. He panicked and moved backwards down the aisle. No woman had ever affected him so quickly.

"What is it that you want?"

Blaine stopped his backwards descent and looked down into the biggest pair of chocolate brown eyes he'd ever seen. For a moment he thought his heart would stop. Despite the woman's cold stare he felt drawn to her.

The sadness that had emanated from her to bring him to her now washed over him in waves. He clicked his tongue against his teeth trying to feel the woman's energy.

She'd placed a block to keep him out. Damn. That had never happened before.

"I'm sorry," he stammered. "My name's Blaine MaDia." He smiled at the woman while his skin began a slow crawl of awareness. It wasn't so much her looks as her aura. In looks she was ordinary with the exception of her eyes. It was the woman's aura that held an intense fascination for Blaine.

"I'm sorry, Mr. MaDia. Am I supposed to know you?"

Blaine tried again to probe gently at the woman's thoughts. When that didn't work he tried more aggressively, but still she held out against him, blocking any entrance. This stirred his curiosity making him wonder what it was the woman was hiding so possessively that she'd thrown up a shield against a stranger.

"Mr. MaDia, did you want something?"

Now he was standing there feeling like a fool, his own psyche open for probing, and his defenses weakened. He knew better than to continue with his questions, yet he felt compelled to press on. Never in all the years since Blaine became a professional psychic had he ever used that gift to seek out females, or to impress. He was now embarrassed and could feel the flush of that embarrassment with the next words he uttered.

"I'm Blaine MaDia, the psychic on television." He gulped. The woman appeared unimpressed. "I was just walking, I didn't want anything." Blaine continued. Still nothing. The woman simply stared at him, her deep-set chocolate eyes turning to liquid cocoa. Now besides wanting to touch her, Blaine wanted to stand there and take a long drink from her eyes.

"I don't know you, Mr. MaDia and I don't mean to appear rude, but I'm very tired. I paid for two first class seats so I wouldn't be disturbed." She tilted her head slightly letting Blaine know she wanted him to leave.

"Sorry I bothered you," he murmured and turned to walk back to his seat. He paused and stuck out his hand toward the woman. "Nice to meet you Miss…Miss…"

He waited for an acknowledgment and a name, but the woman looked at him with mere curiosity, ignored his outstretched hand and cast her gaze back on the book in her hand.

Surely the woman had to be a psychic, Blaine thought. In the very least, she was familiar with psychic gifts because she was using them so effectively to keep him out. And he wanted in.

He set back in his seat amused and peeved. He was behaving like a hormonal teenager, trying to impress a girl into giving him her name. Still, knowing something and having emotional feelings about it were two different things.

The very thought of not knowing bugged him, when less than an hour ago all he had wanted was to be able to tune out the emotions and the thoughts of the people around him. Now, more than anything, he wanted to know what the woman four rows ahead of him was thinking. And why she'd thrown up a defense against him.

Blaine took his glasses from the perched position on the bridge of his nose and folded them into the clear plastic container that hung around his neck. He smiled to himself. He loved the three inch case and the glasses that bent like spaghetti to fit into the case. He'd found them at a cheap boutique and thought they were cool.

He gazed around the cabin ignoring an inner command to rest. Sure he knew what he was doing. He knew that soon everyone in his section would recognize him and they would ask for readings. There would be a flurry of activity. Something in his experience no woman could let slide. Then, he thought, the woman with the chocolate eyes would drop her defenses.

He was fully aware his thoughts and actions were wrong. He had no right to violate another person's mind without their explicit invitation. And the code of conduct governing legitimate psychics prohibited such behavior. Still, he found himself smiling at no one in particular.

The need to know this woman was erasing his moral code. It only took a moment and a bit of gentle mental persuasion before the passenger across the aisle turned to him.

"Aren't you Blaine MaDia?"

"That's right I am."

"Wow. I can't believe it. I've been watching you on television for over a year and listening to you on the radio. I heard you wrote a book. Is it out yet?"

"No, it will be out in a month or so. Thanks for the support."

Blaine smiled more deeply at the man, resisting the urge for further tampering. He could easily give the man a hypnotic suggestion to carry the fuss up an octave or two, but that wouldn't be necessary. Nor did he want to cross any more barriers than necessary.

Soon everyone in the first class section were clamoring, begging Blaine for a reading, telling him how much they admired him, watched him, believed him. Everyone that is, with the exception of the lone woman occupying two seats.

Blaine tried again. She kept the invisible fence around her thoughts. In fact she'd fortified it and this time he knew it wasn't to keep out a stranger. This time it was personal. It had been structured to keep him out.

Taking out a small piece of paper from the notepad he always kept tucked in his shirt pocket he scribbled a few words on it and handed the note to the passing flight attendant who wrote on it and gave it back.

Cassandra Boozer. Smiling his thanks at the woman he handed her his card. "Call me. I owe you one."

He didn't care that the woman thought it odd that he didn't just approach his fellow passenger, or as most people thought, his being a psychic he should automatically know the name of every person he met.

Sure that happened on occasion, but most of the times it didn't. Sometimes there was someone with such a strong personality that they would literally shout their name into his subconscious, much like the spirits he preferred to deal with.

There was only one other woman, one other person period that had ever had a draining effect on him. And that woman was his mother from his only other lifetime. This feeling he had for this woman was extremely weak compared to the massive energized connection that had summoned him to his mother's side.

Still as weak as it was, Blaine was intrigued. He didn't feel she was someone from his past, either in this life or the one before it, but there was something about the woman and for some reason he knew he wanted to know her.

He stopped the thought as quickly as it had come wondering if it had anything to do with the cryptic message his mother's shadow-self had delivered to him. He remembered Michelle's words clearly now. *"You'll find someone, Son."*

Could this Cassandra Boozer, the mysterious woman who feigned no interest in him or his reputation be the one he was looking for? He thought of her disinterested voice and cold stare. If she was the one, Blaine sure as hell hoped that her demeanor was just a psychic front. He had no wish to become involved with a woman with ice in her veins. No, with a woman like that he would only offer his professional services.

Again he felt the sudden tightening in his pants and lowered the paper he was reading to cover the bulge. Oh yeah, he thought, All I want to give her is professional services. With nothing left to do, he decided to return to his seat and catch a quick nap.